WHAT NEXT?

SHARI LOW

Boldwood

First published in Great Britain in 2022 by Boldwood Books Ltd.

Cover Design by Alice Moore Design

Cover Photography: Shutterstock

This book is a work of fiction and, except in the case of historical fact, any resemblance to actual persons, living or dead, is purely coincidental.

Every effort has been made to obtain the necessary permissions with reference to copyright material, both illustrative and quoted. We apologise for any omissions in this respect and will be pleased to make the appropriate acknowledgements in any future edition.

A CIP catalogue record for this book is available from the British Library.

Paperback ISBN 978-1-80048-735-2

Large Print ISBN 978-1-80048-734-5

Hardback ISBN 978-1-80415-981-1

Ebook ISBN 978-1-80048-737-6

Kindle ISBN 978-1-80048-736-9

Audio CD ISBN 978-1-80048-729-1

MP3 CD ISBN 978-1-80048-730-7

Digital audio download ISBN 978-1-80048-732-1

Boldwood Books Ltd
23 Bowerdean Street
London SW6 3TN
www.boldwoodbooks.com

To my own bucket list pals, Liz, Lyndsay and Jan, for the annual adventures, the laughs and the gin.
And to my brilliant editor, Caroline Ridding, because once again, this book wouldn't exist without you.
Love, Shari x

BEFORE YOU TURN THE PAGE...
A NOTE FROM SHARI

Dear chums,

Huge thanks, as always, for picking up one of my books. If you've read some of them before, welcome back. And if you're new to them, hello! I'm so chuffed you found your way to this one.

Either way, there's a bit of a story behind the pages you're about to read, so let me catch you up.

Twenty-one years ago, in January 2001, my first novel, *What If?* was released. It was the chronicle of Carly Cooper and her merry band of friends, Kate, Sarah, Carol and Jess, all of them in their late twenties and navigating their way through life, love and the occasional disaster.

In that book, Carly was having a pre-Millennium crisis. Single and restless, she quit her job, her home and her life and set off to track down the six men she'd almost married, determined to see if she'd accidentally said goodbye to her soulmate. I won't give away any spoilers, but all that matters is that you know that, in the end, Carly found her match and as the new century dawned, she celebrated with her rekindled flame, her best friends and cocktails. Lots of cocktails.

What If? was a bestseller for the second time, when my publisher, Boldwood Books, released an updated and re-edited special anniversary edition in 2020.

And then came the next chapter in Carly's life.

Over the two decades since the first version of *What If?* many readers had asked what happened next to the gang of pals. I was curious too. Did Carly and her husband go hand and hand into the sunset? Did Sarah find happiness after escaping a destructive marriage? Did Jess ever recover from her scandalous affair? Did Carol's marriage to Carly's brother, Callum, go the distance? And did Kate get a sainthood for being the cool, loving voice of reason in every situation?

Well, I had to know. In 2020, I laughed, cried and drank endless cups of tea at my laptop as I delved back into their world and in 2021 the sequel, *What Now?* was released. Set twenty years after the first book, it found the friends older, but not so much wiser. Over the years, they'd stuck together through marriages, divorce, love, heartbreak and tragedy and there was still more to come. When I typed The End on that story, I thought I'd maybe look in on them again in another decade or so.

But then the strangest thing happened. They refused to pipe down and leave my head. They're bolshy that way. When we turned the last page of *What Now?* the women were all on the cusp of new lives, new futures, new happy ever afters and they all knew for absolute certain that 2020 was going to be their best year ever.

Sigh. We all know how that turned out.

Curiosity got the better of me once again, and I couldn't resist dropping back into their lives. After more laughter, more tears, and more endless cups of tea at my laptop (yes, I have the strangest job ever), here's what I found. *What Next?* kicks off at the end of 2021. Plans have been scrapped, relationships have changed, and some of the women are about to face a couple of those curveballs that life chucks at you when you least expect it.

Read on to find out if they caught them or let them fall.

And thank you again – I'm so grateful to every single reader who lets me tell stories every day.

Much love,

Shari xxx

THE WORLD OF 'WHAT NEXT?'

Carly Morton (formerly Cooper, then Barwick) – jobbing writer, grateful mum, unfailingly loyal friend, wife of Hollywood megastar, Sam Morton, and survivor of more bad relationship decisions than she can count.

Sam Morton – Carly's husband. They first dated back in the nineties, when they both worked in a Hong Kong nightclub. Later, Sam moved to LA when his tale of being a high-class escort got made into a movie. That catapulted him into a life of fame and fortune, but now he's a producer who stays firmly behind the scenes.

Mac Barwick – 19 – Carly's wild, driven, adrenaline-junkie, 6 foot 4 inch son, loves basketball, working out and partying. He occupies 50 per cent of Carly's maternal heart and causes 90 per cent of her maternal worry.

Benny Barwick – 17 – the other 50 per cent of her heart. A laid-back, caring bloke whose common sense and maturity is clearly a throwback to a latent gene in the family line.

Mark Barwick – Carly's ex-husband of nineteen years, now a co-parent and much-loved friend. Most of the time. Except when he's being just a bit uppity or judgemental about her life. A corporate lawyer who always plays by the rules.

Tabitha Hendricks – Mark's thirty-year-old live-in girlfriend, a legal shark who is making a name for herself in the field of Human Rights. Gym obsessive with abs that could double as speed bumps.

Val Murray – Carly's aunt, born and bred in Glasgow, a woman who never misses an opportunity to laugh, to call people out on their behaviour, or to eat a caramel wafer. Val has suffered two huge losses in life – the deaths of her daughter, Dee, and her best friend, Josie.

Don Murray – Val's husband of fifty years, the only man she has ever loved or lusted after (if you don't count George Clooney and Tom Jones).

Kate Smith – One of Carly's gang of lifelong friends who all met in primary school in Glasgow, and who, one by one, moved to London in their twenties. Kate and Carly have been next-door neighbours for the last twenty years, and Kate's architect husband, Bruce, knocked up a natty waterproof shelter joining their back doors because Kate's hair turns to frizz in the rain. Her offspring, Tallulah, Cameron and Zoe are all in their twenties.

Carol and Callum Cooper – Carly's brother and his wife, another of Carly's pals since childhood. Married for twenty-two years, Callum is now an in-demand silver fox model, while former model, Carol, has built a new, very successful career as a blogger and influencer on social media.

Charlotte and Antonia Cooper – Carol and Callum's twin daughters, now twenty and already more responsible than their parents. After being humiliated in a public revenge-porn incident, Antonia (Toni) is now an influencer and spokesperson on cybersecurity, anti-bullying and mental health. Charlotte recently announced that her childhood abbreviation of 'Charlie' is no longer appropriate now that she's working towards a career in the legal sector.

Jess Latham – the brains of Carly's friendship group, she's brutally honest, unfailingly blunt. Jess now runs a company that specialises in crisis management and her skills frequently come in handy. Her son, Josh, is at uni, her only child from a duplicitous and bitter marriage. She's finally left her loathing of her ex-husband behind, now that she's fallen in love with...

Arnie Deluca – Sam Morton's former stunt double and right-hand man. Jess is living with Arnie at Sam's estate in LA, and they're planning their wedding (her second, his third).

Sarah Russo (deceased) – one of the original gal pals, Sarah and her husband, Nick, were killed in a plane crash in 2016. They are survived by their adult children, Hannah and Ryan, who both remain close to their mother's best friends.

Estelle Conran – Sam's ex-girlfriend, a Hollywood goddess and Oscar-nominated actress. Gorgeous on the outside, bitchy to her soulless core on the inside, the kind of woman who smiles convincingly at you while she's secretly planning your death.

Hayley Harlow – a client of Jess's crisis management firm – a British model who claims she's pregnant by a sleazy Hollywood talent agent, Dax Hill.

CARLY MORTON

PROLOGUE – DECEMBER 2021

Set You Free – Kelly Llorenna

'My TripAdvisor review of this place isn't getting five stars,' one of my cellmates mutters. 'Not even a bloody minibar.'

Yep, cellmates.

Things I learned today:

1. The American dream is only a couple of twists away from the kind of nightmare they make movies about. Right now, *The Shawshank Redemption* and *The Great Escape* come to mind.
2. I really need to brush up on my driving skills as at least one hospital admission in the Los Angeles area today was my fault.
3. Right now, out in the world, there's probably a lawyer already planning a court case against me that will destroy my life.

4. Oh, and a Los Angeles jail cell isn't that different from a
   London one. Four walls. A locked steel door. And
   despite ample padding in the posterior area, my arse is
   not designed for a concrete bench.

A wave of anxiety makes my stomach churn and my skin crawl.
Apart from the buttock area, which is comfortably numb. But that's
not the point. I'm in jail. Again. And in the words of the cowboy
with chafed thighs, this ain't my first rodeo.

A couple of years ago, I found myself in a London police station,
after a video of me threatening to take a cheese grater to the balls of
a scumball who was blackmailing my eighteen-year-old niece, Toni,
went viral. Of course, I'd never have actually done that. I like my
cheese grater too much. My electric sander though...

Anyway, that time around, the charges were dropped and I ran,
arms wide in celebration, shouting 'Freedom' in the streets. Okay,
that might be a slight exaggeration. I actually scurried out, flushed
with mortification and hightailed it home before they changed
their minds.

But this time?

Oh bollocks, another gut wrench of anxiety. This episode of
incarceration in the clink is so much worse on way too many levels.
For a start, as aforementioned, I'm in the USA. Sunny California.
Although my chances of getting a suntan are currently zero unless
my one phone call is to St Tropez Spray Tan to ask them to smuggle
me in a face mist in a natty shade of deep caramel.

There's also an element of public interest in this case, given that
my fairly new husband is someone who shares the stage on talk
shows with guys like Brad Pitt and George Clooney. Pretty sure any
hopes I had of George's missus, Amal, inviting us to their home for
a starry barbeque have been scuppered after this performance by a

lead perpetrator in a real-life crime drama. Although, she is a hotshot lawyer, so perhaps she can give me some pointers.

The last time I got jailed, Mark Barwick, my then-husband of twenty years was furious. It wasn't the reason for our divorce, but it didn't help. This time around, I've only been hitched to my current matrimonial partner for eighteen months, and although that's a lifetime in Hollywood relationship years, there's a real possibility that his crisis-management team are already leaking divorce rumours to the *Daily Mail*.

Another twinge of dread. If that happens, it's a sure-fire bet that my sons back in the UK will read it on their Twitter feeds over their morning protein shakes and get straight on to Loose Women to share stories about my parenting fails. I've gone from the mother who preaches good decisions and accountability at all times, to 'the accused'. My slide down from the moral high ground has been swift and bumpy.

That thought makes me glance to my left, where one of my alleged accomplices is brushing some imaginary dust off her bright pink palazzo pants, her blonde bob – the size and consistency of a motorcycle helmet thanks to her daily application of more hair product than the average boyband – decidedly unruffled by our current predicament. Even her pink lipstick and blue eyeliner are still flawless. Granted, I've never seen her any other way. She could go through a car wash and she'd still come out looking like RuPaul's immaculately groomed, more flamboyant granny.

Yep, I've landed my Auntie Val in the slammer with me. Val Murray. Aged sixty something. She refuses to discuss her real age and I'm too scared to ask for written evidence. Born and bred in Glasgow, she's a woman who has overcome the kind of heartbreak and devastation that could make some people bitter, cynical or defeated, yet she somehow manages to love life, love her family and

friends, and love a bit of adventure. Although, I'm not sure this is
going to be in her top ten lifetime highlights.

Sensing my gaze, she unpurses her pink pucker to speak and I
brace myself for profound words of wisdom.

'I suppose there's no chance of room service popping in with a
gin and tonic and a Toblerone. Or a packet of cheese and onion
crisps.' She lifts her legs and nods in the direction of the totteringly
high pink sandals on her feet. 'I'd give one of these furry mules for
a Greggs steak bake. I'd be walking in circles for the rest of the day,
but I don't s'pose it would matter in here.'

Our third cellmate closes her eyes and, for a second, I wonder if
she's upset or trying to contain her anger, but then I realise that
she's actually just committing every detail of this to memory to be
recounted later to her fans and followers. My sister-in-law, Carol. I
know the whole Carly and Carol thing can be confusing. But when
we met as kids, on the first day of primary school, we had no idea
that our friendship would last a lifetime, or that she would marry
my brother, Callum, and make the whole damn thing even more
befuddling. I didn't change my name when I married my first
husband, so for a long time we were Carly Cooper and Carol
Cooper. But now that I've remarried and changed my name to
Morton, it's a bit less of a situation. It's a relief to be honest. It does
things to your ego when your name is confused with a size 10,
utterly stunning former model, who retired from the catwalk and
then became one of the original Instagram influencers, with 1.2
million followers and counting. Although, I'm not quite sure how
her followers will feel about the fact that I've now landed her in the
kind of exclusive club that qualify for their very own prison tattoos.

The fourth felon in our criminal gang shakes her head. 'Just
remember, say nothing without a lawyer,' Jess says, because she's
always been the smart one and because she feels she qualifies as a

legal expert as she always guesses the correct outcome on *Judge Judy*.

'I'm so, so, sorry about all this,' I bleat, for the 234th time since the metal door banged shut. 'I promise that somehow I'll make it up to you all.'

'An invite to George Clooney's house for a pool party might just about do it,' my Auntie Val demands. 'I know you've got connections there.'

I decide now isn't the time to let her in on my certainty that I'll be about as welcome as a sausage at a vegan restaurant in A-list circles after this. I appreciate her trying to inject some levity into the situation, but it isn't working. The reality is I've seriously messed up. I've undoubtedly shamed my husband. Been a shit example for my sons. Pissed off my friends. Enraged my brother. And served my ex with the perfect excuse to call me irresponsible and feel smug about our parting of the ways.

I can't see how it could get any worse.

'Morton!' A shadow is cast across the floor as a muscle-bound guard the size of a Portaloo appears in front of the bars on the door.

'There's someone here to see you.'

He stands to one side and there is one of the best lawyers in the business – according to the role he once played in five series of an Emmy Award-winning legal drama.

In real life, he's Sam Morton, former actor turned movie producer. And my husband. The man I'd vowed to love in sickness and health. For richer and poorer. I just wished I'd written in a line about 'in times of happiness, in sorrow, and when you're looking like an extra from *Orange Is The New Black*.'

Our eyes meet and I'm not sure what I see there, but the muscle that's throbbing on the side of that perfect jaw of his tells me it's not happy thoughts.

This is it. Our first major test as a married couple. If you don't count my cooking.

'Are you here to get us out?' I ask weakly, deciding this isn't the time for small talk or sweet endearments.

His beautiful brown eyes darken, that muscle in his jaw throbs faster, and his head goes into a slow-motion, loaded shake. That's when I realise our score on that marriage test is about to be an epic fail.

1

VAL MURRAY
TWO WEEKS EARLIER

Always Remember Us This Way – Lady Gaga

Dear Josie,

Well, doll, this is it. Last-chance saloon.

All these years I've been writing to you and we both know I've been avoiding bringing up the list. The thing is… when we made it, it was supposed to be for both of us and I couldn't face it on my own. I can hear you right now. 'Val Murray, get your big-girl pants on and woman up. It's time to grab life by the balls and don't waste a single fecking day.'

So that's what I'm going to do, because if it doesn't happen now, it never will. If you can see what's going on down here, and what we know lies ahead of us, you'll understand why.

Wish me luck, pal. I've got you up there. I've got the memories. I've got the list. And I've got a bloody brilliant woman in mind to go on this ride with me. She just doesn't know it yet. I'm flying to London to see our Carly today – she's got a big heart that one, so I'm hoping she'll go for it. If not, well, I'm going anyway. I'll be buggered if I'll let us down.

I'll keep you posted, ma love.

Keep dancing, keep laughing… and be happy up there.

Love you,

Val xxx

2

CARLY

LONDON, NOVEMBER

Umbrella – Rihanna

Sometimes this motherhood stuff can be like a kebab skewer through the heart.

'Right, you two, let's go over the ground rules again before everyone gets here,' I said, my voice cracking halfway through.

Over at the kitchen table, my two man-children groaned, then flopped on the well-loved oak slab and played dead.

'You're hilarious. Honestly, my sides are splitting,' I drawled sarcastically, while trying not to laugh.

My firstborn, Mac, slowly raised his head. 'Sorry, Mum, had a blackout there. Happens every time you mention rules. I think we're still traumatised at the prospect of you abandoning us. Casting us aside like yesterday's pizza box.' He finished the sentence with a fake sob, making his seventeen-year-old brother, Benny, crack into giggles.

I froze. It was still a sore point and it made my heart hurt, but my maternal defences wouldn't let it go. 'Are we doing this again, Mac? I am *not* abandoning you. You know we want you to join us next spring when your basketball season ends. And you, my little chuckles...' I turned my gaze on Benny, 'you decided you wanted to stay to finish your A-levels and I respect your wishes. Even if they rip out my soul and make my ovaries ache.'

'Get out while you can,' Mac deadpanned to his brother. 'She's on about her ovaries again. It'll be the hour by hour stories of the days we were born next.'

It was a struggle not to laugh as I swatted him on the shoulder. Labour stories aside, they weren't the only ones who could play the guilt game. I came from a mother with a PHD in martyrdom. There was no situation that I couldn't milk for sympathy if required, although it was a superpower that I used sparingly and only in jest. I switched back to the more familiar territories of teasing and pointing out the obvious.

'Besides, I'm hardly leaving you destitute on the streets. You're living in a swanky penthouse in Battersea with one of those boiling water taps and a yoga room.'

It had taken a while for us to get to these living arrangements. When Sam and I married almost two years ago, he moved post-production of his new movie from Los Angeles to Pinewood Studios in Buckinghamshire, and the plan was that we would live in the UK until that was complete, giving him, me and the boys time to get used to living as a family before we all uprooted and moved back to California with him.

Hang on, I just had to repeat that, because I still can't believe this is my life. Three years ago, I was a middle-aged, lumpy and bumpy mother of two teenagers, who alternated between school runs and endless drop-offs and pick-ups for two sport-obsessed teenagers who had better social lives than me. I'd been married for almost twenty years to my first husband, Mark, and it was pretty fair to say we'd grown apart. Like 'need binoculars to spot each other on the horizon' kind of apart. Mark is a good man, but he's also a workaholic lawyer, who slogged eighteen-hour days for two decades, and when he did join us, he was preoccupied with whatever case was loading up his desk. Meanwhile, I juggled motherhood with writing novels and a weekly column about family life in a totally pretentious, obnoxious magazine that's now gone, deservedly, bust. I'm not proud. Working for that mag was my equivalent of a side-gig in porn. I started when I was young, I needed the money and I'll always feel like I need a shower when I think about it.

Anyway, eventually something had to give and for us it was the till death do us part stuff. If there was any silver lining, it was that Mark re-evaluated his priorities and his first gesture as a divorced dad was to take the boys off on their first ever solo holiday. To keep me from staring at the door for a month, waiting for my offspring to return, my pals surprised me with a trip to Los Angeles to stay with my old pal, Sam Morton. And by 'old pal', I mean someone I used to have sex with when we were engaged back in the nineties. In those days, he was a skint bouncer working on the door of a nightclub that I managed in Hong Kong. When I got cold feet and called time on the relationship, I had no idea that Sam's career path would go like this (I'm giving the abridged, pamphlet edition of the story here):

1. Twenty-five years ago, he was a bouncer in an exclusive nightclub while teaching martial arts during the day to kids and bored housewives. (That's where I left the picture.)
2. His job description then dramatically changed direction when a favour for one of those bored housewives graduated into a very lucrative career as a

full-time escort. My jaw still drops when I think about that bit.

3. He then wrote a book about his raunchy career, that I refused to read because I don't want to remember how sensational he was in bed. Especially with someone else.

4. That was picked up by one of his illustrious clients, who passed it on to a friend in LA.

5. A movie company bought the rights, and after a dedicated regime of acting training, Sam landed the lead role, playing himself.

6. That led to a blockbuster career as a leading man, when he ultimately became one of the top action stars on the planet.

7. His business brain then shifted him to a new role behind the camera.

8. Now, he's produced several of the biggest hits of the last five years and has a few more in the various stages of the production pipeline. Yet, somehow, he manages to still be the sweet, caring, libido-stirring, sexy guy that he was when we were first together.

Throughout all this, Sam and I maintained our friendship with regular calls and texts. When he was in London for work, he'd stay with us, and I even made a couple of trips to LA with the boys. Maybe that's why, by some fricking miracle, when my pals and I landed at his Pacific Palisades house after my divorce, he didn't see a knackered, jaded, cynical, defeated, comfort-eating, broken-hearted, very sweaty and sweary hot mess. Actually, he did see all that, which makes what happened next even more astounding. The bloke who played poker on a Thursday night with the kind of names that are on billboards at our local multiplex also saw someone he used to love, someone who'd been a friend for three decades, and the crazy guy fell in love with me all over again. I have absolutely no idea how that happened. None. It's like the stuff I write about in my romcoms. Actually, if I wrote that story, it would get rejected as being unrealistic. Especially when he followed up the love stuff with a proposal, and we ended up hitched and happier than I've ever been.

My boys grew up loving Sam as an uncle, and they were thrilled he was now their stepdad – largely, I suspect, because he would take them to events where they'd meet Ariana Grande and Zendaya. My sons have definitely dipped their toes in both sides of the gene pool. Up at the deep end, they got their father's sporting prowess, motivation and metabolism, before visiting me at the shallow end for some laughs, appreciation of Marvel movies, superficiality and a fondness for cake.

So all was well. Sam and I were married. We were a happy family of four. With Sam doing post-production of his latest movie at Pinewood Studios, we knew we'd have at least a year before we had to make the move to the USA. As these things do, it ran over schedule, and they decided to do a load of reshoots at Pinewood, which suffered from scheduling conflicts and delays and a lot of movie terminology things that I don't understand. All I can tell you is that Sam, the megastar producer, ended up spending almost two years in my semi-detached, slightly ramshackle house in Chiswick. He had the good grace not to mention that the whole property could fit in his ten-car garage back in sunny California.

I loved every laid-back, blissful minute of it. While Sam was at work, I wrote a novel based on my trip to the USA with my chums (available in all formats next year), took care of my boys and in every school break, we'd go over to Sam's house in LA and live his life for a week, or two, or six in the summer.

The deal had always been that we'd all move back to the USA when Sam's movie was done, but the fact that it overran came with pros and cons. The pro was that we got to spend more time living our lives in my home, my happy place, surrounded by everyone who was in the life that we'd built. The cons were that in summer the boys had to make decisions about what to do next. When Mac finished school in June, he had moved to a sport-specialist college, where he could pretty much play basketball all day, while playing with a semi-professional basketball team in London. He figured he'd play basketball for at least a year while he was working out what he wanted to do with his life. Now that I was going over to the USA, he was moving into his dad's swanky flat until the end of the season next spring, then he'd decide where his future lay. And Benny had started another term at his old school in September and was just six months off sitting his A-levels, so he'd also opted to stay with his dad until they were done. There was massive separation anxiety. All of it mine.

My ex was delighted that he was getting the opportunity to actually live with the boys again, especially as his messed-up work/life balance had made him fairly absent when we were all still together and living under the one roof. He saw it as a last chance to make amends and develop the kind of closeness that would be great for them all as the boys moved into their adult lives.

My current husband thought it was all going swimmingly too. Sam flew back over to California last week to sort out his house and catch up with some work stuff. He adored my boys, but he was excited to be finally living back in his home, and looking forward to spending some alone time with his wife and getting into the swing of our married future together.

My friends were all thrilled for us. They knew what a long road Sam and I had travelled to get to this point – almost thirty years of detours, wrong turns and a few crashes along the way – so they thought it was wonderful that I was getting another shot at love and adventure.

And, of course, Mac and Benny were happy about it too. It was a new adventure to them, a chance to spend time with their dad and to live in Mark's high-gloss, high-tech, very chic flat in the centre of London.

The thought brought me back full circle to our kitchen table, where I could see Benny was still digesting my comment about living in his dad's flat, with the boiling water tap and the yoga room.

'Tabitha works out in there at five o'clock every morning,' he informed us, with his usual matter-of-factness.

I bit back my first reaction, which was *'wow, what a motivated, disciplined, powerhouse of a woman she is.'* Under oath, I might have to admit that was actually my second reaction. The first being, *'wow, what a motivated, disciplined pain in the finely toned arse she is'.* Please don't judge me. I'm sure she's lovely on the inside. But when your husband rebounds from your admittedly amicable, mutually agreed divorce with an Alpha female who's brilliant, beautiful, twenty years younger, and who gets out of her bed at 5 a.m. without the aid of a crowbar and the aroma of bacon rolls, it's hard not to be cynical. Although, granted, I rebounded with Sam Morton. I think both Mark and I traded up.

I poured my twenty-third cup of coffee of the day, checked that none of the high carbohydrate snacks in the oven were on fire (nothing worse than a charred sausage roll) and slid onto the bench beside Benny.

'Okay, before I get pathetically clingy, tell me the ground rules again.'

Benny slung his arm around my shoulder. 'Mum, sorry if this is a newsflash, but you're already pathetically clingy,' he teased.

I dug him in the ribs, making him laugh again. God, those dimples. And the messy, wavy brown hair. And eyelashes that, since he was a toddler, have been so long and dark that they could have come straight from an advert for Max Factor mascara. And now, all of that was on a 6'2" tall swimmer's body that had shoulders the width of a sunlounger.

Across the table, an even more muscle-bound, broader version of his brother, Mac was nodding in agreement. The two of them worked out together most days and although their personalities couldn't be more different, in the last couple of years they'd managed to get over the usual brotherly squabbles and establish a new closeness as mates. They even occasionally backed each other up in arguments. Sometimes I missed the old days when they bickered from noon until night and once broke a mop and my good floor lamp in a lightsabre fight to the death.

I wasn't letting the 'clingy' comment slide.

'Eh, I prefer "hands-on and involved, with a slight hint of overbearing",' I countered, before putting them right back on the hook with, 'Okay, go. Tell me all the things that are going to make your beloved mother happy when she's thousands of miles away from you.'

They surrendered. Mac took a slug of some gunky protein shake thing, then kicked it off with...

'We have to text you before we go to sleep, to let you know we survived the day. We have to text you as soon as we wake up to let you know we survived the night. You want a minimum of one FaceTime call a day. If we have any problems, we've to call you at any time of the day or night, whether we think you can help or not.'

Benny took over. 'And if we turn off the "Find My Family" on our iPhones, you're calling the emergency services, Dad, all our aunts and you'll be on the next flight over to track us down.'

'That just about covers it,' I admitted sheepishly, aware that it was perhaps a tad on the dramatic side. They were grown men, seventeen and nineteen. But to me they were still my kids, and I reserved the right to overdramatise every situation. Case in point... I leaned forward, elbows on the table. 'Let's just do the quickfire round. Who do you call if you get arrested?'

Mac had that one covered.

'Dad first, because he's closest, and you second, because if we've messed up really badly Dad might disown us, and you'd be able to talk him round. And also, you want to know quickly so you'll have more time to plan out how you're going to kill us.'

'Give a coconut to the bloke with the muscly pecs,' I announced, glad they'd taken in that message.

'Alcohol?' I asked next.

'I can have a cider at the weekends, but only if Dad's around,' Benny said correctly.

'And I'm nineteen so I can get wellied off my tits and sleep in a gutter,' Mac grinned.

'Only if you don't want to see twenty,' I countered, worried that he was only half joking. The boy loved his sport, but he loved a social gathering and a bit of fearless adventure too. When they were kids, Benny would come home from school, eat some fruit, do his homework without prompting and then read a book until dinner was ready.

Mac would come in right behind him with six pals he'd invited for dinner, a ripped shirt because he'd been climbing trees, a Curly Wurly dangling from his mouth, bouncing two basketballs simultaneously and asking what was for tea.

'Okay, and what happens if you meet a girl you like...?' The very idea set off panic alarms in my soul. I didn't want anyone anywhere near their hearts. Or any other parts of them.

Mac went first this time. 'I have to introduce her to at least one of our aunts and one of our cousins to make sure our attraction to her isn't blocking out red flags.'

I nodded. 'Excellent. And finally, if things progress in the relationship and you both consent to intimacy, you have to use condoms and wear two layers of bubble wrap pants because I don't want to be a grandmother yet.'

Mac put his head on the table and groaned.

Benny wasn't letting that go either. 'Ah, Mum, how sensible were you when you were our age?'

I cleared my throat. 'Extremely,' I said, brazening it out.

The two of them howled with hilarity. That was the thing about still having the same friends that I'd had since I was a teenager – nothing was sacred. The boys had heard all the stories of our teenage antics: the relationship disasters, the sneaking into bars and clubs, running off to Amsterdam when I was the same age as Benny is now, not to mention six broken engagements to other men before I finally got married to their father. It's a long story. I had commitment issues before they'd even been invented. The thought made me shudder. Thank God we didn't have social media and mobile phones back then, and we could make our endless mistakes in private.

The back door opened, and Kate staggered in, hair flying behind her. 'Bloody hell, it's gusting a gale out there. I think my hair extensions just got blown on to the whirligig.'

Kate Smith. Another one of my closest friends since we started school in a little town on the outskirts of Glasgow. There had been five of us back then and we'd stuck together through primary school and high school, before life took us all in different directions for a few years. Jess went off to uni in St Andrews, Sarah moved to Edinburgh and got tangled up in a horrendous marriage, Carol sashayed down to London to pursue her modelling dreams and Kate ended up here too, working as a junior hairdresser in a trendy salon. Jess and I migrated south a few years later, and Sarah came back into our lives when she escaped from her husband. We all stuck together again, through marriages, children, divorces, celebrations, dramas and disasters. Until...

I swallowed again. It still ached to think about it. Until we lost Sarah, and her husband Nick, in a plane crash a few years ago. We'd miss them until the end of time. We also knew, though, that Sarah would want us to move on and to suck every possible moment of joy from life, so although the pain of missing her never left us, that's what we did.

'Aunt Kate, Mum's trying to tell us she was angelic when she was our age,' Mac grassed me up.

Kate plonked the huge baking tray she was carrying on the worktop and then turned, eyebrows raised. 'Sounds about right. She was the Patron Saint of Oh Dear God What's She Done Now?'

That set the boys off again. Like I said, having lifelong pals had its drawbacks.

Thankfully, my attention was swiftly diverted, as I peered over to see the contents of Kate's tray. Mini banoffee cheesecakes and tiny apple pies. 'I was about to refute your slanderous claims, but when you come bearing gifts like that, you're forgiven,' I told her, as she grabbed a glass from a kitchen cabinet, a bottle of wine from the fridge and joined us at the table. None of us stood on ceremony in each other's homes. We'd been mates for way too long for that, and with the waterproof shelter that Kate's husband, Bruce, had knocked up to join our back doors, it was basically like communal living.

'How are you doing?' she asked me warily, knowing that the question could set me off on the emotional equivalent of those huge bumpy slides you get at water parks that leave you breathless, a bit bruised and tugging out a wedgie.

'Like I'm about to leave my home, my family, everyone I love and move to the other side of an ocean,' I replied dolefully, red heat rising up my neck at the very thought of it.

'Oh, you poor thing,' Kate said, oozing compassion. I was almost taken in by her sympathy until she added, 'It's going to be awful for you. Maybe you can take your mind off the hardship by doing ten laps of the pool in your back garden, then pulling on some Gucci and doing a trolley dash down Rodeo Drive with Gwyneth Paltrow.'

My new life was every bit as ridiculous to my pals as it was to me. Good to see they were intent on keeping me grounded. Her dismissive chuckle reinforced the point though. Every single person in my life was happy about my move to Los Angeles. Everyone.

Right now, more of my friends and my extended family were on the way over for a goodbye gathering. My boys were packed and ready to go. My new husband was counting the hours until I joined him. I would be leaving here in... I checked my watch... Twenty-four hours, thirty minutes and twenty-seven seconds.

There was just one slight problem, one that I hadn't admitted to anyone.

Not to sound ungrateful, because I was very aware that this was the kind of life many people dreamt of having.

But I didn't want to go.

3

CAROL COOPER

Pretty Hurts – Beyonce

Callum's voice bellowed upstairs. 'Carol! Are you ready to go, babe?'

'Give me ten minutes,' I replied, as I pulled my straighteners through another sheath of my long platinum hair. All those magazines that say hair should be cut to a more appropriate level when a woman reaches middle age could kiss mine and Gwen Stefani's tight fifty-something buttocks.

I knew that right now Callum would be rolling his eyes and my girls would be muttering something about spending their whole lives waiting for me. If only. There was no point reminding them that I'd spent every single day of their lives waiting for them to get up in the morning, waiting for them to eat their breakfast, to get ready for school, to get out of school, to eat their dinner, to...

I stopped myself. I was doing it again. Losing myself down a dark spiral of negative thoughts. I wasn't sure when that started, but it was all too frequent now, every day, more than once. The irony was that not a single person had noticed. How could they? On the face of it, my life was perfect. Peachy. Couldn't be better. I'd been married for over twenty-five years to the love of my life. We had two wonderful girls. We had enough money to have a comfortable life. And I had a gazillion internet followers who trusted my opinions, despite the fact that I could barely trust myself to remember my Instagram password. And yet... I'd never felt more miserable. Or sadder. Or like I wanted to crawl under a bush and hide.

What the hell was wrong with me? Why didn't I wake up every morning with a warm fuzzy feeling of contentment?

'Mum, come on!' Charlotte's echoes of her dad's sentiments bellowed upstairs. She'd always been the more impatient of my twins. Charlotte and Toni were twenty now, beautiful, smart, about to leave home and... was it okay to admit this? I was dreading them leaving, but at the same time I felt the time was right for them to go. Not that I didn't love them, because I adored them both, even when one was screaming at me to hurry up.

By the time I was their age, I'd been living in London on my own for two years, learning about life, working my arse off in a bar while going to every modelling go-see I could find, getting rejected, sometimes getting lucky, but I was figuring stuff out and learning about myself. Back in the day, Carly, Kate, Jess, Sarah and I had no cushions. Nothing to fall back on except friendship and hope. That kind of risk built the strength and smarts that you needed to survive the crap that life throws at you later. So, much as I knew that giving the girls independence was the right thing to do – God, this was so hard to admit to myself – I envied them living the young, free, optimistic life that we used to have.

I felt my chest start to tighten again and took a deep breath. Maybe I was just feeling especially low today because Carly was leaving. I'd never say anything because I loved my sister-in-law too, but I was more than a little jealous. Her husband, Sam, is such a good guy, and he comes with a package that's pretty freaking incredible. A stunning home in Los Angeles. An interesting job. A star-studded social life. Carly was going to have everything and anything she could ever want, and she'd never have to worry about anything else again. I was thrilled for her, I really was. She's grafted all these years, pretty much bringing the kids up on her own, working long hours, looking out for everyone else. She deserved this. There was just a part of me –I couldn't believe I was admitting this even to myself – that wished I was going on that flight to a new life. And there was another part of me that didn't know what I was going to do without her here.

'Carol!' Callum again. Agitated. He hated being late. Which was ironic, given that Carly is his sister and she's late for everything.

'I'm just coming, darling,' I bellowed back. Darling. Saying that was just a habit now. Like everything else in my life. Gah, I knew I was being pathetic, but it was just... where's the joy? Every day, I went through the motions, thinking 'Is this it?' Callum Cooper used to set my knickers on fire with just a smouldering glance and I used to feel that I was the most desirable woman in the world to him. Now he crashed out in front of *Wheeler Dealers* every night and I got every shred of excitement from watching the latest episode of *Real Housewives of Beverly Hills*. Or New Jersey. Or Atlanta. Or any group of women whose dramas could provide some mindless escapism.

Our sex life was down to once a fortnight, and even then, it was over in ten minutes and the heart monitor on my Fitbit barely raised a beat. It was all just so... bland and punctuation. No, that's the wrong word – I meant perfunctory. Fuck, my brain was in some kind of fog and it was like I had to work twice as hard to make it fraction. I mean, function.

I flicked off the straighteners. They were from a brand that I endorse, and a shiny new set arrived every couple of months, along with whatever hair products they're adding to their range. I used to model for them in my heyday – endless hours of back-breaking work. There was the irony. Now I got paid more for a few internet posts than for a whole week of standing in sub-zero temperatures in a bikini filming a summer hair campaign. The world was going mad. And I was pretty sure I was too.

As I stood up, I felt my legs shaking a little. It was the anxiety. I'd read up on it online when it first started happening. The hair loss. The dark thoughts. The confusion. The feeling that my ribcage is too small for my lungs to breathe. It was like my body and my mind weren't my own any more. On the inside, I'd turned into a person I didn't recognise. In our group, I'd always been the most laid-back. The one who refused to get flustered. But this anxiety had come out of nowhere and I had no idea why it had arrived or when it would leave. Maybe it was some sort of midlife crisis? Worry that I was running out of time, nearer the finish line than the start?

A last glimpse in the mirror. I could see the years. I wondered every day how long it would be until the work dried up and the industry decided I was past my sell-by date. Tick. Tock. Right now, the lighting in this studio room was doing me a favour – it had been an investment, as it was where I filmed all my vlogs and promos – so, as always, I took a quick pic and loaded it up to my Insta, along with hashtags highlighting all the products I'd used on my look today. #bobbybrown #revlon #browpower #liplove #hairbyflatiron #palmerscoconutoil

The sweet comments started coming in immediately. Once upon a time that would have thrilled me. Now I felt… numb. Which wasn't a bad thing, because at least I didn't let the trolls bother me any more either. Last week, someone informed me that it was time I started advertising Tena lady and day-care centres. I didn't even bother deleting it. What was the point?

'Mum!' Charlotte again. She was clearly in some kind of Time-Police Tag Team with her dad.

Okay, here goes. Smile. Make it reach the eyes. Deep breath. Steady. You've got this.

'I'm coming, honey,' I chirped back. Even my cheery responses were fake. Just like everything else in my life.

I pulled a cream-coloured shawl over my white T-shirt and ripped blue jeans. Tossed my hair back. Grabbed my bag and slung it across my shoulder, then skipped down the stairs.

Toni was lying on the ivory sofa, typing something in her phone. Charlotte and Callum were at the dining table, but got up as soon as they saw me.

'Sorry!' I said with the appropriate apologetic grin. I had that down to perfection now too. 'Takes me longer every day to get this face.'

Charlotte rolled her eyes, while Toni led with kindness. She's learned a lot over the last couple of years, since the dickhead she was dating tried to ruin her life with some revenge pics. Her Aunt Carly put an end to that situation with an eye-watering threat of ball grating. Now Toni was in the family business and had turned the cyber nightmare into a successful career as a blogger and podcaster. She was a measured voice of support on the kind of subjects that her generation have to deal with: things like revenge porn, social media pressure, mental health, sexism and bullying. I couldn't be prouder of her. She was a badass, strong, independent woman – and she had more substance to her than I've ever had.

'Don't worry about it, Mum. I don't think they will have noticed we're late. Benny just texted and said Aunt Carly is having a freakout about leaving and she's told them three times that they can't ever leave home without a condom. He's mortified.'

For the first time today, I laughed.

Callum was grinning too as he reached for my hand. 'Gotta love my sister. Always the calm, sensible paragon of reason.'

He was teasing. Callum and his sister were as close as any

siblings could be, and they genuinely liked each other too. They had that weird thing going where they always knew what the other one was thinking and feeling. Callum and I used to have that too…

The thought must have cast a shadow on my face, because a flicker of concern crossed his brow. 'You okay, babe?' he asked, throwing his arm around my shoulder and giving me a hug.

Why did such a simple act of sweetness to me make me want to cry with relief and rage on the inside all at the same time? I adored my husband. He loved me. Yet sometimes, these days, all he had to do was walk in a room to irritate me. Why? Where were these feelings coming from? He didn't deserve any of this. Maybe that was why I couldn't tell him: 'Hey, husband, don't want to worry you, but sometimes when I'm with you, I just feel numb. Dead inside. I don't even love myself any more, so how can I possibly love you?'

'Of course,' I wittered, hoping he'd buy it.

He did. There was no doubt he would. He had absolutely no reason to think that I was anything other than okay.

'I love you, gorgeous,' he whispered, making Charlotte roll her eyes. For years, she'd been thoroughly disdainful of our tactile affection. Problem was, on the inside that's how I felt now too.

'I love you back,' I murmured into his chest. *Come on Carol, get it together. Do not show how you're feeling.*

I'd thought about sharing everything with him, but something stopped me. Probably the same thing that stopped me telling my girlfriends. I was… I could hardly even bear to say it to myself. I was terrified that I was going mad. That something was wrong with me. That it could be something really bad and my life was going to change for ever. The logical part of my brain told me that everyone would support me and they'd help me put myself back together, but I couldn't do it. Not while I could still hide how I was feeling by slapping on a smile and going through the motions. I was Carol Cooper. Perfect family. Perfect life. And today, and every day, had to be business as usual, because I was scared beyond words that if I admitted how I felt, my perfect life would crumble to dust.

I had this. Let's go.

I pulled my phone out and everyone automatically went into their roles. I flicked a few buttons, then pressed record on Instagram Live. Beaming smile. Come on.

'Hi everyone! Carol here and I just wanted to check in on you guys. Hope you're all having a great day and, remember, make some time today for a bit of self-care and do something you love. I'm sending a virtual hug to you all from the Coopers.' I panned the camera around and Callum waved, then the girls did the same. They didn't love this, but it was how I'd made my living since they were kids, so they knew the deal. It was normal. Business as usual, selling the dream.

Back to me. 'And remember, tune into my YouTube channel tonight, for the latest episode of my Christmas pressie early-buying specials. It's Gifts for Granny tonight, so don't miss it. Take care, love you all, and happy weekend!'

With another wave, I stopped the recording, checked that it had uploaded correctly and then slipped my phone in my pocket. Job done. I'd pushed my brand out there for another day – a brand that portrayed me as the happiest person, with the perfect husband, perfect kids, perfect everything.

Those 1.2 million followers had no idea that on the inside all I felt was imperfectly broken.

4

CARLY

Family Affair – Mary J Blige

I was on my second of Kate's little banoffee tarts when the back door opened again and in trotted the rest of her family: her husband, Bruce, their daughters, Tallulah and Zoe and their son, Cameron. We'd always been a gang of pals who'd formed our very own framily (apologies for the psychobabble terminology, but the trendy word for friends who lived like a family suited us perfectly). Now, our communal approach to life had an extra bonus, because we could watch how that had filtered down to the next generation. Between me, Carol, Kate, Jess and Sarah, we had ten kids who were all in their late teens and twenties now, and they were all like one big, crazy bunch of bickering, loving, hilarious, decent people who genuinely adored each other, when they weren't fighting over what to watch on Netflix or whose turn it was to buy a round at the pub. Benny was the youngest, and the girls all had a soft spot for him, demonstrated now by Tallulah, who was standing behind him with her arms around his neck. With her long brown waves pulled up into a messy ponytail, and her off-the-shoulder pink sweater and retro Reeboks, she looked identical to Kate circa 1988.

'Aunt Carly, why are you forcing them to go stay with Uncle Mark when they could just stay here and we'd look out for them.'

I raised my overworked right eyebrow of cynicism. 'Because the last time we left you lot together you had a party where someone spilled Blue WKD on my cream shagpile rug, two phone chargers went walkies, my drinks cabinet got emptied and someone ordered a hundred quid's worth of food from Just Eat on my credit card.'

'Ouch,' Mac gasped, buckling over. It didn't take a genius to work out that Benny had kicked him under the table for ordering all that food. This was why I wasn't leaving my boys without a parent in close proximity.

'But that isn't going to happen this time, is it, Tallulah?' I asked, the eyebrow up again.

Her sister Zoe answered for her. 'Nope, not a chance, Aunt Carly. I promise we'll take really good care of everything.'

At twenty-four, Zoe was the youngest of Kate's children, but like Benny, she was the most sensible. That's probably why I'd offered to let her house-sit for me while I was away. She was a nurse on the neonatal ward at Great Ormond Street and London rents were impossibly high so she couldn't afford her own place. Our arrangement suited us both: I wanted to have someone in the house, and Zoe wanted some rent-free independence. Although, when she first floated the idea, there had been a convenient omission that Zoe came in a package deal with her sister, Tallulah, and my twenty-year-old nieces, Toni and Charlotte. Sarah's daughter, Hannah, was going to be over in the UK for a few weeks doing some work for the restaurant chain founded by her late dad, Nick Russo, so she would be bunking here too.

The girls had been talking about living together for years, so they were all ecstatic about finally getting the chance to do it – and even better that it didn't come with pesky things like bills taking a chunk out of the food and wine budget. However, I was now torn between going to the USA to be with the love of my life, and staying here, hanging with the young ones and reliving those brilliant times in my twenties when all that mattered was going out, falling in love, being with my pals and having nothing but wine in the fridge. This felt like history repeating itself, and that gave me a warm and bubbly glow. Or maybe that was the heat from the... Shit, the sausage rolls!

I flew out of my chair and pulled the charred remains from the depths of the abyss, then dropped the tray on the draining board, just as, in perfect timing, the fire alarm began to wail. After a good few minutes of waving the kitchen towel at it, it finally stopped.

'Aw, I'll miss that sound coming through the wall,' Kate said wistfully.

'Me too. We're going to have to develop an appetite for food that doesn't taste of charcoal,' Mac sighed.

'Exactly,' Benny added. 'I mean, how are we supposed to do that at our age? It's too late to change our ways. We'll starve.'

I ignored their cheek, distracted by the back door opening again. This kitchen was about to be standing room only, and that was just the way I liked it. God, I'd miss this. My pal, Carol, was the first to make an entrance, followed by her husband, who also happened to be my lovely brother, Callum, and my nieces, Charlotte and Toni. Individually, they were pretty spectacular. Carol and Callum had been models in their twenties and thirties, and Callum still made his living as the ultimate middle-aged mannequin. If you flicked through a magazine or a website and there were adverts for country living, knitwear, beer, gin, whisky, underwear, or visiting Scotland, with a grey-haired, square-jawed hunk of male gorgeousness in it, chances were that was my brother.

He got every physical attribute my parents possessed and many that they didn't. Thankfully, I'm not bitter, because I love him to bits. Okay, I'm a little bit bitter about the fact that he got a super-fast metabolism, but I'm only human. While Callum still makes his living in front of the camera, Carol diversified and became a social media influencer right at the start of the trend. Apparently, she's got 1.2 million followers on Instagram who hang on her every word and cheesy endorsement. Which is unbelievable, as we haven't followed her advice since she got us all arrested in the great underage drinking heist of 1986. It's a long story. All I'll say is that for the sake of our blood pressure, I really hope that Charlotte and Toni's apples of common sense fall pretty far from their mother's tree.

Mac and Benny got up to hug everyone, then emitted some kind of psychic signal that could only be received by people who haven't turned thirty yet, and all the offspring trotted out to the firepit in the gazebo in the back garden. It was our favourite part of our home. No matter what the weather was like, out we were, wrapped in blankets, firepit blazing, pizzas cooking in the pizza oven that Sam and the boys had built from a DIY video on YouTube. It also came with the added bonus that there was no smoke alarm in the gazebo, so when I inevitably burnt the pizzas (I preferred to call it 'thoroughly cooked'), our ears avoided the trauma.

'Dear God, what is that?' Carol asked, transfixed on the sausage rolls. Before I answered, she whipped out her phone and I knew that, within seconds, she'd have up some witty post about her sister-in-law's cooking, along with a contest to identify the remains. Her 1.2 million followers would then feed on the frenzy, and the funniest answer would win whatever product she was endorsing this week. My heroine, Nora Ephron, used to say everything was copy. For Carol, everything was a chance for her to earn a hand-some pay cheque and a year's supply of detoxifying foot pads. Or a free trip to the Seychelles. Or the kind of jewellery that doesn't go green when you wear it in the bath.

Her phone started to ping like crazy, so she switched it to silent and shoved it in her Gucci backpack. The thing was, it would be easy to be jealous of her too, but Carol Ann Bernadette Sweeney (her mother still gave her the full maiden name when she was irate) was the most down-to-earth, generous, lovely person underneath that fine layer of designer clothes and jewellery. She also adored my brother, their children and her pals, and she'd be happy on a desert island as long as she had the people she loved with her. And maybe Wi-Fi and her Clarins Flash Balm.

Callum joined Bruce over in the corner of the kitchen where the beer fridge lived, while Carol grabbed a glass and joined Kate at the table, watching as I scooped forty-eight crispy sausage rolls into the bin.

'Are you sure you're okay with letting all the girls live here while you're away?' Carol asked, and I could hear there was a slight tightness in her voice.

'Oh no. Are you getting separation anxiety too?' Kate asked knowingly, with a side glance at me.

'Nope, it's just Charlotte is flat out denying that she's dating a lawyer in the company she interned for last year, which means she definitely is,' Carol countered, taking a handful of salt and vinegar twirls from the bowl in the middle of the kitchen table and popping one in her mouth. 'I goggle-stalked him and he's thirty-nine. She's twenty. What's a thirty-nine-year-old guy doing going out with a girl who thinks Britney Spears is ancient?'

'Have any of the others confirmed or denied this?' I asked, my glance going from Kate to Carol and back again.

Kate shook her head. 'First I've heard of it. But I promise, if Tallulah or Zoe get wind of it, they'll make sure she's okay. The best thing that could happen is for them all to live together. If Charlotte won't take relationship advice from any of us...'

'Because we're even more ancient than Britney...' I interjected.

Kate went on, '... She'll confide in the girls and they'll steer her in the right direction and help her figure it out.'

Carol's shoulders rose a little as she thought that through and realised that Kate was right. The older ones in our collective brood always looked out for the younger ones. And no matter what mistakes any of them made, the others would pitch in to put the pieces back together. A couple of years before, when Toni had her private moments splashed over social media by a vengeful ex, my boys and Kate's brood all took turns in hanging out with her, holding her chin up, making her feel good about herself again. Now she was a force of nature and she'd turned the whole situation round to her advantage. We've always told them that climbing back up is easier if you've got a pal with a ladder.

'I'll keep an eye too,' Kate promised. 'If I see anyone fitting the description coming in here, I'll get my catapult out.'

I took my oven gloves off and gave up trying to add anything edible to the gathering. Instead, I plucked another banoffee cheese-cake from Kate's tray, a can of gin and tonic from the fridge, and a glass from the cupboard and joined them at the table, sliding in beside Kate.

There were three empty chairs and every time I thought about that, I had to swallow a lump in my throat. We'd all sat in the same seats in each other's houses since the beginning of time. Force of habit. In my kitchen, I always sat next to Kate, and across from Carol. If Jess were here, she'd be sitting across from Kate and Sarah... I swallowed again. Before we lost her, our friend, Sarah, used to sit at one end of the table, opposite my ex-husband, Mark's usual seat at the other end. Neither Sarah nor Mark had sat in those chairs for a long time.

Carol took a sip of her wine. 'Thanks, Kate.' Another sip. Weird. She still seemed tense. Carol was normally the most chilled of us all. I was about to probe a bit more, when she cut me off with, 'Anyone heard from Jess? I was on FaceTime with her last week. She was positively giddy with happiness. And she never does giddy. She only does sharp and brutal.'

'Yeah, I think maybe she's on drugs,' Kate piped in. 'Or Arnie has some kind of magical powers. She grinned for a whole hour the other day on a Zoom call. I'm starting to think she's possessed. She's going up to Napa this weekend to start making arrangements for her wedding. When are you seeing her, Carly?'

Jess was the fourth friend in our little quartet. She'd stayed in LA throughout the quarantine with her bloke, Arnie – who was also Sam's best mate. They were the other couple to come out of that trip to California a couple of years ago and they were still going strong. She was my only hope for salvation, my only pal over there, but she travelled so much with work that I knew she couldn't fill the hole left by losing my whole wide world here.

It wasn't that I was making rash judgements or jumping to unreasonable conclusions about life in LA. I'd spent a fair amount of time there and I knew, without a shadow of a doubt, that it wasn't for me. I didn't do fitness. I didn't want to get up at 5 a.m. to do a morning meditation. Everyone we met there was 'in the business' and I had zero in common with them. And much as I utterly adored my husband, he worked long hours and rattling about in a big house behind humungous gates just wasn't for me. I loved familiarity. I loved hugging my boys at night and going to their sports events at weekends to cheer them on, even if they pretended they didn't know me when I suggested, with volume, that the referee nip out for an eye test. I needed to see their sleepy faces in the mornings and hear all the gossip they chose to tell me about the night before. I liked walking to the corner shop for a bottle of tonic to top up my gin. I wanted my Friday night takeaway and my Saturday morning coffee with Kate and Carol. I wanted the laughs that I had now when I caught up with my pals every couple of days for a gab. Mark had been so absent in our day-to-day existence, that I'd built a life apart from him that I truly loved and, selfish as it sounded, I wanted Sam, but I didn't want everything else to change. Perhaps in my twenties, or even thirties, I'd have been up for a brand new adventure and starting over, making all new friends and building a different world, but I didn't want to live in an ageist, body-conscious, frequently fake, ruthlessly ambitious society drinking green juice and sitting on my own in Coffee Bean playing spot the facelift.

When it was far in the distance, and just a vague plan that Sam and I discussed, I went for denial and optimism. Now that it was here, though, it filled every pore of my body with dread.

Bugger, I'd drifted off on a mental tangent again. Snapping back to real life in the hotbed of excitement that was my kitchen, I realised the others were waiting for an answer about Jess.

'I'm going to meet up with her next week,' I told them. 'Unless Sam has any plans for us to do something else. You know, this will be the first time we've been alone since we got married.'

'Cheers to that,' Kate chirped, raising a banoffee cheesecake toast, that Carol met with her wine glass.

I reluctantly joined in. They clearly didn't sense that anything was amiss. And okay, it didn't help that I hadn't said anything. I've no idea why. We usually shared our deepest darkest feelings like they were breezy incidentals. Nothing was off the table and there was no judgement. I should just blurt it out, tell them that I felt like a crap mother for leaving my boys. That I didn't want to live thousands of miles away from my pals. That I loved Sam, but I didn't want that life. I wanted my life here, but with him in it. I wanted everything to stay exactly the way it had been since our wedding. Just us. Me. Sam. My boys. Living here. In our little bubble.

Now or never. I took a breath. Made the decision.

'Listen,' I began, interrupting Kate, who was wondering out loud whether there was anything in the freezer that we could rustle up to replace the sausage rolls. 'I need to tell you something.'

'Oh, crap,' Carol eyed me warily. 'You're chewing your bottom lip. That's always the calm before the hurricane.'

My sister-in-law had displayed a lifelong affliction when it came to accuracy in metaphors. A bird in the hand had always been a sure sign that there were too many cooks in the kitchen.

'The thing is...' I paused.

Say it. Come on. Say it. I. Don't. Want. To. Go.

'The thing is, I. Don't. W—'

I didn't get the rest out, because that's when the back door flew open and in came the surprise arrival of the day.

One who would change everything.

5

VAL

Miranda Lambert – Smokin' and Drinkin'

'Did someone order an aunt?' I asked, throwing my arms wide open. I thought jazz hands might be a bit too much, but, sod it, I threw them in anyway. Might have been a mistake. That, combined with a push-up bra that had no business being on my bosoms (I bought it from a catalogue and ran out of time to send it back, so I'd decided to get my money's worth despite the fact that it gave me boobs like rugby balls), threw my centre of gravity off and I came close to toppling forward and face-planting in Carly's kitchen.

Thankfully, Carly prevented that happening because I'd barely got my cream suede Biba boots over the door (vintage – I'd bought them in 1979, they were back in fashion and thankfully – unlike the rest of me – my feet hadn't got any bigger over the years) when she jumped up and threw her arms around me.

'Auntie Val!' she screeched, causing temporary deafness in one ear. Over her shoulder, I could see Carol and Kate sitting at the kitchen table and I had a pang of longing. What was it with us and kitchen tables? Over the years, I'd discussed every happy thing, sad thing, heartbreak and crisis at the battered old mahogany table in my kitchen. And it had seen far too many of the heartbreaks and crises in recent months.

Carly eventually released me from her squeeze. 'Why didn't you tell me you were coming? I'd have picked you up at the airport.'

This wasn't the time for honesty. The truth was that I didn't tell her, because right up until the very last minute, I wasn't sure I'd be able to leave. I didn't know that I could go through with it. Until the plane actually pushed off from the gate at Glasgow airport, there was a possibility that I'd unclip my seatbelt and beg to get off. But then I thought about what this trip meant, and as my dear departed pal, Josie, would no doubt have suggested, I pulled up my big-woman pants and managed to make it here. I was so glad that I had. If anything was going to stick some of the cracks in my heart back together again, it was these three women and all their extended families – and the favour that I was here to ask of one of them.

'Och, love, I'm perfectly capable of getting here by myself from the airport,' I brushed off the question, an avoidance tactic that was helped by Carol and Kate taking their turns to hug me too. I was here. I'd done it.

Now breathe, Val, I told myself, *and slap a smile on yer face.*

'Right, before we get started, let's take care of the important stuff.' I opened up the huge bag that was over my shoulder and began to remove the contents. 'Here you go...' I began, slapping down a block of Lorne sausage (a Scottish breakfast treat that was, in essence, flat, square sausage meat), followed by a packet of Morton's rolls, two packets of tattie scones and a box of home-made tablet. It was my granny's recipe and contained so much sugar that social services would be at the door if I fed it to a child these days. These women might be Londoners now, but they were born and bred in Glasgow in the seventies and eighties, a place and time when square sausage and high-sugar snacks were in the DNA.

Carly groaned. 'Ah crap, I just gained three pounds looking at that.'

Bag empty, I plonked myself down on the empty chair next to Kate, feeling the tension of the last few hours, days, weeks, months rise into my pores then slowly dissipate, like a pressure cooker with a loose valve. Just a little bit at a time, and, oh, it felt so good.

'Did you two know about this?' Carly asked Kate and Carol.

'No, I swear!' Carol rightly protested her innocence.

Kate's face was blank too.

'I didn't tell anyone,' I assured her as I lifted the stem of the wine glass that had materialised in front of me, and a little more of that pressure fizzled away at the sight of the bubbles popping in the glass.

On the plane down here, I'd prepared an explanation that I thought would get me through this, and I'd rehearsed it in my head a dozen times, in between nudging the snoring bloke next to me off my shoulder and defending my pretzels from the woman on the other side.

I made a start on assuaging Carly's curiosity. 'I didn't say anything to you because I know that you've got enough to think about, and it was by no means certain that I'd get here. I hope you don't mind me landing on you like this?'

'Mind? Aunt Val, I'm thrilled. Honestly, I can't believe you came all this way just to say goodbye.'

I swiftly lifted my glass. Those pressure bubbles were building up again. Time to say something. Get it out there. Rip the plaster off.

'That's the thing, ma love,' I began. 'I didn't come to say goodbye. I came because I've got a huge, bloody great favour to ask you. You see...'

I paused, took a slug of wine.

'I'm hoping you'll take me with you.'

6

CARLY

Pick Me Up – Gaby Barrett

Kate reached over and lifted my chin back up. Did I hear that correctly? 'You want to come with me? To America? For a holiday? Or have... have you left Uncle Don?'

Even as I was saying it, I knew the latter couldn't be true. Val and my Uncle Don, who was my late dad's brother, had been married for a lifetime and although they were two very different people – he was a typically strong, kind, West Of Scotland man who kept his emotions to himself, while she was a loud, raucous woman who loved fiercely and wore her heart on her sleeve – they adored each other and they'd weathered every storm life had thrown at them.

'Eh, naw, love – some of us got the memo about sticking with the happily ever after stuff,' Val retorted with a cheeky glint in her eye, her rock-hard platinum bob twitching as she shook her head.

'So it's just... a holiday?' I asked, still trying to grasp what was happening here. I knew Auntie Val. Her pre-holiday regime consisted of six weeks of preparation, fourteen new pairs of shoes and a fake tan the colour of her garden hut. This seemed so much more spontaneous.

With another shake of the blonde bob, she began to explain.

'Not quite. You see, our Michael is over from Australia for a few weeks, and he's taken his dad off for a blokes' trip. They've always wanted to trace my Don's family roots up north, so that's what they're doing. It got me thinking that this would be the perfect time for...' Her words trailed off as she delved into her white tasselled handbag and emerged with a folded piece of A4 paper, which she unfurled and turned around so that we could see it. '... For this.'

I didn't have my specs on, so I had to squint to read the elaborate, old-school print. It wasn't Val's writing. I would have recognised that after a lifetime of birthday and Christmas cards. That's when I saw the title.

JOSIE AND VAL'S USA BUCKET LIST

Underneath was a scrawled:

And feck anyone who says we shouldn't do it

Kate, and Carol and I all came to the same conclusion at exactly the same moment. That turn of phrase threw up a flashback to a million laughs, a thousand hilarious conversations, a dozen adventures and one dearly missed woman. My Aunt Val's best pal, Josie. She'd passed away a few years before. The light in Val's life had dimmed that day and I wasn't sure it would ever burn as brightly again.

A warm flash of nostalgia made me laugh. 'Josie?'

'God, I loved that woman,' Kate murmured. 'Even if she was mildly terrifying when provoked.'

Carol nodded in agreement. 'Remember that time you two came down for the weekend to see *Les Mis* and she roasted the politician she bumped into in the bar of the St Ermin's Hotel?'

We all smiled at the memory. Val and Josie had come down from Glasgow for a theatre break and we'd joined them and hit the sights. We'd stopped for a drink in the bar of the St Ermin's Hotel, and there was the member of Parliament for Josie's Glasgow constituency, in a very obviously flirtatious, handholding moment with a young woman sporting bright red lipstick on lips that had been filled to the rough size of a sink plunger. Before we could stop her, Josie was off, a septuagenarian with her spiky grey, punk era hair, dressed all in black, like a retired ninja warrior, sticking her finger in his chest as she berated him for a list of failings that went on for a good ten minutes. The closure of the recreation centre for the elderly. The reduction of resources for the homeless. The rise in council tax. The bin collection being reduced from weekly to two-weekly. The mandatory cost for a new wheelie bin. The increase of the price of vodka in the last budget. In fairness, that probably wasn't his fault, but he was accused of not using his political sway on the Chancellor.

On and on it went, while the rest of us clutched our shopping bags and kept a lookout for approaching security. Eventually, drawing a deep, ominous breath, she ended with, 'So consider yerself on notice, son. Instead of galivanting down here thinking yer something special, get back up the road and start doing the things we pay you for.' We exhaled, as she began to walk away, then cut short the relief when she stopped, turned. 'Oh and, son, she's not with you for yer looks or yer personality, so unless yer willy is as big as yer ego, I'd question whit she sees in an arse like you. Apart from yer wallet, that is.'

With that, she strutted back over to us, leaving the politician looking decidedly Les Mis, picked up her Jack Daniel's and Coke, and chirped, 'Right, ladies, how about a wee afternoon tea? I could murder a scone.'

If you'd asked any of us, we'd have said that Josie was indestructible, so we were heartbroken when we discovered that she wasn't. She and Val had been inseparable until lung cancer became the only fight Josie ever lost.

'Aye, he slashed the price of a wheelie bin a month later,' Val said, a couple of tear droplets appearing on her bottom lids. She took a deep breath.

'The thing is, me and Josie had plans. It all started when we watched that *Thelma and Louise*. Or was it when we watched *Sleepless In Seattle* for the seventy-fifth time? Anyway, we decided we were going to go to America and we had a whole list of things we planned to do, but that bastard disease took her before we got there. We'd been putting fifty quid a month away for years, and that money is just lying in the bank. Josie would hate that.' As she paused to blink back the little pools of tears, my heart ached for her. I knew how it felt to lose a best friend. And Josie, well, we'd all adored her. She was the kind of huge, hilarious personality that left a chain-smoking, raucously-laughing, life-loving crater in Val's world. She took a sip of wine, then carried on. 'She'd talk all the time about how we deserved a bit of fun after all those years of grafting. I know if she's looking down on me that she's mighty unimpressed that I haven't followed through on the dreams. I feel like I'm letting her down, so I'm thinking... now's the time. I want to honour my pal by going on the trip and ticking off everything on the list. For Josie, and for me, too. I know I could do it myself, but you heading over there this week, at the same time Michael arrived to keep Don company, well, it just seemed like Josie was lining up the ducks for us. I know you were planning a bit of alone time with

Sam, but I was wondering if I could steal you for a couple of weeks first. But, ma love, I won't be offended if it doesn't suit you. I'll steam ahead on my own and get as many things done as I can because, one way or another, Josie will be with me. And, let's face it, without her actual presence, there's less chance of us starting a riot or getting arrested.'

'I'll come with you!' The outburst was so sudden and loud, I had to check for a moment that it hadn't come straight from my gob. But no. The fact that Kate and Val's heads swivelled to face my sister-in-law identified the source.

'Are you sure, Carol? What about your work? Not that I understand any of that internet nonsense. I only use my iPad for watching *Call The Midwife* if Don's got the football on.'

Carol shrugged, and it was odd, but I could swear her eyes suddenly seemed brighter than they'd been five minutes ago. 'It's no problem. I can work from anywhere, Aunt Val. I'll just schedule my posts and make sure I cover all my commitments. To be honest, it'll give me some great new content too, so you would be doing me a favour. Callum's working away for most of the next couple of weeks anyway, so I was going to be on my lonesome.'

'Och, yer a gem, Carol Ann Bernadette Sweeney!' Like Carol's mum, Val always went for our full childhood titles in times of high emotion.

'As long as you don't mind keeping an eye on the girls?' Carol checked with Kate. 'I know they're old enough to look after themselves, but like I said, Callum has loads of jobs on this month, so I'll feel better if I know you're watching out for them.'

Kate gave her a reassuring nod. 'Of course. I wish I could come too, but I'd never get time off work at such short notice. I'll hold things down here though. It helps that they'll all be living right next door. Don't worry, they'll be absolutely fine. Remember, I've got a catapult and I'm not afraid to use it.'

Carol gave Kate's hand a squeeze of thanks, then three heads turned in my direction.

Oh, bollocks. This was a terrible idea. Awful. My husband was waiting for me. He'd been so good about moving here when we first got married, and taking on the chaos of family life, and now he had all sorts of romantic, belated honeymoon stuff planned for us. I'd even had a bikini wax. I couldn't delay it further by saying I was off on a jolly with my pals. He was an understanding guy, but after almost two years of putting my life priorities above his, it was my turn to embrace his life. Our life. The new one. In Los Angeles. With a swimming pool. Next door to a bloke that looked like Matthew McConaughey who did naked yoga every morning. This wasn't about me, it was about my marriage.

For a whole three and a half seconds, I convinced myself of that, before my gob provided a reality check. This wasn't about me or my marriage. It was about my Aunt Val, a woman I adored, and she was asking something of me, something that would, admittedly, delay the inevitable and allow me to hang on to much-loved pieces of my life here for a little bit longer. Even if that hadn't been the case, though, my answer was never in doubt.

My words came out with slow certainty. 'Oh, I'm so in.'

That earned simultaneous cheers from the others.

'But what about Sam, love? Won't he mind us stealing you for a couple of weeks?'

Yep, I was pretty sure he would, but I shook my head anyway and picked up my mobile.

His number was on my favourites list, so his phone rang with just one quick press of the screen.

'Hey, gorgeous,' he bellowed, before I could warn him that he was on speaker.

'Honey, you're on...'

A delay on the crackly international line meant that he didn't register my interruption before he barrelled on. 'I can't believe you'll be here in twenty-four hours. I'm counting them down. Shit, I can't wait to get you here on your own. I hadn't realised you came in a package deal with a dozen other people. I love them all, but you realise that we still haven't had any time together, just us. Prepare to be naked, Carly Morton. A lot. Because I'm going to—'

'Sam!' To my relief, that stopped him before he said things that would make Val's hair defy two cans of solidifying spray and turn up at the ends. She adored Sam, but there were some things that she didn't need to hear.

He registered the urgency in my voice. 'What's up babe? Are the boys okay?'

Val answered for me. 'Aye, but I'm clutching my pearls and need smelling salts after those last comments, Sam Morton.'

My husband covered up his surprise with a chuckle. 'Val! I've missed you every moment of every day since I saw you last,' he said, piling on the charm. Those two had adored each other since they first met twenty odd years ago at Callum and Carol's wedding. Their relationship consisted purely of inappropriate flirtation, cheeky banter and love.

'Well, I might be able to do something about that,' she quipped.

It became immediately obvious that he thought she was joking.

'There's always room here for you,' he bantered. 'You know you're my favourite. I only married Carly because you were taken.'

'Well, funny you should say that...'

A pause. Val clamped her mouth shut, and glanced over at me, realising that she'd almost blurted out information that should probably come from me.

Bollocks. This was like one of those runaway trains at Disney. It was speeding down the wrong tracks and I wasn't sure how to get it back on course.

Sam hadn't quite caught on. He was still chuckling, oblivious to the undercurrents. Time to go for total derailment of the Sam Morton honeymoon train.

'Sam, I'm counting the hours too. I can't wait to see you.'

'Okay, babe, well, I'll let you go and spend time with everyone before you leave. Love y—'

I knew he was about to hang up, so I cut him off. 'The thing is, honey, I'll be there soon, but... I'm not coming alone. A couple of people in that package deal are coming with me.'

Much as he loved my family and friends, his silence told me he wasn't thrilled that this wasn't going to be quite the honeymoon he had planned.

7

VAL

Dreams – Gabrielle

I thought Sam took it quite well, all things considered. He didn't say anything for a minute or two and then he came out with something about having to go into a meeting, and that he loved us all and would call Carly back later. But then, as Carly pointed out, he was a world-famous actor. If he could play a lead role that called for him to get three blokes off death row with his legal prowess, he could hide the fact that he was raging about his romantic honeymoon being gatecrashed.

Anyway, hopefully, when I explained everything, Sam would find it in his heart to forgive me for stealing his wife for a couple of weeks. Not that she put up much of a fight. Call me her out of *Murder She Wrote*, but I had a weird feeling that Carly was... I struggled to pinpoint the right word. Relieved. Yep, that was it. She seemed relieved that I was running a steamroller right through the start of her new life. Maybe it was something in the water, because my spider senses were tingling every time I looked at our Carol too. She'd been Carly's pal since primary one, I'd known that lassie all her life, long before she married my nephew, Callum, and I had a real sense of unease that something was off with her.

For once, I stopped myself opening my mouth and storming in with a barrage of questions. Maybe I was reading them wrong, or just being overly suspicious about their emotional well-being (that was a personality trait – I blamed Oprah), but if something was up with the two of them, I was going to let them tell me in their own good time, even though keeping schtum went against every iota of my being. Josie used to say that I had the kind of interrogation techniques that the KGB used in the Cold War. And that came from a woman who could make anyone spill their deepest secrets with just a raise of her right eyebrow.

'What are you smiling at, Aunt Val?' Carly asked me, with a nudge.

I didn't get time to answer because the air hostess appeared at that moment with my champagne. Aye, champagne. And not the stuff out of the Co-op that doesn't cost much more than a good Lambrini.

'I'm just thinking Josie would love this,' I told Carly over the partition separating her bed from mine. I only had the budget for an economy flight, but – God love them – the girls had upgraded me, so I had one of these flat-bed thingies with the free socks. It wasn't that they were being flash. Sam had already paid for Carly's ticket, and Carol had some kind of deal with British Airways that meant she got a walloping great discount on all her bookings as long as she posted about the flight on that social media nonsense. Speaking of which...

'Right, Val, are you ready?' Carol asked, crouching down so that her head was next to mine.

I grabbed my lippy and slapped on a fresh coat of baby pink, which matched the gobstopper baubles around my neck and the two-inch flamingos dangling from my ears. A holiday wasn't a holiday without tropical bird earrings and a mid-flight cocktail.

'Guys, this is my Aunt Val,' Carol said into the screen. 'Well, Val, what do you think of British Airways Club Class?'

'Och, it's fantastic, love,' I said into the camera, with my very best smile on my face. 'The seats are comfy as anything, but I've already downed half a bottle of fizzy stuff, so I could be sitting on a hedgehog and I'd feel no pain.'

A bloke in a suit to my left threw me a look that could only be described as horrified. Stuck-up git. I blame him for what came out of my mouth next.

'Only thing is, it's not a barrel of laughs. Nothing a wee sausage roll and an ice-breaking game of bingo wouldn't sort out. Oh, and maybe a bit of Tom Jones or the Beach Boys.'

Carol slapped a palm to her forehead when she switched the camera off, but next to me, Carly was having a good old giggle. 'Right, Catherine Zeta-Jones,' she said to me, clearly appreciating my talents, 'enough of the filming and let's get organised. Dig out the list and let's make a cunning and devious plan of how we're going to tackle everything.'

Carol perched on the edge of my seat, and Carly kneeled on hers and stretched across the partition, so we all had full view of the paper I spread out on my wee flight table. Yesterday, after the girls had agreed to come along, I'd filled them in on the reasons for every item on the list. At least once a week, Josie and I would have a wee movie session, where we'd try whatever new film was on Sky Cinema, or rewatch an old favourite. That's where most of our ideas came from – the movies that we'd watch again and again because – for one reason or another – they were the ones we loved. My original VHS of *Thelma and Louise* had been watched so many times the tape had burst.

To be honest, there used to be more things on the list, but we'd scratched skydiving (*Mission Impossible*), paragliding (James Bond), swimming with sharks (*Jaws*) and a high-speed car chase (*Fast & Furious*) when we realised that getting down ASDA's frozen food aisle without contracting hypothermia was a death-defying feat at our age.

JOSIE AND VAL'S BUCKET LIST

1. Go to a line dancing bar and snog a cowboy. (A cross between Urban Cowboy, Saturday Night Fever *and the end bit of* Dirty Dancing)

It was the closest we'd get to synchronised dancing without any sexy, hip-thrusting stuff pulling a muscle. Plus, we were determined that twenty years of line dancing down the community centre wasn't going to be wasted. And Josie once had an erotic dream about Tim McGraw that had given her hot flushes for weeks.

*2. Act in a TV show or movie (*A Star Is Born – *the Barbra one)*

Josie was absolutely positive that even at the age of seventy-something, her big break was just around the corner. 'Look at that Harrison Ford bloke,' she'd mutter on a regular basis. 'That one is so old he should be making Indian Jones and The Hip Replacement of Doom.'

*3. Gamble a month's pension on a blackjack table in Las Vegas (*Casino)

Josie fancied herself as a bit of an aging Sharon Stone. Neither of us had ever had two pennies to rub together, so she was convinced she could outmanoeuvre the odds and win enough for a

Caribbean cruise with her winnings. I had visions of her gambling in her pants after literally losing the shirt off her back, but I was up for the adventure.

4. Shop on Rodeo Drive and stay in that hotel from Pretty Woman

And while we were there, we were determined to recreate one of the scenes from the movie. Big mistake. Big. Huge.

5. Have breakfast at Tiffany's, then skate on the ice rink at the Rockefeller Centre in New York (Breakfast at Tiffany's *and every rom com ever set in New York)*

Breakfast was just to stock up on the carbs we'd need for going to the ice rink. And if she needed reconstructive surgery after a skating fall, she'd finally get something from the travel insurance she'd been paying into for five decades of zero claims.

6. Run across the Malibu sands in slow motion à la the original Baywatch *series*

Back in the nineties, she'd loved that show and whenever she got drunk, she'd play David Hasselhoff songs to piss off the grumpy old git who lived next door to her.

7. Sing 'Sweet Caroline' on top of a bar (Coyote Ugly)

Because that was Josie's very favourite song in the world and she believed Neil Diamond topped Mozart and Beethoven in the history of musical greats. She also loved all that sexy strutting on bar tops in *Coyote Ugly*, so she'd decided to combine the two. We hadn't quite worked out how we were going to get our bones up on the bar without a set of ladders and a safety harness. Or how we were going to get ourselves into the leather trousers Tyra Banks wore in the film.

8. *Snog a stranger at the top of the Empire State Building* (Sleepless In Seattle)

Sleepless In Seattle was one of her favourite films and she claimed that as long as her arthritis wasn't playing up, she could shag Tom Hanks until the sun came up. I pointed out that due to my happily married status, I couldn't snog a stranger or shag Tom Hanks, but I was up for watching the first of those two events.

9. *Ride a motorbike* (Top Gun) *and drive a convertible* (Thelma and Louise)

She'd insisted on keeping the motorbike one in, despite my objections that there was no way I could throw my leg over a bike without pulling something. And I didn't mean a leather-clad, long-bearded, bike-loving Hells Angel called Bubba Joe. And the convertible? I quite fancied that myself. As long as we went nowhere near a cliff edge or had to use a SatNav. Last time I tried one of those it took me twenty minutes to get out of Tesco's car park.

The list stopped there. The truth was that there were ten things on the original list, but I'd folded the bottom up so they wouldn't see that last one because I didn't want to put them off coming with me. It was a daft one anyway. Totally unrealistic. And it had been all Josie, so I was happy to lose it. I'd tell the girls about it when this was all over.

'Okay, so I think we need to separate them into cities and start ticking them off that way,' Carly suggested, whipping her phone out and beginning to tap away on her keyboard. 'I'll put this on my notes and send you both a copy, so we know what we're doing. Right, I think we should start in LA. That will give me a chance to grovel to my husband and make up for bailing on our honeymoon.'

'Just blame me, sweetheart,' I told her. 'I'll remind him that I don't have many years left on this earth, and this is you doing some community work with the elderly.' I was grinning as I said it, but something made my gut tighten just a little, and it wasn't these bloody Spanx I'd poured myself into. It was the thought of my Don, of what he was going through, of what was ahead of us, of what it meant for him, for us, for…

'Malibu Beach and Rodeo Drive are both LA, so let's put them at number one and two,' Carly said, her eyes on the screen and her fingers tapping away. 'We might be able to get Sam to pull some strings and cross off acting in a TV show too. Right, that's three. Vegas next, for the gambling one, maybe the line dancing and singing on a bar too. Then we can go to New York for the Rockefeller Centre Ice Rink, Tiffany's, and the Empire State Building. That leaves driving a convertible and riding a motorbike to fit in wherever we can. How does that sound?'

'That sounds perfect, love. Och, yer a gem, you really are,' I said, squeezing her hand.

'Tell that to my husband,' she quipped, before sliding back down on to her chair. Her hand was still in mine. 'We've got you, Aunt Val. And Josie too. We'd do anything for you both.'

Aw bugger. Tears sprung to my bottom lids and threatened my blue eyeliner as a weird feeling came over me. It was hard to pinpoint what it was. There was excitement because I was finally carrying out Josie's wishes. Gratitude that these women were coming along for the ride. And a huge bloody great pang of longing because Josie wasn't right by my side. I blinked back the fluid rush and took a sip of my posh champagne to calm myself.

Carol had gone back to her own bed thingy and had slipped in her earphones, while Carly was now typing away on her laptop. I'd already checked out the in-flight movies and there was a new action flick with that Liam Neeson chap. If it wasn't for my dodgy knees, I'd do some raunchy things to that man. Anyway, that was my next couple of hours sorted, but first…

I slipped my notebook out of my bag. Or rather, Josie's notebook. Leopard-print covers and corners turned down on loads of the pages. I'd found it on her kitchen table after she passed. In it were notes and thoughts and reminders, all in that flamboyant, curly handwriting of hers. That's where I'd found our bucket list. Every daft thing we'd talked about, on the back page. She'd taken it all in, written it down as if that would ensure it happened.

Apart from that, there was nothing of importance in the notebook, yet it was one of my greatest treasures. 'Tell Val about the sale in Marks and Spencer's this weekend,' one entry said. 'Get frock for the wedding. Make sure hat is fecking huge,' said another. Loads of the later notes were about the wedding she was planning the night she died, for Cammy, a bloke she'd worked with for years. There had been high drama that day, but in the end, the couple had made it up the aisle and we'd laughed, we'd sung and we'd danced until dawn. She didn't crack a light about the appointment she'd squeezed in that morning, but it was right there on the page. 'Saw doc for results of biopsy. Not good. Feckers.' He'd told her then that it was incurable cancer, but she'd kept that to herself, organised the whole day, had a rare old time, and then, after her and I drank a final glass of champagne, our shoes off because our feet were sore from dancing, she'd gone to bed and she hadn't woken up. And no, telling me that's how she would have bloody wanted to go doesn't help. It's true, but it doesn't make it hurt any less.

I flicked the page over to a clean sheet and began to write.

Dear Josie,

We're on our way, ma love. Carly and Carol are with me. Took no persuading at all, which was a bit of a surprise. Think neither of them are exactly skipping through daisies in their own lives, but I'm not sure what's going on. Just got a feeling that something's off with them both. I'll find out more and see what I can do about it and I'll keep you posted.

Oh, and doll, they've got me in business class. There's free socks and cocktails that would blow yer knickers off. Our Carly has everything all sorted and planned out, so I feel like it's finally happening. Four years too late, and without my partner in crime, but I know yer watching, doll. First stop, Los Angeles. Then Vegas. Then… I can't remember what was next, but Carly will get us there.

Do me a favour, pet. I know you can't be in two places at once, but keep an eye on my Don for me. Just make sure he's okay and if I need to get back home pronto, send me a sign. And a return ticket with more free socks.

Anyway, that's all for now. I miss you more than ever, pal.
Keep dancing, keep laughing… and be happy up there.
Love you,
Val xxx

I closed the book. I'd got over the first hurdle. We were on our way. Now I just needed to deal with the most pressing problem ahead of me: the very sudden urge to pee. How was I supposed to get in and out of these bloody Spanx in an airplane toilet?

Compared to that, tackling the bucket list would be a breeze.

8

JESS

Better Man – Little Big Town

The midday California sun was piercing my Ray-Ban Aviators as I headed to Los Angeles International Airport. The first time I'd flown into LAX, I was so excited to see what the city had to offer. Now that I knew, I couldn't wait to get out of here.

I was supposed to be miles away from the pollution and the chaos of the LA traffic today. Right now, I should have been in a Napa vineyard, checking out the function suite and picking colour schemes for the table arrangements for my wedding. Change of plan.

And I wasn't someone who handled change particularly well. Organisation. Structure. Commitment. Without them, everything went completely fucking haywire. Which pretty much summed up my life right now.

I slammed my hand on the horn to ward off a dickhead in a Maserati who was trying to cut into my lane. He gave me the finger and it took every ounce of discipline I possessed not to ram the back of his penis-extension vehicle with the front of my car. If I wasn't in a rush, he'd be counting the cost of his car repairs and wishing he hadn't been an arse to the nice lady in the Jeep. Today wasn't the day. Hopefully, next time, someone in the sisterhood would slay him for me.

The handset attached to my dashboard flashed and sent a persistent ring through the truck's onboard audio system. My gaze went to the display. ARNIE. I used the button on the steering wheel to decline the call with shaking hands.

Breathe. Come on, Jess, just breathe.

My eyes caught the sign approaching on my right. LAX fifteen miles. That was fifteen miles of thinking, and no amount of Lady Gaga on the radio was going to save me from the pull of the flash-backs that were tugging at my mind.

Shallow. Turns out that pretty much summed up our rela-tionship.

Shame I didn't realise that two years ago. Or was it almost three? Sentimentality wasn't my thing back then. Arnie and I met when I came over here with Carly just after her divorce. God, she was in pieces. While Sam was scooping her up and putting her back together again, I was sneaking out for hot nights with his right-hand man and former stunt double, Arnie. I'm biased, but I still stand by the fact that he was one of the most attractive men I'd ever met in my life. African American. At sixty-two, he was over a decade older than me, but didn't look a day over fifty. He'd been a college basketball player, served in Vietnam, a martial arts expert and, thanks to his lifelong intensive fitness regime, every muscle in his body was honed to perfection. The square jaw, the contours of his face, the laughter lines at the sides of his eyes, the easy smile, and those deep, deep brown eyes... oh, dear God, he was perfect. It was his laid-back attitude that got me though. He'd finally persuaded me to slow down, to chill out, to live in the moment. Plus, he was sensational in bed and, to be honest, that's all it was ever supposed to be – a few quick hook-ups on holiday. That was my mantra for life in those days. No commitments. No ties. No expectations. Just great casual sex whenever I came across someone who made my libido perk up and come out to play.

In hindsight, maybe there were a couple of red flags. Two marriages behind him: one to his childhood sweetheart, with whom he shared two daughters in their thirties, and the other was a Vegas dancer that he'd married a month after meeting her.

When we met, he was single at almost sixty, he was living in an admittedly pretty cool apartment above the garage at Sam's home, and he made no secret of his avoidance of any kind of commitment. Maybe I should have steered clear.

However, Sam loved Arnie, and I respected Sam's judgement, so I treated the red flags like javelins and tossed them into obscurity. The bottom line was that I trusted him. After a crap marriage and several long relationships with guys who had PHDs (Pretty Horrific Douchebags) in Cheating Bastardom, Arnie was one of the good guys. Until he wasn't.

I switched lanes, causing an over-Botoxed woman in a minivan behind me to throw her hands up and make gestures that I caught in my rear-view mirror.

Lady, you think you've got problems. Let me tell you about problems.

For the last two years, I'd been over here, happily shacked up with my man. Sam was in England with Carly, so we'd moved into the main house and had endless, gorgeous months of solitude, great sex and box sets. I already worked on both sides of the Atlantic, and had the kind of job that didn't require an office, so now that my son, Josh, was at uni, it was easy to run my life from LA instead of London. My PR company specialises in crisis management. You know, the high-profile people in entertainment who get caught buying crack down a back alley. The politicians who are exposed by the press with photographs of them getting whipped by a six-foot dominatrix in a leather peephole bra and thong. The sports stars who get fingered for placing illegal bets because they're trying to win back the millions they've lost at the bookies. Those peaches are my clients, and it's my job to minimise the carnage, turn public opinion around and rehabilitate their reputations.

Nowadays, it was all about un-cancelling the cancel culture and most of the communication work and messaging was done online. I missed the old days when I'd have that nervy excitement on a Sunday, waiting to see which of my clients the tabloids were slaying that weekend. These days, it was all TMZ and celebrity websites and trolls out of control on Twitter. It wasn't nearly as much fun as threatening to sue *The News Of The World* every Monday morning. It was a different kind of gutter. Still deep, and still overflowing with the dregs of humanity, but far more brutal because when a story was online, so many people jumped on the bandwagon.

Right now, I was representing a British model, Hayley Harlow, who was facing a relentless smear campaign by a very married talent agent called Dax Hill, who'd got her pregnant, then dumped her. Now he was paying a company overseas to plant endless negative tweets and false stories about her, in the hope that she'd disappear and scurry off into obscurity before his wife found out. I also had a football player (the British kind, not the American ones with the shoulder pads) who had been cancelled because one of his former team-mates was trying to pay off his own gambling debts by selling false stories about non-PC antics from the past that never happened. Then there was the candidate for congress who knew his opponent was about to release details of a shoplifting charge from 1986. It was my job to fight back and drown the story online so that it would get buried before the next news cycle.

Sleazy stuff aside, I loved my job and I felt lucky that it was the kind of work that could pretty much be done from anywhere in the world, as long as I had an internet connection and a phone line to badger newspaper editors, TV commentators and celebrity bloggers. However, and I wasn't playing the victim here, it was also the kind of job that chipped away at your faith in human nature. You saw the worst of people. You saw them at their lowest, their most degraded, and you witnessed first-hand the carnage that some people's secrets and lies wreaked on the lives of the partners or families who loved them. I thought I was way too smart to let that happen to me. Apparently not.

I veered into the off ramp at LAX and followed signs for the terminal building. The car park was full, but I managed to stalk a bloke in a suit all the way to his yellow classic Mustang, and then slid into the space he vacated, giving evils to a young guy in a bandana with face tattoos who was ready to claim the spot in his pimped-out Cadillac. Not today, son. I gave him a stare that said, 'try me', and he made the right decision to back off and do another circuit of the car park. Wise move.

I left the engine running while I checked my phone. Four missed calls from Arnie and one from his daughter, Talia. That one made my teeth grind. On her thirtieth birthday last month, Talia had showed her willingness to embrace her new stepmother by blocking me from the guest list. She'd given her father an ultimatum. Come alone or don't come at all. He went alone. I should have known then that something wasn't right.

The voicemail envelope appeared in the top corner of my screen, so I pressed 1 to let it play. Arnie's voice immediately flooded the car, causing me to buckle as if I'd been punched in the stomach.

'Jess, I'm sorry. Look, we need to talk. Let me explain. Let me make this okay, babe.'

I flicked it off. Sod him. I didn't need him to explain. Didn't need to talk. I'd heard everything I needed to hear when I'd walked in on him in the bedroom and listened to him on the phone to his ex-wife. Those same gorgeous dulcet tones were saying something completely different then.

'Baby, it's always been you,' he was whispering. I couldn't hear her side of the conversation, only his, but what he said next made me gasp. 'Honey, we'll work it out. You and me. I'll come back and we'll be together again... I just need to sort some things out here first... I'll speak to Sam and work things out... he'll understand... No, baby, I'm not with anyone here... I told you, you're the only one for me... no one else matters...'

No. One. Else. Matters. It had taken everything I had to trust a man again, to give my happiness and my future over to someone and this was how it had turned out. After everything, I should have fucking known better. And yes, I was aware that I couldn't get a cohesive thought out without using at least one 'fuck'. Blind fucking fury and the memory of that guy taking a mallet to my heart did that to me.

I jumped out of my car. Technically, it was Arnie's car, but I'd been driving it since I got here. I quickly texted him four words. 'Car is at LAX'. He could use the spare key to come and collect it. I had no idea how or when he was going to find it, but that wasn't my problem. Grabbing my case out of the boot, I tried not to think about the fact that I'd been in LA for over two years and everything that mattered to me now could fit in a single suitcase. I'd left behind the photos, the gifts he'd given me, the mementos of everything we'd shared. On top of the pile, I'd left the engagement ring, the one that he'd made himself from a piece of silver he'd bought from a tiny artisan jewellery store on a trip we'd taken up the coast to Carmel. When we got back, he'd spent days in the garage, battering it, moulding it, shaping it, but I had no idea that's what he was doing until a few nights later.

It was a while after dusk and I was sitting on the bonnet of his pickup truck, my back against the windscreen, my legs crossed, mug of coffee in my hands. We often sat there after dark, on the balmy nights, looking out over the endless stream of flickering lights on the Pacific Coast Highway, to the ocean beyond it, all the activity such a contrast to the perfect stillness and silence. Before Arnie, I'd never appreciated peace. Or contentment. Or sitting still long enough to properly breathe. He had taught me to notice those things, to put the crazy stress of corporate life to one side and leave it there long enough to appreciate the moment. It was hard to explain, but there was an authenticity and a wisdom about him that I'd never known before. He didn't buy into all the shallowness of this city or the fake bullshit. If you'd asked me then, I'd have said I'd never known anyone with more integrity, more decency, than Arnie Deluca, and I couldn't get enough of it. Of him.

I'd just pulled a blanket around my shoulders and drained the last of my lukewarm coffee when he'd sauntered out of the garage a few metres away.

'Hey. I was about to send out a search party,' I'd told him, wondering if the urge to smile when I saw him would ever leave me. This was the kind of goofy stuff that happened to Carly or Carol, not to me. Yet one glance of his brown eyes and that casual swagger triggered inexplicable happiness.

His boots were dusty and his battered jeans rippled as he climbed up on to the truck and lay next to me, his black T-shirt exposing the round curves of his biceps as he reached over and took my hand.

'Just keeping busy,' he'd said in the New York drawl that made me want to slide that T-shirt off him there and then. His thumb was slowly grazing the inside of my palm, the softest of touches, again and again, as he leant on his side and stared at me.

'What?' I'd asked, intrigued. 'Were you smoking a joint in there, because you look decidedly weird. You know, sixty isn't too late to pick up a new habit and go off the rails.'

That had made him grin again.

If anyone had told me that a sixty-year-old man could make me feel this way, I'd have thought they were the ones smoking the dodgy stuff. Arnie wasn't just any sixty though. He was Denzel Washington sixty. Jamie Foxx sixty. Samuel L. Jackson sixty. Utterly gorgeous, libido-stirring, beautiful-soul sixty.

'You're my only bad habit,' he'd teased. 'And I think I'm about to go right off those rails.'

'Oh, yeah? How's that then?' I'd replied, thinking naked outdoor sex. Maybe a few beers under the moonlight.

That's when he'd flicked a silver ring, one I hadn't noticed, off the tip of his pinky and held it out to me.

'Marry me,' he'd said simply. 'Just because you love me. And I love you. I don't ever want there to be a day that you're not next to me.'

It wasn't like the movies. Blindsided, my chin dropped in a way that definitely wasn't attractive. 'Did you make that?' I'd whispered, staring at the ring. 'Is that what you've been doing in there all week?'

'Yeah. And it's gonna last forever. Just like us.'

The roar of my trolley wheels on the airport car park concrete interrupted the memory and I tasted the droplet of salt water that had found its way to the corner of my lip.

Do not cry. Do not, I told myself. I was not going to fall apart.

I checked my watch. There was enough time to detour to the arrivals hall, as planned. Hopefully Carly wasn't stuck in immigration, or I'd miss her altogether. Maybe that wouldn't be a bad thing. I had no desire to share my trauma in the middle of crowds of people rushing through the terminal. Especially with someone who was landing here, thrilled to be starting off a fabulous new life with the man she loved. The one who – unlike mine – loved her back.

I'd seen Sam a few days ago, when he arrived back here and he was so excited that Carly was following on and joining him today. He'd arranged loads of things for them to do: a few days over on Catalina Island, dinners at Craigs and Nobu and Mr Chow, and a cook out in the garden with all his LA friends, to welcome her. She was going to have an amazing life here, and I was pretty sure that it wouldn't be dented by my desertion. Much as I wanted to see her face, I knew she'd understand that I'd bolted back to the UK. When we were in our twenties, she was a woman who'd flaked out and done a runner more times than we could count. I knew she'd hoped we could catch up while she was here – after all, Arnie and I were back in his apartment on the grounds of Sam's home, so we were neighbours – but I couldn't. I had to go. We were passing ships, but we could FaceTime when I got back, and I could fill her in on what had happened. Yeah, maybe that was a better idea.

As I scanned the arrivals board, I was surrounded by eager relatives, kids with excited faces, men in suits holding up cards with names on them. Flight from London Heathrow. Arrived 1.20 p.m. Almost two hours ago. Either she was stuck in immigration, still waiting at the baggage reclaim, or she was already through and on her way to Sam's house right now. Actually, that must be the case because otherwise Sam would be here waiting for her and I couldn't see him anywhere.

No point in waiting around then. My check-in down in the departures terminal was already open so I could just go on down there and be on my way.

'Jess Latham, ya big darling!'

Oh my God, I was so traumatised that I was hearing voices now. Was this how split personalities started? One minute I was a grounded, sharp-minded woman, and the next I was imagining that

I could hear the voices of people I loved? Because that voice almost definitely came from Carly's Aunt Val, and I was pretty sure I had to be hallucinating.

But no. I turned to see three very familiar, expectant faces rushing towards me in a flurry of excitement, suitcases and duty-free bags. Despite my internal raging storm, I couldn't help but laugh. Val was indeed there, and she had her arms outstretched, the fringes dangling from the sleeves of her white Elvis faux-leather jacket quivering as she moved. Carol was just behind her, and Carly was bringing up the rear, pulling two trolley cases.

Val wrapped me in a hug, and rocked me from side to side. 'What are you doing here? Carly said you were away this weekend, so we were going to surprise you by appearing at yer door when you got back from your trip.'

There was something so comforting about seeing them, about feeling Val's arms around me, about knowing these people would hold me up no matter what. But still, I wasn't going to air my dirty laundry all over LAX. I went for nonchalance and matter of fact-ness.

'Change of plan. Don't freak out, but I've called things off with Arnie. No big deal. It just wasn't working. I'm flying back to London today and I just stopped by here to say hi and bye to Carly. My flight leaves in two hours.'

The three of them froze, suspended in time, staring at me. Carly was the first to break the game of statues. 'What? No, no, no. You don't get away with dropping a bombshell like that and then just brushing it off like it's nothing. What happened? Are you okay? What can we do? And not that it's all about me, but don't you bloody dare leave me.'

I felt the most alien sensation, and realised that it was an urge to cry, bubbling up from my gut and into my throat. I never cried. Falling apart wasn't in my DNA. I was a fixer. A solver.

'Nothing major happened,' I deflected her questions. 'It's fine, really. Anyway, I love you all, it was great to see you, but I need to go check in. Carly, you'll be fine without me because I'm pretty sure Sam will have you locked in a love suite for the next year. Val, Carol – let me know when you get back and I'll hear all your stories.'

The urge to crumble was stronger now. Like a river pushing against a dam, desperate to find a way through. I needed to get out of there pronto, so I grabbed the handle of my case, ready to zip off while the fake smile was still on my face and my tightening chest was still allowing me to breathe.

I didn't even get one step away.

Val grabbed me again, enveloped me in a hug that was unbreakable. 'Yer not fooling me for a single second, ma love. Don't you dare move. I'm not letting you go anywhere like this, because you're ours and we've got you. We've got you, sweetheart,' she repeated.

That broke the dam. The one thing that slayed quicker than a broken heart was someone you loved showing sympathy and care. Val's compassion and empathy kicked the crap out of my defensive barriers, and before I could stop them, huge fat tears were sliding on to the arm of Elvis's jacket and my chest was heaving as I gulped for air somewhere between her shoulder and the rock-hard entity of her blonde bob.

'Aw bugger, Jess. What's happened?' That emotional sigh came from Carly, who was wrapping her arms around the two of us.

'We're here, honey, it's okay.' That was Carol, who joined the group hug.

There we were. Four independent, cosmopolitan, grown-ass women, standing in a huddle in the middle of the arrivals terminal at LAX, clinging on to each other and crying silent tears as the whole world rushed around us like we didn't exist.

'Yer not going anywhere, love. Yer coming with us and we're

going to take care of you. You don't get to deal with this on your own,' Val crooned.

I could name four people in my life who'd ever been able to make me change my mind or do something I didn't want to do. Top of the list was my son, Josh, who only had to look at me with his big brown eyes and I surrendered to whatever request he threw out there. Of course, they were few and far between now that he was in his third year of uni, and had inherited his mother's self-sufficiency genes. Next was Arnie, and he'd already been scored right off the list. The final two were Val and Josie. In Josie's case, I knew my limits – she was a woman who had taken fierce to a whole new level. No one and nothing stood a chance against her – except the cancer that eventually took her. And the final person was Val. I'd adored her since she used to bring sandwiches to all our childhood netball games and use sweary words to describe the opposition. When you're twelve, that leads to instant adoration and lifelong devotion.

'You hear me in there?' Val murmured into my hair.

What else could I do? I didn't want to stay here in Los Angeles. I wanted to get as far as possible away from Arnie and the life I thought we were going to have. I wanted to get on that flight, get back to London and lick my wounds.

But this was Val. And Carly and Carol too. Which meant that three of the very best people in my life were here.

In the midst of the huddle, I nodded.

'I'll stay,' I agreed. 'But only if you promise to take my mind of all of this.'

Val responded by nodding, then looking upwards. 'Oh, we'll have no problem doing that, ma love. Josie has it all planned out.'

9

CARLY

You Give Good Love – Whitney Houston

'Do any of you ladies need a ride?'

I recognised the voice, but not the person. The guy in front of me was wearing thick glasses, a baseball cap with long dark hair sticking out of the bottom of it and he had exceptionally dodgy teeth that protruded over his bottom lip. On second glance, I recognised the hair as my Cher wig from Halloween a couple of years ago and the teeth Sam had used for a part in which he played a serial killer with a distinctive overbite. The sloppy plaid baggy shirt, gardening jeans and (deliberately) stooped posture added to the insignificance of his existence. Sam Morton, A-list actor, producer, and all-round hunka burning love was standing in the middle of a packed terminal and no one had a clue he was there.

I threw my arms around him. 'Oh Cher, I've always had a thing for you,' I murmured, laughing.

Val hadn't quite caught on. Behind me, I heard her gasping,

'Dear God, she's lost it. What was she drinking on the plane? Do you think someone could have spiked her Prosecco?'

'You're next, Val, so pucker up,' Cher said, his face mask slightly displaced by my enthusiastic snogging.

Val's penny dropped. She'd come here with us a couple of times before and she'd loved the disguises Sam pulled to make sure he didn't have to deal with the constant scrutiny of cameras flashing in his face and people taking note of everything he was doing, or approaching him relentlessly looking to chat, to tell him how much they loved or hated his movies.

'Sam, ma love!' Val stage-whispered. 'God, son, you gave me the fright of ma life there. I thought Carly had finally lost the plot.'

I chose not to point out to her that she might be right. I'd wondered how I'd feel when we landed here. Would I suddenly realise this was where I should be? Would it feel like home? So far, despite the drama, the pals, and the absolute gush of love I felt for the man in the Cher wig, the answers were no and no. Right at this moment, I wanted to live my life with Sam, but I still didn't want it to be here.

I shut the thought down. Nothing to be gained from that right now. Val had bought me a couple more weeks with my pals, so the best thing I could do was just live in the moment and resist stressing about what was coming. If Sam thought it was strange that Jess was there, he didn't mention it, probably figuring she'd just caught an Uber here to join the welcome party. On the way out, I filled him in under my breath, watching his eyes widen with surprise. He clearly knew little or nothing about the drama going on above his garage for the last twenty-four hours.

On the whole journey back to Sam's house in Pacific Palisades, the gorgeous neighbourhood of multimillion-dollar homes just inland from Santa Monica, Val, Jess and Carol chatted in the back of the minivan, while Sam and I held hands in the front. Jess's car – or rather, one of Arnie's cars – was still at the airport, because apparently, she'd already texted Arnie to tell him it was there and didn't want to have to contact him again. She also seemed to be very open to the idea that it would inconvenience him to go get it and he'd be left with a large bill to get it out of the car park. Hell hath no fury like a woman in her cheating fiancé's Jeep. I listened in as Jess filled Val and Carol in on everything that had happened with Arnie. It was shocking. Unbelievable. I'd known Arnie for years and I'd have bet the last pound in my overdraft that he was a decent man, yet, as Jess was now recounting, she'd heard him whisper sweet nothings to his ex-wife. Why? Why would he do that? Why would he hurt my friend? Jess had been through some pretty tortuous relationships in her life, and she was as close to bulletproof as it was possible to be, but I really thought she'd found her happy ending. And not that this was all about me, but shit, she was the only pal I thought I would have here and now she was leaving. If I wasn't already going to punch Arnie for hurting her, I'd be doing it for chasing her away.

I cast a side glance at Sam. 'Did you honestly not know about this?' I asked, my voice low so the others wouldn't overhear.

'No idea. This morning he called and asked me for time off, said he had some personal stuff to sort out. I didn't ask. You know I don't pry. I just told him to take whatever he needed.'

Arnie had worked for Sam for at least fifteen years. They lived across the courtyard from each other and Arnie spent most hours of the day by Sam's side, so they were as close as brothers. Unfortunately, it was the kind of brothers who loved to hang out, who appreciated each other, but who rarely talked about anything deeper than Monday night football.

Sam continued to explain, 'He said he'd arranged for Eliza's daughter, Selena, to move into the house to take care of things while he's away, and she's happy to stay indefinitely. That's as much as I know.'

Eliza had been Sam's housekeeper when I first came here thirty years ago. She'd adopted him and was fiercely protective of him, like a cross between a helicopter mother and a third-world dictator. If Eliza didn't like someone Sam brought home, she made it known, and more than once had 'forgotten' to pass on messages. I'd adored her and thankfully it was reciprocated, otherwise I'm pretty sure she would have found a way to have the US government cancel my ESTA. When Eliza retired, Sam bought her a gorgeous little house near her six daughters and now the eldest, Selena, filled in when Arnie wasn't around, managing the house, cooking and generally taking care of Sam's life.

'Have I told you how glad I am that you're here?' Sam asked, swiftly changing the subject. 'Feels like we can finally get some kind of normal life. You realise that we've never actually lived on our own as a married couple?'

The glasses, hat, teeth and Cher's hair were gone now, and all I could see was Sam. My husband. This gorgeous man I'd loved back in the nineties, and then found love with all over again. I should be so grateful to the Gods of Mid-Life Miracle Romances for delivering him, but all I could feel right now was my stomach churning at the thought of what he'd just said. Him. Me. Alone. Here.

My turn to change the subject. 'So are you pissed off that I came with the gang in tow?'

He had one hand on the wheel and the other was on mine. 'How could I be pissed off with that lot? No, I've waited this long to get you here, so another two or three weeks isn't going to kill me. Although...' he lowered his voice further, 'I'd like to make an official request that you're naked and in the shower with me within five minutes of getting home. Do you know how long I've been thinking about that?'

'I've put on ten pounds of banoffee cheesecake this weekend. I don't know that we'll both fit in the shower now.'

His laugh was low and husky. 'We'll squeeze in and get really close together. Think that's the whole point.'

My pelvic floor muscles got a bit excited at the thought. 'In that case I'm cancelling my Weight Watchers subscription,' I answered, laughing. It still shocked and stunned me that Sam Morton was surrounded by specimens of sublime beauty every single day, some of the most stunning women in the world were on his phone, and yet he didn't give two hoots that his wife had stretch marks, thirty or forty extra pounds, and boobs that – when untethered – pointed at her shoes.

An hour after we left LAX, we pulled into his huge circular driveway, then parked outside the massive Spanish-style mahogany front doors.

'Welcome home, babe,' he murmured, squeezing my hand again.

I kept my mouth shut. This wasn't home. Home was my slightly weathered semi in Chiswick, with the dodgy seal on the washing-machine door and the kitchen cutlery drawer that frequently stuck so we had to eat our meals with whatever knives, forks and spoons were on the draining board. This had been so much easier to deal with when it was just a faint notion of something that would happen in the future. Now it was real. I was here. I should feel like the luckiest woman in the world, but... I did a quick mental check on my emotions. My heart was bursting with joy that I was with Sam but, yep, still wanted to turn round and take the first flight back home to my boys and my ordinary life. LA was the land of the quick fix. Maybe there was a hypnosis program that could sort my head out. Or a large mallet that could cause temporary amnesia until I settled into life here.

I disguised my internal anxiety by leaning over and kissing him.

'I love you, Sam Morton,' I murmured truthfully. I really did. With every bit of me. Except the bit that missed my boys and getting the train into Covent Garden to wander round the Christmassy shops in December.

'For God's sake, put that man down,' came a chuckle from the background. I turned to see Val harrumphing her bosoms. 'Or at least unlock these doors. I need at least ten minutes' grace time to sort out these Spanx when I get to the loo and I've got a feeling I'm cutting it fine.'

Sam unlocked the doors and Val, with the kind of bicep strength usually only possessed by people who worked out three times a day in the gym, wrenched the door open and jumped out, squinting into the sunshine. She'd been here before and knew her way around, so with a cheery, 'Hello luvly!' to Selena, who had come out to greet us, she swerved in through the open front door and headed for the nearest bathroom.

I followed her out of the car, stopping to hug Selena. 'It's so good to see you,' I told her with absolute honesty. 'How are you and how's your mamma?'

'Great to see you too.' She had the sexiest Latin accent, to match her long, jet-black waves, beautiful white smile and her mother's indomitable DNA. 'My mamma is great. Still terrorising the whole street. Anyone steps out of line and she's in there like a rottweiler.'

That made me laugh. 'I wouldn't expect anything less. Please give her my love.'

'She sends hers too. She always said you were the one for Sam. Although she does say, many times, that she wonders why it's taken you both so long to realise it. She says she told you this many years ago.'

I had a sudden flashback to fifteen years ago, when I brought my boys over for a visit. Things with Mark weren't great and he'd been too busy working to come along, so I'd packed the boys up, brought them here, and Sam took care of us all while I went for meetings with producers, hoping to sell the film or TV rights for one of my books. It was a resounding failure – my movie dream never transpired – but we all had a great time and for a moment, just a moment, I considered staying. Eliza knew it too, and she made a few well-placed comments about Sam and I belonging together. It had taken me more than a decade to discover she was right.

'I realise now that I should have listened to her words of wisdom. I'll tell her that as soon as I get a chance to go visit her. I'll pop over once my friends have gone.' Stomach flipped again. *Once my friends have gone.* Even thinking that made me feel a bit sick.

Behind me, Jess and Carol had alighted from the minivan and were making their way towards us. I noticed Jess peering over at the garage and Arnie's apartment above it. It looked empty. We knew Arnie's Jeep was at LAX, but his pick up truck, which usually sat in the space to the side of the building, was nowhere to be seen.

Like Sam, Selena showed no surprise at seeing Jess, although her gaze of sympathy hinted that she knew something wasn't right.

'Selena, you didn't see me here, okay?' Jess suggested with a loaded but sad smile.

'I've no idea who you are,' Selena replied as the two women hugged with genuine fondness, before Jess introduced Carol, who did the same.

'Sam, you have a guest inside,' Selena threw out, just as Sam pulled the last suitcase from the back of the van.

Sam glanced towards the door, at exactly the same time as Jess, who was clearly wondering if Arnie was here after all. No. Arnie practically ran this place, so Selena would never introduce him as a guest. It must be someone else. Hopefully someone that would set Val's heart a-flutter and give her bragging rights down at her weekly coffee morning in the community centre every week. *'Well, you can imagine my surprise... I walked into the living room – did I mention it had one of those great big cinema screens on the wall – and Tom Cruise was sitting on the sofa. Aye, he's not as braw as he looks on the telly. And much shorter. He must wear those things in his shoes to give him an extra couple of inches.'*

That mental image released anther knot of tension from my shoulders. Okay, forget the future and concentrate on now. So far, damage limitation seemed to have worked. We were all here. We'd persuaded Jess to come back and we would support her through the situation with Arnie. Val was palpably happy that we were doing something important to her and fulfilling Josie's wishes. My gorgeous sister-in-law was along for the ride. And my ever-patient Sam wasn't outright furious and seemed to be onboard with the Val-shaped spanner in our works.

Live in the moment, Carly, I told myself. And right now this moment was good.

'Well, look who it is, the gang is all here!' came an exclamation from the new arrival at the front door.

My teeth automatically went into the grind position. Hell, no. She had one of the most recognisable voices in the free world. One of the most adored faces. One of the biggest acting careers as a leading lady. And some of the biggest box-office hits of the last five years.

She was also my husband's ex-girlfriend, the one he'd ended things with so that we could rekindle our relationship.

Estelle Conran was in the building.

Suddenly this moment wasn't looking quite so peachy.

10

CAROL

Malibu – Miley Cyrus

The sun was rising on the Malibu sands as we congregated down at the shore. There were already a dozen or so surfers out on the water, despite the early hour and the chill in the dawn air.

Callum had called me at 2 p.m. his time, which was 6 a.m. here.

'Hey, baby, I knew you'd be up and working out by now.' I could see why he thought that. I'd always been an early riser, one of those annoying people who liked to run at 5.30 a.m. while the world was still quiet. Not today. Today I'd barely crawled out of bed and I'd only made myself do it because I had to get some content up on my Insta.

'No workout today. I'm way too jet lagged,' I'd croaked, trying to sound something close to human.

'No worries, I'll let you go then,' he'd said, and I could hear in his voice that he was smiling.

'No, it's fine. I've got five minutes before we leave for the beach.'

'Urgh, don't make me jealous. Anyway, I just wanted to let you know we're all good here. The girls spent their first night over at Carly's house last night, and when I called them today, they answered, so I don't think they're in jail or a gutter. I think we're good.'

'Glad to hear it. How is your day going?' I began, then tuned out while he spoke. Why didn't I feel that familiar warmth that talking to him used to give me? Why was my stomach churning, my legs shaking, the hairs on my forearms tingling? And why couldn't I tell him that I was feeling this way?

'Carol? Babe, are you okay?' He sounded sleepy. Or bored. That was it. He was bored with me. Or annoyed at me for something.

'Yes! It's just a bad line,' I'd lied. The insecurity that was making my fingers clench took over the conversation. 'Callum, you didn't mind me coming here, did you? Just taking off like this?'

There was a pause and, again, the logical side of my brain rolled its eyes and muttered expletives, just as it did every single time this new weak, pathetic side took control of the conversation. Logically, I knew that question would have surprised him. All our lives, Callum and I had travelled for work, booked jobs in different countries, given each other loads of space to come and go. It was normal to us.

'Of course not,' he'd answered, puzzled this time. 'I'm working away most of this month anyway, but even if I wasn't, why would I mind?'

I'd tried to sound like I was brushing it off. 'Oh, you know – maybe you suddenly realised you couldn't live without me.' My laugh didn't sound convincing to me, but somehow I got away with it.

'Goes without saying, but I'll fight through the despair,' he'd chuckled. 'I love ya, babe. I'll call you tomorrow.'

'Love you too.'

Sigh. I was acting crazy. I was sounding crazy. My stomach swirled with anxiety again. I was feeling crazy.

Now, half an hour later, with the sand in my toes, I tried to take my mind off it by focussing on what I was there for. I swept my phone around, making sure I got in the gorgeous shades of sun coming up on the horizon, then turned the camera to face me. I'd planned out this shoot before we'd left the house this morning, getting up even earlier than everyone else to apply 'no make-up' make-up and then spent twenty minutes making my hair look perfectly tousled in a 'just out of bed and shoved up in a ponytail' kind of way. I'd pulled on one of the new ensembles from the Yawn & Yoga line I'd been promoting for years. It was a company that specialised in cosy sleepwear and sassy workout gear and in the beginning, I'd been thrilled to head up their marketing campaigns. Now there was definitely a bit more pressure and a bit more effort to make sure the body did justice to the clothes. No pizza or pasta for me last night – I was too busy knocking back water and vegetable juice to try and flush out the post-flight bloat.

I flicked my camera on and began recording. Smile. Energy. Positivity. Joy. Aspiration. Enthusiasm. And go. 'Morning, guys! Hope you're all doing great this morning... or I guess it's already afternoon if you're in the UK. I just wanted to show you my workout outfit this morning – from the new range by the brilliant Yawn & Yoga...'

On I went for another five minutes, at one point slipping into the downward dog as I convinced everyone who was watching that I'd switched the camera on half an hour into my workout, and that this was the very, very, very best part of my day. After signing off with a link to buy the outfit I was wearing, I slumped on to the sand, just as Carly plonked down beside me and gave me a travel mug filled with coffee.

'Urgh, all that chipper energy and Spandex first thing in the morning is making me feel faint,' she groaned, gesturing to my outfit. 'You know, if I didn't love you so much, you'd put me right off my morning muffin.'

'The less I know about your morning muffin, the better,' I quipped back, putting my head on her shoulder. We sat like that for a few moments, just staring at the sea rolling back and forwards. Carly was the first one to break the silence.

'Honey, are you okay?'

'Of course!' I shot back, with my eternal cheeriness. 'Why do you ask?'

She shrugged, forgetting my head was on her shoulder and almost giving me whiplash.

'I don't know. I think I've just had a vibe off you for the last while that feels a bit different. I know being married to my brother might make it a tad difficult to share everything with me, but you know I'm here for you, no matter what. Actually, scratch that – if your problems have anything to do with my brother's dangly bits, I don't want to know. But please don't tell Jess either, because she's so pissed off with the entire male species right now that she'll just suggest you chop them off.'

'I'm rubbish with a pair of scissors, so Callum's bits are safe.' I didn't want to add that I saw them so rarely these days that there wasn't much of a window of opportunity. Lately we'd gone from having sex two or three times a week to a solid twice a month and even at that I tried to avoid it and he didn't push it either. I don't think either of us cared much about it any more. 'But thanks, Carly. I'm fine though.' Best smile back on again. 'If I wasn't, you'd be the first to hear about it.'

In past days, that would be true. But now? I just couldn't face listening to myself spilling my guts out, especially when she was so excited about starting her new life with Sam. I wasn't going to be the Donna Downer. Or was it Dina Downer? Debbie? Whatever. I wasn't going to be the one to come in with the negative energy and make this all about me. Whatever I was feeling would pass. It had to.

Besides, Jess was being negative enough for all of us.

'Is it just me, or should Arnie be worried about her developing homicidal tendencies?' I asked, doing a swift pivot of the focus on to our pal, who was walking along the sands towards us, deep in animated conversation with Val.

Carly nodded. 'He should probably hire security. And if she's feeling murderous, I should have pointed her in the direction of Estelle Bloody Conran last night. I swear that woman gets on my hooters like no one else in the free world. Was it my rampant insecurities and general dislike of her, or was she really being a complete cow to us? Those gift bags were like the passive-aggressive version of putting her feelings about me on a billboard.'

I could see Carly's point and I say that as a completely objection bystander. Shit, I mean objective. Aaaargh. I tried to focus back on the conversation. Where were we?

Estelle. Yeah, that was it. Estelle, who clearly still had issues with Sam rejecting her in favour of my non-celebrity, non-A-list, not-thirty-something, not-size-zero sister-in-law.

First, she'd ushered us all in as if it was her house, a sure sign that she was trying to irk Carly. The outfit was another giveaway. Ripped jeans that exposed more tanned legs than they covered, and a tiny, white cropped Bardot top, and long caramel waves, centre parting, that any half-trained eye knew were the very best in hair extensions and had been done that morning for the occasion. Definite power play. Then, in Sam's huge, and very stunning industrial-style kitchen, she'd perched at one of the islands and handed out gift bags to Carly, Val and me. Sam had obviously told her that Carly was bringing us and she'd gone all out to impress us. Or him. Or maybe just to make a dig that would piss Carly right off.

I took another sip of my coffee, while idly making lines in the sand with my toes. 'Do we even know why she was there?'

Carly shrugged. 'She told Sam she wanted to welcome us and say hello. She said we'd all been such great friends last time we were there. And he's a male who knows nothing of the workings of the female mind, so he bought it.'

'Fool,' I said, shaking my head, making Carly laugh. We both knew that was a lie. The first time we met Estelle, she was living here with Sam and despite the sugary sweet parade… not parade. What was the word? Façade! That was it. Yeah, despite her sugary sweet façade, it was clear to us all that we were about as welcome as an itch that required an antibiotic. The fact that Sam had then broken off their relationship to rekindle things with Carly had made it even worse and none of us were buying her 'friends and co-workers' act with Sam. Estelle Conran was a sniper at the side, ready and waiting to take Carly out. She had to get through me, Jess and Val's Elvis jacket first.

Last night, she took her first shot.

'Just some things I thought you might need after your journey,' she'd purred, with a flick of the hair as she handed over Carly's gift. Carly had opened the bag and pulled out a bag-reducing eye mask, some Gaviscon for heartburn, a detoxifying, weight-loss juice, a set of exercise bands, a book on manifesting 'the best version of you' and a pot of extremely expensive anti-aging cream 'for mature skin'.

Carly continued to vent her irritation. 'I wouldn't have been surprised if she'd popped in a packet of Tena lady just to ram home the point that it was a rescue kit for knackered old bags. Maybe some menopause supplements and a battery fan for flushes.'

'You still getting those?' I asked her. 'I thought they'd passed.'

'They have, thanks to all that is holy. I think menopause is like pregnancy. You forget how bad it is when you come out the other end. It was ropey there for a year or so with flushes and night sweats, but I feel totally fine now. See what you've got to look forward to,' she grinned, nudging me.

We were the same age, but I still had periods every month, twenty-eight days on the dot, so I hadn't hit the menopause yet. I wasn't looking forward to it. Yet another sign that my youth was gone and my best years were behind me. My breathing began to speed up and I had to close my eyes and focus really hard to make it slow down again. Carly didn't notice, because she was still on a roll, bemoaning Estelle.

'Anyway, you know I'm all about lifting up the sisterhood, but if I ever ask you to help me hide a body, it's a pretty fair bet it'll be hers. The worst thing is, Sam's completely oblivious. He thought it was a sweet gesture and I knew if I moaned, I'd come off like a complete bitch, so I let it go.'

'Didn't Sam say they're working together this week?' I asked, another memory of last night's conversations dropping in out of the blue.

'Yep. They're reshooting a couple of scenes for the movie they worked on three years ago. There was some kind of distribution delay, so they're reworking some storylines now that it finally has a release date. He'd planned to work on it remotely because we were supposed to be doing the belated honeymoon stuff, but now that Val has kidnapped us, he's decided to get fully involved on set. I'm going to be absolutely fine about it. I will not be jealous. I will not be jealous. I will not be jealous.' She sighed. 'This mantra stuff is shit. It just makes me think about the problem all over again. Sod it. I'm going to be jealous and I'm going to make a catapult with the exercise bands and shoot walnuts at her arse instead.'

'Good plan. Sensible. Intelligent. I'm so glad I married into your family and carried on your gene pool,' I barbed back, making her giggle.

Val reached us. 'Right, you two, get these on, then come save me from Jess. She's going through the stages of grief. Yesterday she did disbelief and sadness. Today she's considering cashing in her ISA and hiring a hitman. I always said that lassie's temper would be the end of her. Remember when she punched that lad at the school sports day? Her mother was mortified.'

Carly got in with a rebuttal before me. We'd both been there that day. School sports day. Primary two. 'Val, she was seven. And she punched Billy Porter because he'd deliberately tripped Sarah up in the hundred-metre sprint. She was just addressing an injustice. And her mother was only mortified because she was shagging Billy's dad.'

'But his dad was married! And he was our vicar!' Val exclaimed. 'Oh Christ, I was relying on him putting in a good word to get me through the pearly gates. If he was shagging around, there's my one religious ally gone. It's too late for me to start being pure of thought and deed. Right, come on – Jess is over there and ready. If we keep her waiting, it might tip her over the edge. Bollocks, I hope she's being friendly to the natives.'

Carly and I both switched our glances over to where Jess was standing, giving something to a man she was talking to. A couple of things clicked. The first was that she seemed to be deep in conversation, and the second was that she'd dropped her towel and now she was wearing a bright red swimsuit on a body that was rock hard, thanks to her daily gym sessions. Beside me, Carly's gaze shifted at exactly the same time as mine, going from Jess's red costume, to the red stretchy fabric that was being revealed inch by inch as Val opened her robe, to the tiny scraps of red fabric that Val had thrown at us.

Realisation dropped like David Hasselhoff in a dodgy lift.

'We've to wear these? I thought we were just recreating the *Baywatch* slow-motion run? I didn't realise there were costumes.'

'Aye, our Josie didn't do things by half. The crotch in these things would cut you in two. Josie told me she was going to get a Brazilian before she did this. I thought she meant a bloke from Rio de Janeiro. Turns out it's something altogether different. Anyway, I brought two with me – that's the ones me and Jess are wearing. Selena managed to track down another two for me yesterday, so you pair get those ones. They're a wee bit smaller than ours, but, och, you'll be fine.'

As Val wandered away, Carly held up the swimwear and nudged me with her shoulder. '"A wee bit smaller"? I think I'm going to have to wear this as a bandana,' she groaned, getting up and wrapping a blanket around her waist so she could maintain her dignity while she was changing.

She wasn't wrong about the size of the suits. These ones were thong-style swimsuits, the kind that Pamela Anderson wore back in the day. I had no problem slipping it on. It wasn't too different from the kind of swimsuit I usually wore on holiday. Carly however… when she opened the blanket she was changing under, the swimsuit was on, but so were a large pair of rainbow-shaded granny pants, sticking out from under the high-cut legs.

'Don't say a word,' she warned me. 'There's no way my arse is going to be exposed to the world, especially if there's motion involved.'

Her eyes went up to the skies. 'Josie, I hope you're having a good laugh up there, because when I see you, we're going to have words.'

She pulled the blanket back around her waist and we padded across the sands to join the others.

The guy Jess had been talking to was now standing, holding up her phone, ready to film us. 'This is Adam,' Jess informed us. 'He lives further along the beach, and was out for a walk, so I've roped him in to catch this moment for posterity.' Now we were closer, we could see that he was holding Jess's phone, ready to video whatever was coming next.

'Brilliant. Photographic evidence of this moment of dignity in my life. I think I'd have preferred it if he were a hitman,' Carly murmured.

'Right, lassies, get in a line. Did I mention that when me and Josie first came up with this one, we were three sheets to the wind on porn star Martinis and she was already fantasising about who we were going to save?'

'The porn star Martinis explain a lot,' Carly whispered, dropping her blanket.

Val and Jess caught a glimpse of the pants and did an adamant job of holding it together. Admirable. That's what I meant. Admirable.

'I'm pretty sure I saw rainbow knickers on *Baywatch* once,' Jess deadpanned.

'It's that or this G-string goes through my lady garden like a Flymo,' Carly argued.

Val ignored the bickering. 'Okay, ladies,' she said solemnly, before looking upwards, just as Carly had done earlier. 'Josie, pal, we miss you.' Then back to us. 'Girls, Tom Jones is out there and the daft bugger can't swim. It's up to us to save him. Ready, steady, go...'

With that, four pals ran towards the Pacific Ocean. We laughed as the sand rubbed against our feet, then we squealed as the coldness of the water took our breath away.

As I began to swim towards an imaginary Tom Jones, I realised that I was the only one going out to sea, yet I couldn't stop.

Because for the first time in as long as I could remember, I felt free.

11

VAL

Dreams – The Cranberries

Dear Josie,

Dollface, you would have laughed until you did yourself an injury. There we were, the four of us, howling with laughter as we ran into the water. Our timing was off though. Might have been a glorious, balmy thing to do in June, but the Malibu Ocean at dawn on a November morning was fecking freezing. Not as bad as that time we took a dip off the coast of Dunoon, right enough. If we'd had balls that day, they'd have turned blue and dropped off.

Anyway, love, it was amazing. And it was every bit as much fun as we thought it would be. We looked just like that lot from Baywatch, if you added a few decades, a few spare tyres, a pair of rainbow knickers and a whole lot of sweary words. We dashed out there like Tom Jones really was drowning in front of us. As soon as we got hip deep in the water, me, Jess and Carly turned *right back round again and bolted back to the sands, where we tried to warm up with a good rub-down and a couple of choruses of 'Delilah'. Some bloke Jess met was filming it for us and that's definitely a video we'll be trotting out at every opportunity until the end of my days. Not that I'll be telling Carly that. She was a picture. What's it called? A wardrobe malfunction. Her cossie was a tad revealing so she wore her pants underneath and it wasn't her finest fashion moment. All those years I told that lassie to wear her best undies every day in case she got knocked down by a bus. She never did listen, that one. Rainbow knickers. She was a cross between a Baywatch babe and a box of crayons.*

Carol was a weird one though. The lass just kept swimming until all we could see was a head bobbing in the distance. I was about to call in big Hasselhoff for some assistance when she finally started swimming back to us.

I still don't know what's going on with these lassies at all, ma love. It's like Carol is in her own wee world. There's a sadness about her, but when I ask her how she's doing, she flips a switch and the smile goes back on. I keep catching her though, when she thinks no one is watching, just staring into space like she's got the weight of the world on her shoulders. I'll get to the bottom of it, Josie, don't you worry. I'm just taking my time and going in gently. Get someone to explain to you what that means because we both know that going in gently to any situation was a mysterious concept to you.

Jess is easier to read. She's on a rager because that man of hers has gone back to his last wife, and I don't blame her. Apparently, there was no warning at all. There she was, planning their wedding when all the time he was sneaking off to phone the ex, so she just packed her case and took off. She says she's blocked him now. Not really sure what that means, but I'm not asking. Some of these words the young ones use have meanings that I don't even want to think about. I know now that I need to be careful who I ask about getting a good teabag, because that one means something that made me blush right doon to ma furry mules.

I've not worked out what's going on with our Carly yet either. I don't mean the pants. Maybe I'm being dramatic – not exactly a newsflash – but I just can't shake the feeling that something's not right with her.

She loves that man of hers, no doubt about that, though. And who wouldn't. If you were still here and fifty years younger, the lippy would be on, the boobs would be out, and you'd be having a go yerself.

That just reminded me – remember that day we bought those Wonderbras in House of Fraser? I thought we'd never stop laughing in those changing rooms. Still can't believe they didn't ask us to leave. Two women our age, in bras that put our bosoms up round our ears. My Don said it was handy having another shelf to put his pint on.

Sorry, smudged a bit there. The tears are tripping me as I write this, pet, and I don't know if it's laughter or longing for us to be able to turn back time. I wish that for me, for Don, for you… I'm just not ready for our stories to be over.

I miss you more than ever, pal.

Keep dancing, keep laughing… and be happy up there.

Love you,

Val xxx

PS: I hope you and our Dee are on good terms with the management and can pull a few strings up there for me, cos I've just found out the vicar is going to be no use in that department. I'll explain when I see you. Nothing to do with teabags though. Lol!

The tears were coming in torrents now, and I wiped them away with the palms of my hands. My eyeliner would be ruined. Sometimes the need for a good sob just came over me and there was no stopping it. Only in private though. I wasn't one for wailing when there were others around.

Another memory pushed its way to the front of my mind, probably because I'd just mentioned my Dee. I did a quick sum in my head. She'd be in her forties now. Maybe that's why I treasured my relationships with these women who were with me now. They reminded me of the kind of bond I would have had with my girl if she hadn't been mown down by a drugged-up arsehole who got behind the wheel of a car. For a long time, I thought that would break me, but even then, I kept my feelings inside. I didn't tell a soul that I would go out in the middle of the night to the twenty-four-hour supermarket and wander up and down the aisles, tears blinding me, then I'd dry my eyes, sort myself out, and go home before Don woke for work and act like I was coping. I'd make meals, I'd clean the house, I'd keep an eye on the rest of the family, and the whole time I'd be counting the hours until everyone else in my world went to sleep and I could go out and wander those aisles, zombied by grief. I'm pretty sure the supermarket put me on some kind of weirdo watch list. Anyway, I kept on going like that until one day, years later, when I finally slept through the night again. Josie once said to me that life closes wounds eventually, but we keep the scars to remind us. Dee is one of my scars. There's one here for Josie too. And soon there would be one for Don…

I picked up my phone and texted our Michael. It would be 6 p.m. back home so they'd probably be stopping off somewhere for tea round about now. It had been his idea to take his dad on a road trip and he'd set my phone up so that I could text him every day from here. He'd said not to call, because it only made things worse.

Hello, son, hope you and your dad had a good day. I'm here if you need me. Can't tell you how much I love ya, son. Give yer dad a hug from me.

I pressed 'send' and put the phone down.

Yep, Don was definitely going to leave a wound. I just wasn't ready to tell anyone about it yet though. And I wasn't sure yet how long it was going to be or how deep it was going to cut.

12

JESS

No More 'I Love You's' – Annie Lennox

Carly had gone up for a sleep in their bedroom, and Carol and Val had nipped out to the shops with Selena to track down chocolate digestives and blister plasters for Val's feet.

There were a dozen things on my to-do list for the day, but all I could manage was to sit at the window seat in Sam's kitchen and stare at the spot across the courtyard, in front of the massive garage and the apartment above it, where Arnie's pickup had been parked on the evening he'd proposed to me. That night, nothing could have persuaded me that we weren't forever. Nothing. Not even the way our lunch with Arnie's daughter, Talia, had gone sideways the following day.

I'd been sitting at the kitchen table, in a heated email exchange with a celebrity blogger who was running a blind, but very obvious, smear campaign against one of my clients back then, a talent show winner who had secured a record deal and a sexually transmitted disease on the night of the live final of the show. Bernie was a good kid, a country music singer-songwriter who had a chaotic background that had left him sofa-surfing for two years after his drunk stepfather kicked him out on his sixteenth birthday. The producer of the series, an old friend, had called me in when the rumours started swirling, just mean-spirited jealousy that I suspected was down to some kind of alliance between the blogger and the runner-up. That morning, I'd persuaded the blogger to drop the story, but I'd lost my second battle of the day.

There was a brief knock at the door, before it had opened and Talia glided in.

Arnie's daughter and I had always been polite and respected each other's place in her father's life. It was rare that she dropped in, preferring to meet her dad for lunch down near the talent agency she worked in on Santa Monica boulevard. It was one of the biggest and best, and as a talent liaison manager, she was the person responsible for smoothing stormy seas between the corporate suits and some of the stars the agency represented. The daughter of her black father, and her white mother, she had dark skin, but pale green eyes and she was simply breathtaking in every way. A basketball superstar who'd gone to Howard on a full scholarship, she walked with the posture and grace of an athlete in full command of her body. I wasn't generally given to insecurity, but this woman would make anyone feel average-on-the-cusp-of-dowdy. Nevertheless, I liked her. And I especially liked the way my fiancé's face lit up when he saw her.

'Hey, this is a cool surprise,' he'd said, coming out from behind the kitchen island, opening his arms wide.

'Yeah, well, I was in the neighbourhood,' she'd replied. 'I was dropping off a client at his home on San Remo. Scooped him up outside the Chateau Marmont this morning, stomach pumped, then home. You know, just another morning in Los Angeles.'

Arnie had hugged her. 'Stay for lunch. I'm just making some pasta and there's plenty for three.'

'Are you sure?' she'd asked, glancing at me. 'Jess, if you're working…'

I'd snapped my laptop shut. 'No, please stay. We'd love it.'

There was a subtle but definite reticence, but she'd relented and pulled out the chair across from mine. We made small talk until the food was served – did I mention that Arnie was an incredible cook? Salmon tagliatelle, beetroot salad and a home-made focaccia. I had to run five miles a day just to make sure I could stay in my clothes.

It was only when I reached for the pepper that I saw her eyes go to the ring on my finger. Like a relay race, I took the baton of her gaze and passed it over to Arnie, who cleared his throat. It was the first time I'd ever seen him exude even a hint of nervousness. At first, I thought he was going to bottle it, and I wouldn't have minded if he did – maybe this wasn't the time or place. To give him credit, though, he went with it.

'Talia, Jess and I have decided to get married.'

Okay, simple, straight to the point. Please be happy for us.

'No.' Was her whispered response. I'd hoped I'd misheard her or imagined it. 'No way,' she'd repeated, louder this time. 'Why? Dad, you're sixty years old! Why the hell would you want to do that? And you know what it'll do to us, to your family. Dad, please. Don't.'

She didn't even glance in my direction and that might be why Arnie's jaw had clenched in irritation. Ironically, he never, ever let anyone disrespect me. As it would later transpire, he had the monopoly on that.

'Talia,' he spoke calmly. 'I'm a grown man and I don't need you permission, honey.' He was still trying to keep it light, to salvage the situation.

Talia, however, was taking a different route altogether. 'Jess, I'm sorry,' she'd blurted in a tone that was anything but apologetic, 'but this can't happen. It just can't.' She was facing her dad again, eyes blazing. 'Why would you do this, Dad? It'll cause carnage. You've no right to spring this on us and if you do...'

'I don't respond to threats, Tal, so pick your next words carefully.' It was as low and as sad as I'd ever heard him.

'Or...' She'd hesitated, then visibly backed down from whatever she was going to say, changing course instead. 'I'm not threatening you, Dad, but we'll never accept this. None of us. Maybe you want to think about that. What's more important to you?'

With that, she'd got up and walked out. I never saw her again, but she was true to her word. Every family event, every celebration, every holiday, Arnie was included, but I wasn't. Although, in hindsight, given what happened, I couldn't be sure if that was his daughter's decision or his. Maybe he'd called her the next day and told her he'd broken off his engagement to me so he could get back with her mother. Maybe they'd been playing happy families all along.

I was interrupted from that cheery thought by the sound of the front door banging, and I unfurled my legs from under me on the window seat. I could tell by the footsteps that it was Sam. I'd been waiting for an opportunity to catch him alone since we got here, and now was my chance.

I'd known him since he and Carly first met a million years ago, and our relationship was firmly based on love, respect and sarcasm. He was the brotherly figure I hadn't realised I wanted until he'd strutted into our framily and never left, first as a friend, and then decades later, to the delight of us all, as Carly's husband. He was also my ex-fiancé's employer and best friend, so that made him my official informant. He just didn't know it yet.

As soon as he spotted me, he put his hands up. 'Oh hell. I know that look. If I've done something wrong tell me now and I'll beg for forgiveness. You know I don't want to be on your bad side.'

'Didn't you once take on a whole platoon of rogue trained killers in a war movie and fearlessly slay them all?'

He popped the top off his bottle of Coors. 'Yep, but they're no match for my wife and her girlfriends when they're pissed off. Beer?'

I nodded and watched as he took a bottle from the fridge, opened it and handed it to me. I took it, then put it to one side for a moment as I pulled myself up to sit on the marble top of his kitchen island.

'I hear you're going after Dax Hill in the press. Brave move. He's a scumball, but he's connected,' he said, referring to the talent agent who was currently blasting out false stories about my client, his pregnant ex-mistress, in the hope that Hayley would give up trying to defend herself and disappear.

'Yeah, well, he's a scumball who is being a prick to my client. Let's see who wins.'

His face broke into the widest grin. 'Go on, Jess,' he cheered. 'My money is on you every time. And if I can help, I'm in.'

He was such a sweetheart. One of the few people in this town who would do the right thing rather than the career-protecting thing when it came to the LA fame game.

'Thanks, Sam. You're not bad sometimes. Only sometimes though. Tell me, are you sick of us all yet? Are you pissed off that we're hijacking your honeymoon?'

He shrugged. 'To be honest, and if you tell Carly, I'll have to kill you, but it's actually worked out for the best. The reshoots are more intense than we'd envisaged and we need to get them finished while Estelle still has a window before her next shoot. If I was away with Carly, I'd just be checking on it every five minutes. But, like I say, don't tell her because I plan to milk the guilt trip for at least a month or two after you've gone.'

'Ah, you make me so proud,' I said, with faux admiration, making him grin. I was glad we weren't pissing him off.

'Thank you. I try,' he bowed. 'And I guess I was worried that Carly would struggle here at first because she'd miss you all so much. This is kind of breaking her into LA gently. Just moving the rug, instead of pulling it right out from under her feet.'

'Sometimes you surprise me,' I teased. 'Every time I think you're nothing but a well-carved body, you come out with something smart.'

'Again, I try,' he laughed.

There was a moment of silence, before he took the lead. It didn't take a genius to work out why I was loitering in the kitchen.

'Go on then,' he prompted. 'Ask me whatever you need to know, and I'll answer honestly. But before you do, I swear I don't know what's going on with Arnie. He called, said he needed some personal time, and then took off. I didn't ask and he didn't tell me. I know you find that crazy because you all confide in each other, but he's a private guy. Always has been. He's been my closest mate for fifteen years and I'd trust him with my life, but don't ask me to tell you what's going on in his head because we don't share that stuff.'

I reclaimed my beer and took a slug while I thought about where to go with that. 'Did you ever meet his ex-wife?'

'Which one?'

That elicited a rueful smile. Arnie's first marriage had lasted ten years, and they'd maintained a relationship for the sake of their children in the thirty years since then. His second one, to the dancer he met in Las Vegas, was like a Sin City lightshow: wild, crazy, but it faded pretty quickly. After that, he'd resolved to stay single, with just casual relationships, and he'd been that way for the last ten years or so. He made no secret of the fact that he'd never been exclusive and had no intention of doing the whole relation-ship and commitment thing again... Until he met me. And I bought it. Was I that idiot who thought she could change a guy? Was I completely deluded about his feelings for me? Clearly, I was, because if you had asked me a week ago if anything could break us up, I'd have sworn that could never happen. And yet…

'The first one. Myrna.'

Sam shook his head. 'No, but I know they kept in touch because of Talia and Joanie,' he answered, mentioning Arnie's other daughter. 'Before you came along, he still spent the holidays and special occasions with them. Did you two never discuss this stuff?'

I put my bottle back down on the marble. 'You weren't the only one who didn't get inside his head. He always said there was no point talking about the past, and, to be honest, I agreed. From the start, his daughters made it clear that I wasn't to be included in their family time. I'm too bloody old to play those games and deal with the petty stuff, so I respected that, and he kept that part of his life completely separate from me. Now I understand why. I guess he wanted me nowhere near his family if he was still involved with his ex. Talia and Joanie must have thought I was just a fling on the side, and they were prepared to accept that because they knew he'd go back to their mother.'

'You don't know that,' Sam argued.

'Sam, you didn't hear him on the phone! He was giving Myrna the full seduction routine. Urgh, just thinking about it now makes me want to hurl.'

'What did you do? Carly said you bolted, but did you ask him about it before you left?'

'Because that would be the adult and mature thing to do?' I checked.

He could see where this was going, and the corners of his mouth turned up. 'Yes, indeed.'

'No, I didn't. Don't you mock my communication skills, Sam

Morton. You're the bloke that was in love with a woman for twenty years and didn't bother to let her know.'

'I had to think it through,' he joked, his rueful grin the same one that made countless women (and men) comment on social media conversations declaring their wish to shag him on every surface in their house. My pal was a lucky lady. She deserved him. He deserved her too. I used to think the same about Arnie and me.

'Nope, I just took off, drove around LA in a fury, and by the time I got back he was gone. I know what you're going to say, Sam, and maybe I should have challenged him about it, but if you'd heard the way he was speaking to her... It was like she was the love of his life and he was desperate to be with her. What's the point in fighting that?'

'I'm the wrong person to ask,' he admitted with a sigh. 'Because, as you so kindly pointed out, I'm the tit who let the love of his life go and then spent twenty years watching her live with someone else. You do realise I'm the least qualified person ever when it comes to relationships? Woefully incompetent.'

With a weary sigh, I nodded. 'You are. Why couldn't Carly have married Dr Phil. Or Oprah. I need someone with a shred of emotional intelligence around here. You're a complete disappointment.'

His laughter made me smile for the first time all day. He ditched his beer, and came over, wrapped his arms around me and gave me a brotherly hug, just as he'd done a thousand times before. 'My wife probably thinks the same thing. I'm going to go check.' Then more seriously, 'Look, I'm sorry, Jess, I wish I had answers, but I don't. But I'm here if you need the important stuff...'

'Hugs and beer?'

'Yep.'

'I'd still prefer Oprah!' I shouted as he sauntered out the door.

I sat there for a few minutes thinking everything through. Sam was right. I'd been too hasty. I should have given Arnie a chance to explain. Sure, he could have waited until I got back and then we could have discussed it maturely and reasonably. Or I could have given him the opportunity to let me down gently. He and his wife had a lifetime of history together. I suppose I just couldn't compete with that. Fuck. I really thought that going out with an older guy would mean that I was with an adult who had their shit together, but I guess I was wrong.

I slid off the worktop, and as I did, my eye caught the keys hanging on the board near the door. Top row, second from the left, Arnie's apartment above the garage. Which makes it sound like a tiny studio, but the reality was that Sam had a twelve-car garage and the flat above it was bigger than my house back in London.

I had my own keys, but I'd left them in the flat when I took off for the airport. Not the best decision in hindsight.

Don't go there. Leave the keys where they are. There's nothing in that flat that would help. All those reasonable points were racing through my head like a ticker tape, as I grabbed the keys and bolted out of the door, across the driveway, and up the steel staircase that curved round the side of the building. I only paused once, when my key slid in the door, and I pushed it open. I listened for signs of life, even though I knew he wasn't there.

Silence.

I slipped my shoes off (force of habit) and crossed the wide-plank oak floors of the open-plan living, kitchen and dining area. Everything was exactly as I'd left it. My yoga mat was curled up at the side of the sofa. The remote control I'd used when I switched on the TV to watch the news yesterday was lying on the steel-grey fabric sofa. That seemed like a lifetime ago. It suddenly hit me that when I woke up yesterday morning, I was happy, in love, and planning to set off first thing for Napa. By lunchtime, I'd caught my fiancé cheating, packed a bag and was storming to the airport to flee back to London. That was so spontaneous, so hasty, so absolutely erratic, that it sounded exactly like something Carly would do.

At our bedroom door, I stopped and scanned the room. Drawers were still open, and empty hangers dangled in the wardrobe, from where I'd wrenched my clothes from their place and threw them in my case. The wedding magazine I was reading in bed a couple of nights ago was still on my bedside table, open at the page that featured the winery we'd chosen... Actually, I'd picked it. Arnie said right from the start that he was happy to let me choose everything and all I had to do was tell him where and when to show up. Another bloody red flag. I now had so many I could guide a fricking space shuttle in to land in the Nevada desert.

My eyes fell on the framed photograph that sat on the bedside table beside the discarded mag, my night cream, and the mug of half-drunk coffee he'd brought me in bed yesterday morning. Bastard. It was a photo of the two of us on Santa Monica beach, not long after we met. I'm pretty sure Carly took it when she was on holiday over here with the boys. We'd been playing volleyball and I'd just landed a shot that had almost taken Arnie's head off. He'd ducked under the net and I'd taken off running, but only got a few yards before he caught me, swung me round, both of us buckled with laughter. That was the moment Carly had clicked the camera. I adored the result. It absolutely summed up the joy of the moment, of the day, of us. Although, apparently it wasn't bloody joyful enough to keep him here.

None of this made sense. How could I have got it so wrong? How could the guy in that photograph, the one who looked so happy to be with me, trash me like this? Was I just a convenience? Just someone to keep him company while Sam was over working in the UK?

I flipped the photo, so it was face-down. Enough. That's what I thought we had. Now I knew better. I was about to back out of the room when I noticed two things. The first was the indentation on the bed, where he'd been sitting when I walked in and caught him on the phone. The second was that the drawer of his bedside table was very slightly ajar. I'd never looked in there before. Not ever. Prying just wasn't my style. I took things at face value, trusted my judgement, stuck with integrity and... Bugger it, look where that had got me. In three steps, I was there, and in two seconds, the drawer was fully opened, and I was staring at...

The shock was like a right hook to the gut. I leant down and began pulling out the photos. Dozens and dozens of them. Every single one was an image of Arnie and Myrna. Some of them had young Talia and Joanie in them, some of them were taken when Arnie and Myrna were almost children themselves, back when they met on the air base they both lived on as kids. Arnie was the son of a soldier, and Myrna was the daughter of the sergeant who headed up Arnie's dad's unit. They were best friends at twelve. Married at eighteen. Divorced at thirty-eight. And it seemed like every single day of that relationship had been captured on an image that was in Arnie's bedside drawer.

I picked up the pile, then scrutinised each photo, one by one, placing them down on the bed when I was done. With every one that I discarded, I became more and more convinced of one thing – against all this history, I never stood a chance. I was right to move on. Whatever was going on here, I wanted no part of it and Arnie clearly didn't want me either. I just wished I'd found that out before I was on the wrong side of infidelity for the third time.

I was about to pick up the pile of images from the bed, and place them back in the drawer, when I heard a voice hollering from downstairs. 'Jess Latham!'

Val. I closed my eyes, inhaled, tried to steady my vocal cords. The last thing I wanted to do was tell anyone about this. I already felt humiliated. Mortified. Of all of us, I was probably the most direct, the most ruthless, yet I was the absolute idiot whose first serious relationship was with a man who lied about being separated from his wife, Then I'd married a serial cheater. Now, I'd repeated history by agreeing to marry a man who'd just left me for someone else. What the hell was wrong with me? For someone who spent their lives sorting out other people's toxic situations, I seemed to be pretty bloody good at creating my own.

'Jess Latham, if you make me come up there, you're paying for ma knee replacements,' Val hollered again.

'I'm coming, Val,' I shouted back. 'Save your knees. You'll need them for line dancing.'

Hastily picking up the pile of photos off the bed, I threw them back in the drawer, but as I did, one of them fell on the floor. When I grabbed it, I realised it was a younger Arnie, a younger Myrna, standing outside a house with their girls, who looked like they were in their early teens. Must have been about fifteen years ago then. I had no idea why I turned it over, but I did. There was an elaborate scrawl on the back.

Our home. 2322 Hillcrest.

I knew that Myrna still lived in the same home that they'd raised their family in, so now I had an address.

And I suddenly had a burning need to find out if my ex-fiancé was back there with her.

13

CARLY

Texas – Put Your Arms Around Me

'Good morning, gorgeous,' murmured the low sexy voice by my side.

'You obviously haven't opened your eyes yet,' I replied. 'And if you don't want to experience mild terror first thing in the morning, I'd keep it that way.' I pushed myself up in bed and caught my reflection in the mirror on the wall to my right. 'Yep, Marge Simpson after a night on carbohydrates and crack.'

Sam let out a low chuckle as he took his life in his hands and prised one eye open. 'The crazy thing is, that in this town, the carbs would be the worst of those two habits.' His arm went around my stomach and he pulled me back towards him. 'C'mere you. Damn, it still feels incredible to wake up next to you. Especially here. Do you know how happy you make me?'

I rolled over so my face was just inches from his, then slid on top of him with as much elegance as I could muster. 'Happier than Marge on doughnuts and crack?'

'Definitely,' he murmured, pulling my face towards his so that he could plant a long, lingering, kiss on my lips. His touch set off a chain of events that transformed my physical state from 'jet lagged and rough as a badger' to 'very horny and having morning sex with my husband'.

It was slow, it was incredible, and it was the very best way to start the day. Afterwards, I rolled over, kissed him again, then watched his face as I ran my finger along his cheek, down the side of his temple, across his eyebrows. I could look at that face until the end of time. I just wished it was in London, with the sound of my sons crashing around downstairs in the kitchen, trying to locate their socks / pants / PlayStation controllers instead.

'We're never getting out of this bed if you keep doing that,' he warned, his voice oozing bliss.

'I don't think that's an option. Val will come storming in here any minute, demanding that I move my arse.'

'True.' He sighed, although his grin gave away his amusement. 'You know, I think this is the first time I've ever considered installing an impenetrable panic room.'

We pushed ourselves up so that we were leaning against the pile of pillows behind us, then I watched as his naked buttocks crossed the room, then returned with two steaming-hot coffees from the machine in the wet bar that delivered a fresh cuppa at the press of a button. Actually, it was more of a suite than a room. The bed was huge and covered in grey cashmere bedding that felt like stroking kittens. Over to the left, there was a pale blue velvet sofa, one of the ones that were almost square, so that you could lie on it and watch the giant TV that sat above the long, glass-fronted real-flame fire built into the wall below it.

In the corner next to the TV was the bar, complete with a

drinks fridge, a wine rack and the coffee machine that could spit out twenty different varieties of caffeine. Sometimes, I still couldn't believe this was his life. Our life. When we first met a million years ago, we lived in his little apartment in Hong Kong, happily surviving pay cheque to pay cheque. His biggest dream was to open a martial arts academy and mine was... I have no idea. I just wanted to live in the moment and travel and meet people and enjoy life. When I left Sam to take a trip home to London, I told him I'd be back, but I never returned. Life got in the way.

I managed a few more years of travelling and embracing life, but then came marriage to Mark and two decades of embracing motherhood instead. I just lost sight of all the other stuff. Now I had Sam back, I was madly in love with him, and we had an amazing life in front of us, so why wasn't that enough? Even this room – it was luxury on a whole different level, like the most gorgeous suite in a five-star hotel. Now that it was my palatial home, I should be happy, right?

So why did the thought of being here with him, just the two of us, fill me with absolute dread? What the hell was wrong with me?

'What are you thinking? You've got that wrinkle between your eyes that always appears when you're worried.'

The bluff came naturally. 'You'd be worried too if you were about to spend a day on Rodeo Drive with Carol "Spend Spend Spend" Cooper, Val "Chat To Everyone" Murray and Jess "Might Punch Someone" Latham. Honest to God, you'd think we'd all have life sussed out by now. There's not a mature, settled one between us.'

'You're not settled? Should I be worried?'

Crap. 'Of course I am! I just mean, well...' I felt my face flushing as I stuttered over my words. Now would be the time to tell him. *Sam, I don't want to move here. I want to stay at home with my boys*

nearby, and Kate through the wall, surrounded by our crazy big dysfunc-
tional framily and all the drama that comes with them.

I took a sip of my coffee, willing myself to get the words out, but they were stuck somewhere between my gut and the big lump of cowardice that was blocking my throat.

Come on. Say it. 'It's just that—'

'Carly Morton, get yerself out of that bed and let's get going. Time's a wasting, buttercup.' Val. Saved by the mouthy Glaswegian aunt on a mission. I could hear the click clack of her high-heeled furry mules on the hardwood floor of the corridor outside as she passed on the way to the staircase. 'If you're not downstairs in five minutes, I'm going to waft bacon sandwiches outside yer door.'

Sam nuzzled into my ear. 'Five minutes? You could get dressed or we could have sex again. Twice. Your choice.'

'Tempting,' I giggled. It's a total cliché but his sense of humour turned me on even more than the rock-hard body, the sexy face and the coffee machine. 'But I'm a woman with places to go, friends to sort out, and hair that needs to be wrestled into submission by my straighteners, so your generous offer will have to wait.'

'Ouch, the rejection!' he teased, as he reluctantly rolled over and picked up his tablet from his bedside table, flicking immediately to his calendar. It was standard practice every morning. He had his first espresso while running through his schedule for the day.

I glanced over, trying not to make it obvious that I was scanning the screen for a mention of Satanelle. Ooops, sorry, my mistake. I did, of course, mean Estelle. I found it halfway down the page. 'Campaign meeting – PR, Estelle and Jazo.' Jazo Brooks was Sam's latest discovery, a brusque Irish actor in his forties, who'd played the main character in the movie. On screen, he was tough, formidable and utterly chilling as a serial killer masquerading as a happily married family man in the New York suburbs. In real life, he was an absolute sweetheart. Shame. If only life would imitate art and he'd pop Estelle off somewhere between her *Vogue* photoshoot and her twenty-minute interview special with Entertainment Tonight.

I had a sharp word with myself. *Do not get jealous. It's work. Sam has no feelings for Estelle. He chose you over her a long time ago. And besides, she has waaaayyyyy too much filler in her lips and could get suctioned to a tile wall at any moment.*

Perhaps it was because I was thinking evil thoughts that karma decided to dish out a swift kick of retribution.

Mirroring my darling husband's actions, I slotted right into my usual morning habits. First things first, I reached for my phone, lying face down and on silent so that we wouldn't be disturbed by calls or texts from people in the UK who didn't realise I was in the USA and living my life eight hours behind them. On my last trip, I'd been woken up at 4 a.m. by a delivery driver who was calling to ask directions so he could drop off a pair of screaming pink espadrilles I'd ordered from a dodgy fashion site. I couldn't get back to sleep and by the time I got home, someone had nicked them from the storage box beside my wheelie bin.

As soon as I flipped the phone over, I saw that I was in demand.

Four texts. The first was from Mac. I had yet another pang of longing, mixed with happiness at the sight of his name. Was he missing me? Was he in need of a comforting chat? An emotional exchange about his feelings? Some profound advice or words of wisdom? Some reassurance or a confidence boost from his biggest supporter and emotional crutch? For the purposes of this little interlude of self-pity, I chose to overlook the fact that he was a fully grown, fiercely independent bloke who hadn't required any of those things since he was eleven and planning to ask a girl to go with him to a school disco. I wasn't letting the facts get in the way of a good old bout of separation anxiety.

I opened the text.

Mum, I'm all for a bit of forward fashion, but I don't think it's a look that will catch on. You're a beamer, but we love you. PS: Changing my name just in case anyone knows we're related.

I was genuinely bewildered. What was he talking about?

The second text was from Benny.

Mum, you're a legend. Were you drunk?

There were a dozen more laughing faces after that one.

What was going on? A legend? I hadn't been any kind of legend in my sons' eyes since... well, ever. I was Mum. Sometimes Ma or Maw. Frequently worthy of eye rolls. And regularly an embarrassment. Never a legend.

Next was one from my brother, Callum.

That's like every picture we ever had taken as kids. #wedgiesrule

What the hell? I clicked the last text, hoping it was someone telling me this was all a bad dream or a wind-up.

No. It was my ex-husband, Mark.

Carly, I'm sure you've seen these photos, but you might want to investigate and take appropriate action. I'll discuss with the boys and make sure they're not mortified by it all.

Whaaaaat?

I clicked on the link he'd pasted underneath and... oh, holy sisterhood of the bloody big pants. It was one of those celebrity websites, the ones that specialise in gossip and scandal. When I'd first hooked up with Sam, they'd printed a couple of highly embarrassing photos of me, with captions that implied I was Sam's cleaner, his masseuse, and a kaftan pic suggesting I was his new-age, fortune-telling, hippy shaman. Or should it be shaman-ess? Shawoman?

This time, there was a brutal headline that screamed, 'Sam's Wife or Rainbow Warrior?'

Was I reading that wrong? Was this some kind of prank? Or did they seriously just compare my arse to the size of a ship that patrolled international waters searching for environmental travesties?

I began to feel more than a little sick. I was all for body positivity and I supported and encouraged every other woman to find happiness in her own skin, no matter the size or the sag. I'd just never managed it myself.

'Sam...'

He raised his eyes from his iPad.

'Yeah, babe?'

I turned my phone to show him the images underneath the headline.

'Why are photographs of me running along a beach wearing multicoloured knickers plastered all over the internet?'

14

CAROL

Miss Me More – Kelsea Ballerini

'Let me see, let me see,' Kate begged. 'Turn the phone round! Honest to God, I'm so jealous, I'm a shade of frog. Why am I not there? Why?'

I'd called her as promised to keep her posted on all the happenings so far. The four of us were a group who rarely left anyone behind, and we were all missing Kate's affection and chat. Carly more than anyone. The two of them had been inseparable for most of their lives, and I couldn't even begin to contemplate how Carly would survive without Kate next door, especially given the emotional drama on this trip so far.

After I'd scanned the street, Carly leaned in so that Kate could see her on the camera of my phone. 'It's not too late. Get on a plane. Please come. We miss you.'

'We do!' Jess and I echoed at exactly the same time.

'I would, but I'm slammed with work. I loved the video of the *Baywatch* stuff though. Carly, can we talk about the pants?'

'No, we cannot,' Carly retorted. 'My lawyer advised against it. My lawyer is also my ex-husband so he's probably in his office counting his blessings that he had a lucky escape.'

'You're doing me proud, ladies,' Kate giggled. 'Now I'm going to make dinner. Try not to do anything in the next couple of hours that will put me off my pudding.'

With that and another giggle, Kate disconnected the video call, just as we turned into our iconic destination.

Our first stop on Rodeo Drive was Chanel. It was one of my favourite spots in the world and, yeah, I know that's shallow, but I grew up dreaming of being able to shop here. I remember reading somewhere a few years ago that Chanel had paid $152 million dollars for this store. Worth every penny.

It was more than just a shop, though. This was the first place Callum and I came to, on our very first trip to Los Angeles, when we were in our twenties and had only just got together. We'd flown economy from New York, where he was shooting a tourism campaign for Tartan Week. I'd gone to visit him in NYC with Carly, and despite knowing him my whole life, something shifted and we hooked up. We then flew to LA for a wild fling, decided to get married and the rest is a fairy-tale romance – if the princess in the story ends up on the pension side of fifty feeling totally depressed and anxious. I was just counting on some retail therapy to distract me.

Before I could step over the doorway, my mobile rang and I fished it out of my cream Chanel 11.12 bag. Callum had bought it for me on our tenth wedding anniversary and I'd cried when I opened it, thinking I was the luckiest fashion victim that ever walked the face of this earth.

'Hey, babe,' I answered, wondering if some kind of psychic force had made him call me at the exact moment I was in one of our special places.

'Hey, just checking in. Has my sister led you astray yet?' Once upon a time, even the sound of his voice made me melt. Now I felt... nothing.

'No, we can't crowbar her off Sam for long enough to lead anyone astray.'

'Yuk, that was a mental image I could probably have lived without. A bit like the photos on TMZ this morning. I'm scared to ask what you were doing.'

'It was one of the things on Val's bucket list. A *Baywatch* kinda moment.'

'Yeah, I guessed that, though the pictures of my sister might just have scarred me for life. I called her to tell her I love her, but we can no longer be seen in public together or my career in fashion will be over.'

His deep, throaty laugh had no effect on me. None. It was like I was dead from the neck down. Had all my feelings just left me? Was this some kind of emotional ceasefire?

'But I figured the whole beach thing was Val's idea. Now you know why our childhood was never dull.'

'I knew that a long time ago,' I tried to match his easy tone. 'Anyway, Carly is mortified, but she's banned us from talking about it because she doesn't want to ruin Val's day. We reckon some random pap took the photos on the beach when he was staking out someone else and just got lucky. There are loads of celebrities down there. Must have been a slow day. Or maybe Sandra Bullock and Kate Hudson weren't out in their granny knickers this morning.'

'I can't understand why.' He was laughing again, but when he stopped, there was an uncomfortable pause. When had those started? Callum filled the space.

'Anyway, everything here is fine. I spoke to the girls again last night...'

'Yeah, I did too,' I replied, and I could hear the slight edge in my voice. Did he think I wasn't checking on them? Did he want a 'Dad of The Year' award for knowing where his daughters were? And why, oh bloody why, was I being such a bitch? I could feel my heart begin to pound in my chest, and the bristles of irritation and anxiety running up and down under my skin. Whose body was this, because I could swear it wasn't mine? I changed the subject. 'Anyway, how's your day been?'

'Pretty good. Just getting ready to head off for that Littlewoods catalogue gig tomorrow. It's an outdoor shoot in the Brecon Beacons. Don't even worry about me getting frostbite. No, really. If bits of me turn blue and fall off, I can stick them back on again.'

I'd always loved Callum's sense of humour. It was so like Carly's, dry and quick, which was a miracle because their mother was a frosty character who hadn't smiled since about 1986.

'Yep, there's always Blu Tack,' I said, trying hard to inject some laughter and redeem myself from the sharpness of my last comment.

'Exactly. Anyway, I'll leave you to it. Love ya.'

'Love you back.'

Then he was gone, and I did an internal inventory. Missing him? Warm bubbles of love on my belly? Floods of happy endorphins in my brain? Nope, just... relief. That was it. Relief that I could stop trying to act like the loving, dutiful wife.

Not that I could stop faking it just yet. Now I just had to pretend I was a cheery, carefree professional influencer.

Okay, suck it up. Face on. Back to business.

I already had my phone out, so I clicked record. This was going to be awesome content for my daily post. Yesterday's video had notched up over 50,000 views last time I checked.

'Hi, everyone, Carol here! Guess where I am,' I gushed, summoning every acting skill I'd honed over a million years of chirpy commercials. I slowly teased the camera around so that the block frontage of the stunning store came into view – each facet of the ultra-modern, corner-position prime real-estate building was tiled with a white background, edged in Chanel's trademark black borders. It was like a collection of giant Chanel 5 boxes, each one nudging into its neighbour.

'Chanel!' I blurted. 'Yes, my mothership has called me home, and, of course, I had to look the part.' I stretched my arm out so that I could scan my outfit. 'The jeans are H&M, because you all know how I love to mix High Street with high fashion. But chums, I couldn't come to my holy temple without paying homage, so here we go. My favourite retro Chanel boots, from the 2014 Winter Collection.' I dropped the view to my feet, then raised the lens higher to focus on the top half of my body. 'A classic Chanel signature tweed jacket in baby blue, a plain white T from Tesco – but I won't tell if you don't,' I whispered conspiratorially, with a wink. 'And, of course, I had to accessorise with my Chanel twenty-four-inch logo necklace and my fave glasses, much loved by Anna Wintour.' My cheeks were beginning to ache from smiling. 'All of these Chanel items came from my wonderful friends at "By Design", the very best website to pick out your favourite new and preloved designer clothes. I've put a link to their website on my reel, so you can get shopping! And don't forget to put my name in the promo box, today only, for a 10 per cent discount. Love you all!' I blew a kiss, gave a wave, then pressed stop and let my whole body deflate.

When I'd first started doing online promotions, I would have to do a dozen takes to get one I was happy with. Now it was second nature. Smiles. Enthusiasm. Paint an image. Stick to my glossy, happy, chic and cheerful brand, the one that came with shiny hair, a blissful marriage and a perfect family. If that's what I was putting out there, it had to be true, didn't it?

'In the name of God, Carol Ann Bernadette Sweeney, will you put that phone away and let's get moving, before Josie sends down a bolt of lightning to hurry you up.' Val teetered ahead of us and we fell in behind her as we went inside and browsed the wares of the shop, with a few exclamations of shock along the way. I was checking out the new season's accessories when I heard a stage whisper of... 'Eighteen thousand dollars for a handbag? For that price, I'd want Brad Pitt to dangle that clutch from his willy in the Bahamas!' If the staff over at the checkout area heard, they had the good grace not to react.

Thankfully, we left before our lovely Val could say anything that would get us ejected. The next couple of hours were spent breezing in and out of stores, oohing and ahhing over the luxuries, while Val exclaimed under her breath about the prices and made pointed, louder complaints about the unavailability of anything above a size 12. 'Is that a jumper or a leg warmer, love?' she asked a bemused attendant at a knitwear rail in Dolce & Gabbana.

We all fell on different sides of the designer argument. Carly couldn't care less. Material things just weren't her bag. Literally. She still used a cross-body leather satchel I got her for Christmas in about 2006. Jess, on the other hand, wore pretty high-end professional stuff for work, so she loved a Jaeger or a Hobbs. And Val... as she had just announced in the middle of Armani, in her view, there was nothing better than a good George at Asda or Florence & Fred at Tesco. But that didn't stop her gliding in and out of every store here like she had buckets to spend. And in her huge bedazzled glasses (Accessorise, but could pass for Versace in a dim light) and kaleidoscope of coloured outerwear, full make-up and platinum hair, she looked like an eccentric movie star who had run through her wardrobe covered in superglue, and just put on everything that stuck to her.

At lunchtime, we stopped at 208 Rodeo for a cocktail and a sandwich, followed by coffee and Jaffa Cakes that Val slipped out of the huge tote she'd been carrying all day, and passed around under the table.

Jess shook her head. 'My God, Val, that bag of yours is like a wonder of the world. What else is in there?'

'I can't possibly reveal my secrets,' she replied, all full of mystery and intrigue. We knew better than to press further, and the contents of her bag had left our minds by the time we reached a small boutique at the end of the street. There were full-length racks on both walls and, as far as I could see, no more than three of each item. In one corner, next to a small but lavish shoe display, there was a large gold throne with a green velvet footstool. We'd kept the energy and the laughter up all day, but now Carly's feet were sore, as was her neck, from looking over her shoulders searching for paps who could catch her at an unfortunate moment, Jess's attention span for frivolous stuff was reaching its end, and Val had a mischievous glint in her eyes.

The shop attendant, a flamboyant, very camp chap in his fifties, strutted over to us.

'Ladies! Ooh, you're all gorgeous! You, you, you, and especially...' He checked out Val's outfit of many colours... 'You.' That made her laugh.

'I know, son. I think that to myself every morning when I wake up looking like this. *Val*, I say, *you did it again. Flipping gorgeous*.'

His lipsticked pout – Hermès Satin Rouge, if I had to guess – widened. 'I have the very same experience,' he confided. 'Some of us have just got it.' He held his arms wide. 'What can I show you lovely ladies today then?'

He was the complete opposite of most of the other people we'd encountered in the stores so far, who had generally been cordial, professional, helpful, but with an air of superior coolness. It was all very much in keeping with the Pretty Woman vibe that had inspired this entry on the bucket list.

I'd already zeroed in on a vintage Azzedine Alaia knitted sweater dress on the far wall. My internal fashion database began to spin like a Zanussi washer until it landed on the right image. Yep, that was it. I was pretty sure Kate Moss wore that on a catwalk back in the nineties. Paris. Maybe 1992. I'd seen it in *Vogue*. How come I could remember every detail of the image, but last week I'd forgotten my pin number for the account I've had for the last twenty years? It was some kind of weird anaesthesia. No, that wasn't right. Amnesia! Christ on a bike, this was getting worse.

The only solace was the force field that was pulling me towards the dress, and when I reached it, I pulled it from the rail, held it up against me and checked out the reflection, as the others chatted to the very sweet man.

This gent was whimsical, loving life, curious and gregarious – and it was just as well, because unbeknownst to us, Val needed a partner in crime.

'Here's the thing,' I heard her say, in the voice that would make a SWAT team put down their weapons and go grab her a cup of tea and a scone from the nearest Greggs. 'That one over there is the only one of us that has buckets of cash and no sense when it comes to spending it, so she'll most certainly buy something,' she said, pointing at me.

'Music to my ears,' he replied, as if this was a completely normal, everyday conversation. 'That's my very favourite kind of customer.'

My mouth was open, but nothing was coming out because I didn't know whether to object or laugh.

'But before she does, I think you're the very man to help me fulfil one of my dearly departed pal's last wishes.'

'I'm listening,' he said warmly. To give him credit, he didn't even seem perplexed. But then, this was LA, the kind of town where people had talking toilets and took their poodles for weekly pedicures.

Before she started to explain, Val nodded in my direction.

'Get yer purse out, Carol, love – this one might cost us.'

15

VAL

Open Arms – Tina Turner

My throat hurt from laughing and I was slightly tipsy as I sat down at the desk in the pure posh suite at the Regent Beverly Wiltshire. It wasn't exactly a Premier Inn, with a Harvester across the other side of the car park. It was a stunning building, with bright yellow awnings right at the bottom of Rodeo Drive, the very one that Julia Roberts' character stayed in when she was shagging Richard Gere in *Pretty Woman*. That's where our Josie had got the idea for this item on our bucket list. We'd seen that film about fifty times over the years and it never got old. Yes, we could have made all sorts of judgements about the merits of a movie starring a street hooker and a rich man who bought her affections, but we didn't. 'We're old bags,' Josie would say. 'Let's just enjoy it for the entertainment value and ignore the immorality of the story. It's fiction, for God's sake. Cruella de Vil hates puppies and nobody calls in the RSPCA.' She wasn't wrong, my pal.

I picked up the pen from the mahogany holder on the desk and took a sheet of hotel headed notepaper from the drawer. I could insert it in my diary later. I'd left it back at Sam's place, thinking I'd update it in the morning, but after a few too many cocktails in the bar downstairs, all the girls were now cosied on the sofa in the other room watching a movie, and I wanted to get this down while I could still remember every minute of it.

Dear Josie,

Oh, pet, you'd have laughed till you passed out. It was exactly as you'd wanted it to be. The shop was on Rodeo Drive, couldn't have been posher, and oh the prices! A T-shirt cost the same as a week in Majorca! Anyway, this lovely lad – Raphael was his name – was the manager, and well, I took to him right away. He was a cross between that chap who sang 'Purple Rain', and Daphne down the laundrette, remember her with the filthy mouth and the laugh you could hear four streets away?

I explained the plan and he was in right from the get-go. His only condition was that our Carol filmed it for her blog. Turns out he was impressed by the fact that she had 1.2 million followers and was prepared to buy a second hand woolly dress for more money that we'd spend on electricity in a year.

The girls parked themselves on the chairs next to the shoe bit, and outside the dressing room, while I got everything ready. Raphael helped by pouring us all a wee glass of something fizzy. It wasn't bad, but it definitely wasn't as good as that cheap champagne you got from Lidl for my birthday that year.

Anyway, off I went outside, took a deep breath, and I raised my eyes in case you were watching. I had a vision of you sitting up there, picking popcorn out of yer teeth while shouting at one of those angel types to get the kettle on…

Sorry, love, I had to stop there for a second. The very thought of that brought a wee tear to my eye and I had to blink it away before my lashes fell off. Och, Josie, remember that time we left our lashes stuck to the dashboard of Don's car after a night out? Next morning, he left for work, then came charging back in, shouting about there being a spider the size of a brillo pad in his car. Who knew a grown man could scream that loud?

Where was I? Ah, yes. Raphael, bless him, was an absolute star and went with it.

He was positively giddy when I left the shop, then strutted back in, channelling my very best 'Julia Roberts as a prozzie' vibe.

'Can I help you?' he asked, like he'd never seen me before in his life.

'Naw, son. Just looking,' I said, all casual.

'I don't think there's anything here for you,' he said, pure snooty. He'd already told us he came to LA twenty years ago to be an actor and never made it. It's a travesty.

I ignored the lassies, although our Carly was trying so hard not to laugh, she was turning purple.

Just like we talked about, I started to stare at the caramel wafer I'd left on one of the shelves.

'How much is that?' I asked, nonchalant like.

'It's very expensive,' Raphael replied, getting right into the role. Turns out Pretty Woman was one of his favourites too.

'I've got at least a tenner to spend in here!' I shot back.

'Well, you're obviously in the wrong place,' he retorted. Honestly, if I didn't know he was acting, I'd have believed every word. Sam should have this bloke in his movies.

I gave him the evils and then flounced out, just like Julia in the film. I waited a minute, pulled the punchline out of ma bag, and then marched back in.

'Remember me?' I asked him.

He peered straight at me. 'No.'

'I was in here earlier and you lobbed me out.' I held up the box of caramel wafers that I'd just taken out of my bag and dangled them in his face. 'Big mistake. Big. Huge.' I told him, then marched right out of there, head high.

Well, I had to lean against the window and cross my legs so I wouldn't do myself an injury from laughing. God, Josie, it was brilliant. And you know what, pal? The whole time I could hear that husky cackle of yours in my head.

When I could finally walk without the risk of breaching my Tena Lady, I went back in and, well, the girls were in hysterics and Raphael was leaning on the counter, howling.

He gave Carol 20 per cent discount on the jumper dress, and she promised to… Hang on, till I remember. Aye, she said she'd tug him on the post. Naw, TAG him. Honestly, Josie, it's like a different language.

After that, we wandered about for a bit longer, then went for a libation in the bar on the ground floor of this hotel. It's the same one that's in Pretty Woman, right at the bottom of Rodeo Drive. The drinks were smashing and the bar was lovely, but the folk were something else. A whole load of preening and posing going on.

After a couple of refreshments, we checked in and came up to the suite and had a wee nap before we phoned room service. It's a two-bedroom suite, so I've got one room, Carly and Carol are in the other, and Jess is on a sofa bed in the living room. It's bigger than my house! Glad I'm on ma own to be honest, because this jet lag is brutal and I cannae guarantee I won't be snoring the minute I close my eyes.

So that was our day, Josie. Just like we planned it. Our Pretty Woman moment.

Oh, and Carol uplifted it onto that Instagram thing and she said it's gone virus. I've no idea what that means, but maybe a wee antibiotic from the chemist will sort it out.

I'm getting tired again, love, so I'll go now. Just wanted to let you know that's the second thing off the list and I laughed more than I've done for the longest time.

Our Michael texted me back today and said him and Don are doing fine. I'm trusting that yer still keeping one eye on them for me. Keep them safe until I'm back there to do it maself. We always were a tag team, you and me, Josie. I wish we still were.

I miss you more than ever, pal.

Keep dancing, keep laughing… and be happy up there.

Love you,

Val xxx

I put the pen down, then took the sheet of paper and tucked it into my bag. It was a lot lighter now that I'd left the box of caramel wafers with Raphael. He said he hadn't eaten sweets or biscuits since the nineties, so he was probably running up and down Rodeo Drive right now on a crazed sugar high. My Dee once followed a bowling ball right up the lane at the sports centre after we gave her a glass of full-fat Fanta.

I slipped into the huge king-size bed. This suite was bigger than my house and Josie's house put together.

My eyes were getting heavier by the second, so I closed them gratefully.

Two things ticked off the list. I was relieved. Happy. Grateful. But on the other hand, I could still feel the tension across the top of my shoulders. That's where worry always got me. Right in the back of the neck, late at night, in the dark.

So far, we were doing great with the bucket list. I just hoped we could get everything else done before it was too late.

16

JESS

You Oughta Know – Alanis Morrisette

If you'd told me a week ago that I'd be lying on the sofa of a two-bedroom suite in the Regent Beverly Wiltshire hotel, staring at the ceiling, while Carly and Carol were passed out in one room, and Val was snoring softly in another, I'd have said you'd lost your mind. Yet here I was. And after an hour or so, a wildly expensive ceiling looked just like every other one I'd ever seen.

I tossed, turned and pulled the blanket up to my neck, only to throw it to one side again, because I was too hot, too cold, too restless... too broken.

Today, Arnie had called twice, but I'd blocked him both times and just put the situation to the back of my mind. I knew what he was doing. He wanted to spin me some story, but I'd been down that road before and I wasn't going back there. I'd given my first love and my ex-husband the benefit of the doubt and they'd shredded my life. Once bitten, twice shy, third time not so bloody stupid.

Thankfully, it hadn't been too difficult to distract myself today, given everything else that was going on. Carly was in a state of permanent embarrassment every time someone looked at her, because she was positive they'd seen the internet photos and were imagining her wearing those rainbow knick-knacks under her jeans. Outwardly I was sympathising and morally outraged, but on the inside I found the whole thing hilarious. Carol wasn't as amusing. She was in a weird fug, which was totally unlike her and I put it down to jet lag and worrying about the fourteen texts she'd received from Charlotte discussing what she was going to wear for a date with a man twice her age tonight. I ended up taking the phone and advising my niece-ish to wear a good spray of bug repellent, fortified steel pants and a blanket in case he got a chill after being out late at his age. She didn't find it amusing and threatened to block me.

Val cheered us all up though. The *Pretty Woman* stunt was priceless and one we'll be talking about forever. Last time Carol checked, it had half a million views and she'd had an enquiry about an endorsement deal with Scotland's biggest biscuit brand. Val said if she didn't accept it, she'd never forgive her.

My phone buzzed and I checked the screen. Another late-night email from Dax Hill's lawyers. The repugnant twat was really pulling out all the stops on this one. The poor little buttercup had somehow got wind of the fact that I was about to release a chain of text messages that had him making extremely lewd suggestions to my client shortly after they met. You know, right before they got together and he impregnated her, then pretended he wouldn't know her if he tripped over her on the shagpile carpet of his $35-million-dollar home in the Hollywood Hills' Bird Streets. Scum. He was now threatening to sue me again, and claiming the images were photoshopped. I knew better, but I was blanking him too. His last stunt was to claim Hayley was trying to extort money from him. A couple of the tabloids, who are strangers to the story, ran it as a blind piece without fact-checking. Fine. It was all more ammunition when we went public with the whole story. Every denial and smear he spat out was another couple of hundred grand on the settlement if Hayley could just hold her nerve and put up with the nonsense for a little longer. It couldn't be easy, but I admired her courage in taking on the bad guys.

My mind took that thought and jumped to another frame of reference with it. Why didn't I have that kind of courage? Arnie had wrecked our lives and what had I done? Faced up to him? Fought back? Nope, I'd scurried off and attempted to leave the country. Now that the girls had persuaded me to stay longer than a couple of days, I'd warned Sam not to tell him I was still here. After the two calls from Arnie's phone this morning, I'd had nothing else from him, so he'd obviously given up trying. Bastard.

I stared at the ceiling some more, then checked my watch – 2 a.m. The person I was a couple of years ago would have got up right now, gone to a late-night bar or club, drank, danced and picked up some good-looking guy for a night of anonymous sex. That was in my defiant phase, when I firmly believed there was absolutely no shame in casual sex or one-night stands as long as they were safe and satisfying. I still believed that. I just didn't have the energy or motivation to do it any more. I didn't want that. I wanted what Arnie and I had. Past tense.

I flipped my leg up over the back of the sofa, then groaned quietly as the frustration of the insomnia got to me. This was no good. I couldn't lie here all night. It was already after two and at five most of this city woke up, did an hour-long session in their home gym with a personal trainer who charged his or her weight in gold, then sat down to scan the web while their personal chef whipped them up an egg white and spinach omelette and a wheatgrass juice.

Arnie was never into that kind of thing. He trained at the respectable hour of 7 a.m., then went for a run at some point during the day, usually with Sam if they were together. I'd never joined him in the gym. The morning was my time for setting up my day, planning strategies, making notes, checking the headlines. It was my work time. My only exercise happened after Arnie came back from the gym and I joined him in the shower.

Something was gripping at my gut, but I wasn't sure if it was rage or grief that our time was over. Rage. Definitely rage. Grief would have to stay on the back-burner for a while longer.

I squeezed my eyes shut, then opened them again. Dammit, it was no use. I was never getting to sleep.

I got up, pulled on a vest and a yellow sweatshirt that Carly had picked up from a street trader down an alley near the hotel. I had to do something to burn off this energy. Had to…

I stopped. Sighed. Conceded defeat. Because since the moment I lay down I'd been avoiding the one thing that my mind wanted to focus on: the address that was tucked inside the bag I'd been carrying around all day. The decision was made before I'd even tracked down my trainers.

I summoned an Uber and slipped out of the door, down to reception. It pulled up just as I got there, obviously scouting the salubrious streets nearby in the hope of a late-night fare and a big tip.

I'd already put the address into the app on my phone, so the driver, in a thick Eastern European accent, repeated it, then pulled off. In the daytime, with LA traffic, the trip to Ojai, roughly halfway between Los Angeles and Santa Barbara, could take three or four hours, but in the deserted streets of the night, it only took an hour and a half. Every now and then, the driver would look at me in the mirror, just to make sure I hadn't bailed out while he was sitting at traffic lights or started rocking back and forth in a deranged state. It wasn't a reach. It was the middle of the night, I was wearing the scent of the tequila shots we'd done before bed and a yellow 'My wife went to Beverly Hills and all she got me was this shit sweat-shirt' top, and I was very obviously unhappy. Not exactly the typical customer he usually picked up in the 90210 or 90212 postcodes.

I didn't say a word until we reached the destination, just stared out of the window, watching the lights of the freeway change to the trees of the suburbs. I knew Ojai was in a valley, surrounded by the Topatopa mountains, and famous for being quaint, with a new-age-y vibe. Arnie had told me once that Myrna refused to leave it for the bright lights of LA, even when he was working in the city full time. That was it. That was all I knew. He was a man of few words, and he didn't waste any of them talking about his past. What an idiot I'd been. I'd put that down to him having moved on. I'd had no idea it was because he hadn't.

The car slowed down and I checked the map on my phone. I hadn't tracked the journey because I didn't want to run the battery down. Now I saw that we were only a couple of hundred metres from the address. One hundred. Fifty. Twenty-five. You have reached your destination.

The house could have been a ski chalet in Aspen or a cabin in the Blue Ridge Mountains. Surrounded on three sides by trees, keeping it private from its neighbours, it was built from a dark timber, maybe cedar, and the roof rose above the porch and the first-floor balcony to a peak in the middle. It belonged on a post-card, or in a movie starring Mark Walberg as an ex-criminal who'd entered the witness protection programme and was now living a quiet life in an anonymous street in a quiet part of a rural town, while moonlighting as a vigilante and tracking down a serial killer. Or maybe I'd just been in Tinsel Town for too long. The point was, it was beautiful, rustic, a little beat-up, but that only added to its charm.

The driver was looking at me questioningly in his rear-view mirror again, waiting for further instructions. My inner dialogue was way ahead of him. *What now, Jess? What's the plan? You didn't think this through, did you?* Even my subconscious was kicking me when I was down.

But it wasn't wrong. What next? Was I going to go knock on the door at… I checked my watch… almost 4 a.m. and demand to know if my erstwhile fiancé was cuddled under the duvet with his ex-wife. Was I just going to sit here and wait until daybreak, to see if he emerged from the front porch with a latte in his hand for his morning stretch? What a ridiculous frigging idea this had been. And I was supposed to be the smartest one in our group. Well, I'd just blown that theory, along with at least a hundred dollars on an Uber.

'Are you getting out here?' the driver asked, his patience running out. I knew he'd want to get back to LA before daybreak and the build-up of the early-morning traffic.

I scanned the house again. No sign of life, and crucially, no vehicles. His pickup wasn't in sight. I could see a garage at the back of the property, another wooden structure that was accessed by a track at the side of the house, but the closed doors gave nothing away.

'Can you move forward a little please?' I said, brushing over the driver's question, but seeking answers to one of my own.

He crawled forward until I blurted, 'Stop'. It wasn't in the garage. At the other side of the house, almost hidden under a corridor of trees, was the pickup. I'd driven it a million times. I'd washed it. He'd proposed to me on the bloody bonnet. We'd even made love in the back, under the light of the moon, after pulling off the road in remote spots during trips up and down the coast. It was definitely Arnie's vehicle, so he was there. Living with his ex-wife. It was real. And so was the pain that was twisting every muscle in my body. Why? Why would he do this? How could I have got him so, so wrong?

'Miss?' The driver again.

Now I had a choice. I wasn't going to go in there like a tornado and wake everyone up, so that left two other options – get out, let the Uber go, and wait until daybreak gave me answers, one way or another.

Or turn back around and go back to LA, lick my wounds and try to find a way to put the pain behind me.

The problem was, now that I'd come this far, the rage was up again. I'd run away last time and it had left me staring at the ceiling, desperate to know how my life had fallen apart.

'You can leave me here,' I told the driver. With Arnie and the breakup, I'd driven down a one-way street. And I couldn't bring myself to put the gears into reverse.

17

CARLY

Never 'Til Now – Ashley Cooke

Every emotion I'd felt in the last two hours bubbled over and exploded the minute the door opened. 'Where the hell have you been? I've been worried sick! I thought you'd been kidnapped!'

Jess's eyes narrowed as she took that last bit in. 'You thought I'd been kidnapped from the couch of a swanky suite in a Beverly Hills hotel?'

Ah. I supposed I could see her point. But I wasn't for backing down.

'It could happen!' I screeched. 'People disappear all the time. That's why Liam Neeson is always losing folk in his movies.'

Now that she was back and my anxiety levels were de-escalating, I could accept the flaw in my reasoning.

'You didn't think I'd maybe gone out for an early-morning walk? Or up to the gym for a workout?'

I shrugged sheepishly. 'Okay, those would probably be slightly more likely options. Which one was it?'

'It was...' Jess's eyes darted to the side for a split second, and I recognised the mannerism straight away. Ever since we were kids, as soon as she contemplated lying, her pupils flicked to the right.

'Don't you dare lie,' I warned her.

She threw her hands up. 'Fine! It was neither. I just spent hundreds of dollars on an Uber to Ojai because I suspected Arnie was living there with his ex-wife and I couldn't sleep so I just went and checked and, yep, there his bloody car was.'

Two things struck me. First, she seemed to have lost all ability to punctuate her sentences. And second...

'Is that my sweatshirt you're wearing?'

'Really? That's where you're going with this?' she blasted.

Again, I could see that wasn't where my mind should have wandered in that moment.

'I'm sorry! I've had three hours sleep because I woke up and you were gone and then I was worried and your phone was dead and... well, you know. The kidnapping thing. I'm not thinking straight.' I crossed the room and wrapped my arms around her, a minor accomplishment because Jess absolutely hated the whole huggy stuff. She said it was unhygienic. 'I'm sorry about Arnie. I really am. I'm going to need more information though. Sit down and I'll make us a coffee.'

I led her over to the dining table in the corner of the room, then went to the drinks area and stuck a Nespresso in the coffee machine. Or it might have been a Lavazza. I didn't have my specs on.

Two steaming mugs later, I joined her at the table. It was obvious she hadn't slept. Jess was always immaculately groomed. Back in the day, she wore her hair in a sharp chin-length bob, but a couple of years ago she went for the chop and switched to a shorter, gelled-back style that matched her piercing indigo eyes, which were usually outlined in black liner. She reminded me of a fiercer version of Jaimie Lee Curtis. This morning, though, her hair was spiked up and resembled a loo brush, and there were deep dark circles under her bloodshot peepers.

'Tell me from the start,' I prompted. 'And don't even think about lying to me, young lady,' I added, aping her mother's voice. Jess's mum had been the poshest of all our parents. Growing up, we'd all lived on council estates near Glasgow, but when we were about ten, Jess's parents had bought a house, which we all thought was the height of sophistication. Now we were all sleeping in a hotel in Beverly Hills. Not quite sure how we got here, but I was grateful and more than a little surprised.

Jess managed a sad smile, then sighed and slumped, as if all the air had left her body. 'I went through Arnie's stuff yesterday and found a photo with an address on the back...'

On she went, recounting the whole story, from finding the address to travelling there in an Uber in the dead of night and telling the driver to leave her there. She'd just got to that bit when my imagination took over again.

'Hang on, you told him to leave you in the middle of nowhere, with a phone that was about to die, and no money, bag or anything? Are you mad?'

'I had a witty sweatshirt that I could have sold for cash,' she joked weakly.

I threw my arms up in despair. 'Bloody hell, I much preferred it when you were the smart and sensible one in the group. You absolutely could have been kidnapped or murdered!' I blurted, returning to my original point.

'But I wasn't,' she countered with a roll of her eyes. 'I changed my mind. I realised that I wasn't prepared, or in control of how I was feeling. I was just going to burst in there, shouting my mouth off, acting on impulse and making a complete tit of myself.'

'That sounds like something I'd do,' I admitted. My aptitude for rushing in and making an arse of myself had always made me the chief tit of our group.

'Exactly! So I didn't. I told Uri – that was the Uber driver's name, by the way, and he has absolutely no background in abduction or grisly ends – to bring me home. Fighting what happened is pointless. Arnie has made a choice and I need to just back off, respect it and move on.'

I put my hand on hers. 'That's extremely mature and sensible of you…'

She nodded sagely.

'… But also complete bollocks,' I went on. 'Come on, Jess. Do you honestly think you can walk away and not fully understand what happened? That'll eat you up. And plus, before you blocked him, he was blowing up your phone, so he obviously has something to tell you. Sam says he's called and asked him if he knows where you are. Only the fact that you threatened to suffocate him while he slept has stopped him from letting Arnie know you're still here. I think you need to call him back and talk to him.'

'No,' she answered, with a fierce finality. 'After I split with Mike the Prick…' Even saying her ex-husband's name made her frown. Mike had been a serial cheater who had absolutely slayed her heart, then walked out on Jess and their son. She had a courteous relationship with him now, but she was the type of person who bore a grudge until death, so they'd never be friends. I tuned back into her rant. 'I swore I'd never put up with a guy lying, cheating or leaving me again. I'd never give him a second chance. Now that I know Arnie is with his ex, we're done. *I'm done*. I'll go home with Val and Carol and I'll move on with my old life back in London.'

This time it was me who flinched, and she spotted it. Urgh, it was that whole lifelong-friend drawback thing again. I really needed a few surface-level pals who couldn't see right into my soul, with or without their specs.

I tried to push past it by forging on with a reprimand. 'Okay, but Jess, no more secrets. I'd have come with you last night. I'd have held your hand. I'd have taken my sweatshirt back because now you've worn it and I can't give it to Sam.' That made her smile. 'But don't keep stuff to yourself. We don't do that.'

I thought I'd got away with it, I really did, but no. She fired back like a heat-seeking missile.

'Don't we? So do you want to tell me what's on your mind, because I've been sensing something is off with you since you got here.'

It was the bit about Jess going home with Val and Carol that had got me. The thought of them all leaving and me staying here made every muscle in my body clench. I couldn't say goodbye to them and watch them go. I didn't belong here.

'I know,' I acknowledged, 'but we haven't had two minutes on our own to talk.' We did have now though, and I couldn't wait to offload to her, to get her thoughts on my shitshow of a situation. However, I didn't get a chance to say another word because at that exact moment, there was a wail from the direction of the bathroom.

'What the hell is that?' Jess gasped. 'Is Val in pain? Is she hurt?'

I listened for a few more seconds as the facts assimilated in my mind. I checked my watch. It was eight o'clock now. Somewhere in the middle of our conversation, the sun had come up and the suite was now flooded with light. It was morning. Rise and shine time. Which meant that my Aunt Val, who was determined not to waste a moment of this trip, had risen from her slumbers, gone to the bathroom and...

The sound we were hearing wasn't so much of a wail – it was more of a karaoke classic.

'It's Val in the bath. She's belting out that Prince song that Julia Roberts sang in *Pretty Woman*.'

'Kiss?' Jess asked, listening intently.

Granted, Val had never been one to hold a tune, so it wasn't immediately obvious. 'Yep. Although, I don't think she realises that Prince sang it first. She thinks it's a Tom Jones classic and he wrote it just for her. I'm putting my hands over my ears when she gets to the bit about not having to be beautiful to turn her on and just wanting someone's body. I can't take that kind of stuff at this time in the morning.'

'I've no idea why Arnie left me,' Jess sighed. 'I mean, I've got such a normal, run-of-the-mill life, with normal, run-of-the-mill friends. I'm a catch.'

Just at that moment, Carol wandered in from the bedroom, her long blonde hair falling in a wavy sheet of gloss over one shoulder, her make-up-free face stunning and utterly flawless.

I groaned at the sight of her. 'How do you wake up like that? It shouldn't be allowed. It should be illegal. Go back into that room and don't come out until you look like an extra from the "Thriller" video.'

She didn't laugh. Not even a smile. That was my first clue that something was wrong.

'What? What is it?'

Carol held up her phone and turned it round. Again, I couldn't see the screen because I still didn't have my specs on, but I could tell it wasn't good by my sister-in-law's stricken expression.

'Have you seen the new photos online? You're carrying all our bags down Rodeo Drive...'

'Don't tell me! Does the headline say something about me being a gold digger?' I groaned.

She stayed silent.

'What?' I demanded.

'You told me not to tell you, but you're absolutely right about the "gold digger" headlines. And you're eating a packet of Jaffa Cakes at the same time.'

'Aw bloody buggery bollocks!' I wailed.

She crossed the room to give me a hug. Jess had already headed to the minibar to get me a drink, despite the fact that it was before breakfast. We all had our roles to play in a crisis.

Carol gave me another squeeze. 'I'm sorry, Carly. I don't know what the hell is going on, but it feels like someone is definitely trying to wreck your life here.'

18

CAROL

Adele – Easy On Me

'Hey, Mum! Wow, you look like that woman out of the *Real Housewives of Beverly Hills*. The one who thought she was a pop star then her life got trashed.' On my phone screen, Charlotte ended that little slice of information by taking a bite out of the large slice of pizza she was holding in her hand.

'Erika Girardi? The one who was married to the lawyer?' I asked, confused, trying to picture the cast of that show while balancing my phone in one hand so I could grab one of those mini bottles of wine from the minibar with the other. How did we ever manage to communicate before FaceTime and Zoom? It was 4 p.m., I was twenty storeys above the Las Vegas strip, overlooking the Bellagio fountains, yet I was chatting to my daughter who was having a thin crust Hawaiian, while poring over some books at Carly's kitchen table at midnight.

'Yeah, that's the one. But you're a much prettier version. And much nicer. I think she's, like, totally snide and obnoxious.'

'Thanks. I think.' That was the thing with twenty-something daughters – you never knew whether the statements coming out of their mouths were genuine compliments or veiled digs. And it was Charlotte, so it could be either. Much as I utterly adored both my girls, there was no denying that Toni was the gentler, more caring of the two. Charlotte could be blunt to the point of rudeness, brutally honest and slightly thoughtless, but she had a brain that was sharp as a hammer. I mean, a saw. Or a blade. Or, you know… something in a toolbox. Anyway, if I was an outsider looking in, I'd have thought she was Jess's kid instead of mine.

'Where are you?' she asked, peering into the camera. 'Have you left Sam's place?'

I nodded. 'We're in Vegas. We left the Beverly Wiltshire this morning, nipped back to Sam's house to change, then flew here this afternoon. It's only a seventy-minute flight and I slept for most of it anyway. It's the next destination on Auntie Val's bucket list. Tonight we're going gambling in a casino and then we're… we're…' My mind was completely blank. Nothing there except fog. '… Doing other stuff.'

Charlotte grinned and took another chunk of pizza. 'You are living your best life, Mum. I mean, Beverly Hills yesterday, Vegas today. And I saw the video you did with Auntie Val on Rodeo Drive. It's at over a million views. How amazing is that? You're rocking it.'

Living my best life. Rocking it. I suppose I was. Shouldn't that mean I was happy? Today, at least a dozen enquiries about endorsement deals and interviews had dropped into my inbox after Val's *Pretty Woman* video went viral. I'd done another video showing the four of us strutting through Vegas airport, all wearing shades and working our swaggers. I was with amazing friends, who loved me.

I'd treated myself to a gorgeous gold bangle in Dior, one of the stores on the ground-floor shopping corridor of this hotel, in the hope of cheering myself up. It didn't. My posts today had thousands of comments, with heaps of them saying how fabulous my life was and how they wished they were me. Yet, here I was, trying to get this bloody wine bottle open so that I could cheer myself up with a drink or two. Aaaargh! All I could think about was that right now, I'd give anything to be that twenty-year old, sitting at the kitchen table, all fresh-faced and eating pizza, living with her girlfriends, with a whole lifetime of excitement and love and laughs ahead of her.

'How's the romance going?' I asked her, then braced myself for the answer.

'Oh, it's done with. I decided he was too old for me. Don't say, I told you so.' Scratch my theory about Charlotte belonging to Jess. She was definitely Carly's child. Back in the day, Carly had gone to bed madly in love, then woken up out of love, more times than we could count. It was like her party trick. Her whole twenties were like a series of romcoms in reverse. Not that I was complaining about my daughter's ability to emotionally pivot, when it involved steering clear of a bloke who came with a middle aged red flag.

'Oh, well, plenty more sharks in the sea.'

'It's fish, Mum. Plenty more fish.' Just as she said that, there was a commotion at Charlotte's end, and Toni and Kate's daughters, Tallulah and Zoe, bounced into the frame, all of them bright-eyed and laughing, wrapped up in outdoor coats.

'Hi, Aunt Carol,' Tallulah waved into the screen, followed by the others.

I double-checked my watch. It was definitely midnight there. On a Wednesday. 'Are you lot coming in or going out?' I asked, confused.

'Coming in. We all took the day off, except this swot here,' Tallulah ruffled Charlotte's hair, 'and went into town to do our

Christmas shopping, then out for cocktails. And look – surprise!' They all shook out some jazz hands as Hannah dipped into the screen.

'Hannah! When did you arrive? Oh, it's so lovely to see you.'

'This morning. But I had to go straight from Heathrow to the restaurant for a meeting, so the girls just came and kidnapped me on their way home.' Sarah's daughter had the same business acumen as her late father, Nick, and had completely taken over the running of his restaurant chain. She also had the same smile, the same aura of calm competence and the same sharp sense of humour as her mother. God, I missed Sarah. The pain of that caught in my throat so it was a relief when Carly sashayed in, wearing black palazzo pants and a sequinned jumper. 'Tell me the truth – do I look like I belong in a bingo hall on a cheap cruise or am I Vegas chic?'

'Bingo hall,' I told her, grinning so that she knew I was joking.

'Excellent,' she quipped, deadpan. 'That's the look I was going for.' She realised I was on FaceTime to home and came closer so the girls on the other end could see her.

'Aunt Carly!' Hannah cheered and the others joined in the wave. If there was a wonderful aspect of the world we'd created for ourselves, it was that we were one big family. Not all of us were actually related, but that didn't matter. There was a saying about it taking a village to raise a kid – or was it a town? – but with us, it was just five pals, four now that Sarah was gone, who had stuck together and raised all our children as communal offspring. My girls loved Carly's boys just as much as they would if they were brothers, and it was the same with them all. No matter what happened to us, they'd always have each other.

I felt a rush of tears to my bottom lids, and I looked away from the camera so the girls wouldn't notice. God, this was pathetic. I couldn't remember the last time I went a whole day without crying for absolutely no reason other than I was feeling maudlin, or stressed, or sad, or down. Thankfully, Carly was diverting their attention.

'Have you lot wrecked my house yet?' she jested. 'Because if you haven't, I'll be sorely disappointed in you. You're supposed to be totally rock and roll and throwing televisions out the window at your age.'

'No, but I spilled a glass of wine on the rug in the lounge last night,' Tallulah admitted.

'Red or white?' Carly asked.

'White. And we cleared it up straight away, so you'd never notice.'

Carly sighed. 'No drunken vomiting in the bath? No visits from the police asking you to turn down the music? No rock stars smuggled into your bedrooms in the middle of the night?'

Toni shook her head, giggling. 'Sorry, Aunt Carly – none of that. Zoe did forget to take her vitamins yesterday morning though, so that was a tense moment.'

Carly shook her head mournfully and nudged me. 'Where did we go wrong with them, Carol? My heart is broken.'

The girls were hooting with laughter. Only Toni, after a few seconds, zeroed in on me.

'Mum, are you okay? You look like you're about to burst into tears.'

That made Carly peer round and look me in the eyes. I brushed her – and Toni – off.

'Of course! My contacts are just irritating me. I'm absolutely fine. I'm in Vegas. I'm having a great time. And the world is my iceberg. What could there possibly be to cry about?' I said, as if it was the most ludicrous question I'd ever heard.

Carly held my gaze for a little longer, then turned back to the screen, radiating happy vibes again. 'Okay, well you lot have a brilliant time together. If you see my darling, angelic boys, make sure they're okay and changing their socks every day. Now go be women we can be proud of and throw a telly out of the window. Make it the one in the spare room. It hasn't worked for years, anyway.'

With a whole cacophony of laughter, loads of 'love you's' and cheery waves, they were gone.

Carly grabbed a can of gin and tonic from the minibar and plopped a straw in it, then joined me at the table.

'Know who they remind me of?' she asked, smiling warmly.

I already knew what she was going to say. The way they all loved each other and did life together was so reminiscent of another time and place. 'Us.'

Her straw flicked a bubble of gin and tonic my way when she took it out of her mouth. It dropped on the table in front of me.

'Yep. They're much more sensible though. Remember us at that age? God, we were so full of excitement, so up for anything and absolutely fearless. We thought we were indestructible, that nothing would ever go wrong. Except my love life. Even then we pretty much knew I was going to be a romantic disaster. I think I was on my third fiancé by that age.'

'At least,' I agreed. Carly had been engaged six times in total. If she'd kept the rings, they could have been her pension.

A couple of seconds of silence passed. 'Is that what's going on here, babe?' she said, her voice gentle.

'What do you mean? There's nothing going on.'

'Maybe on the outside, but I don't know... you just seem... sad.'

'Didn't you already ask me this on the plane?' I challenged her. 'Maybe the only thing wrong is that my pals keep asking me what's wrong. I promise I'm fine.'

Why couldn't I say anything to her? Why couldn't I admit that I felt rubbish, sad, lonely? Because it was ridiculous, that's why. I had absolutely no right to feel any of those things. I was hashtag blessed, as the Americans liked to say. Hashtag lucky. Hashtag living my best life. Didn't my 1.2 million followers tell me that every day? Weren't they always commenting that they aspired to my life, my career, my marriage, my wardrobe? Hashtag fricking perfect, that's what my life was. And if I admitted that it wasn't, then they'd all pitch in and I'd be forced to confront whatever was wrong with me. I couldn't do it. So yes, this was going to be the first time in my life that I hadn't shared something with my husband or my friends, but that was how this needed to be because I couldn't bring myself to make it real.

For a second, I thought Carly was going to bite back at me, but she clamped her jaw shut, put both hands up in a surrender gesture, and then surprised me by leaning over and wrapping me in her arms. 'Okay, pal, but know that I love you. And I'm here, no matter what. And there's nothing you could say or do that would change that. Except maybe if you shagged Sam Morton, in which case I'd have to kill you.'

'Ooooh, why are we killing Carol? And can we do it soon, because I want her Louboutin boots,' Jess said, coming into the room with her old veneer of sleek killer boss bitch restored. Her hair was slicked back. Her red lippy was on. She was wearing a black Mugler dress with shoulder pads the width of a deckchair.

'You look like you've just escaped from... from...' Aaargh, what was it? My mind had gone completely blank again. I kept grappling for the thought, but it stayed just out of reach.

'Robert Palmer's "Addicted To Love" video,' Carly interjected, verbalising the exact thought I'd lost.

'Thank you,' Jess said, twirling around. It was good to see her back to her normal state of togetherness. She had me worried this morning in LA, when she got back to the hotel and she was so utterly dishevelled and miserable. After we'd left the Beverly Wilt-shire, we'd gone back to Sam's house to pack new bags, then come straight to the airport for the flight to Vegas, so there had been no time to talk to her properly. By the looks of things though, she'd either rallied or she was slapping on a smile and putting her troubles to one side for now. If she could do it, so could I.

'You okay, Carol? You look like you're about to cry.' She was the second person to say that in five minutes. Clearly, I was shit at rallying.

'It's my contact lenses,' I murmured for the second time.

Val came in just as I said that, and she was a vision in a floor-length silver lamé kaftan. 'Aw, pet. A good wash out with some of that extortionate water in the minibar will sort that. And get a hustle on. Those roulette tables won't wait all night.' She raised her eyes. 'Don't worry, Josie, love, we're on the way. But if there's anyone around that could rustle up a quick miracle, can you ask them to get our Carol's arse off this chair and into the shower?'

19

VAL

Spotlight – Jennifer Hudson

I put my chopsticks down and leaned towards my niece.

'In the name of God, Carly, stop swivelling yer head from side to side. You'll end up at the chiropractor and last time I was at one of those he charged me fifty quid and cracked bits of me that no man has touched except my Don. Pure mortified, so I was. I've never been able to talk about ma bruised coccyx since that dark day.'

Don't get me wrong, I understood her worries. The first photos on the beach in Malibu were a bit embarrassing, but these ones were downright nasty. Carly, on Rodeo Drive, holding everyone's bags because we'd all nipped into the toilets in Louis Vuitton for a pee. Her hair was blown about, and she was a bit torn-faced because she was still fretting over the Malibu pics. Of course, folks ogling the pictures wouldn't know that. They'd just see the headlines and jump to conclusions:

WHAT DOES HE SEE IN HER?

The caption said.

SAM MORTON'S WIFE SPENDS, SPENDS, SPENDS THE HEART-
THROB'S CASH

'Sorry, Val. It's just that...'

I put my hand up, nearly knocking my spare ribs off the burny warmy thing in front of me. 'Stop there, pet. Have I not been telling you since you were a wee one not to give a toss what anyone says about you?'

'Easier said than done when it's the entire internet that thinks you're a gold-digging old boot.' She sighed. 'Who would choose this? Who would actually want to put themselves in the public eye for people to criticise and judge every single day?'

All of us immediately swivelled our heads towards Carol, who, bless her, just shrugged. 'I'm shallow,' she replied, as if that was an explanation. 'And I'm qualified for nothing else.'

'True,' Jess agreed. 'It must be so tough. Is that watch Gucci or Armani, you poor soul?'

Carol didn't rise to it, just kept on eating her noodles. We were having dinner in the super-fancy Chinese restaurant at the Bellagio hotel and, well, who'd have thought I'd ever be here. I was more of an egg-fried rice take-away from the Happy Dragon on the Weir-bridge High Street kinda woman.

'Anyway,' Jess went on. 'I'll put my professional hat on and make some calls tomorrow morning and see if I can suss out what's happening. It could just be some random pap trying to make a bit of money, but it feels more like someone is coming for you. I just can't see who would have any interest in doing that. I also have no idea who could possibly have known that we were going to be at

Malibu beach the other day. I mean, we didn't know ourselves until the night before.'

I reached for a chunk of chicken and then it dropped back on the plate. Bloody chopsticks. I'd never got the hang of them. If I'd a pound for every meal me and Josie had started to eat with them, then ditched the notion halfway through and swapped them for a fork...

'Still think they were trying to get me, and they got you instead. I mean, I'm a dead ringer for Sharon Stone,' I said, keeping a straight face. 'I believe Sharon Stone also slipped on the ice outside Aldi last Christmas and bruised her arse.'

That made them chuckle.

A crowd of blokes in suits at the next table turned to see what all the laughter was about, and I gave them a wee wave. They didn't look impressed.

Right, back to business. Time to get this show on the road and get another number ticked off the bucket list.

I rushed them through dinner and then out to the casino floor, keen to get on with it. That was one thing about Josie, she didn't waste time on this earth. My pal crammed in every single thing she ever wanted to do and more, and even in her last years she had more energy than women half her age. The night before she died, we were up on that dance floor and then she persuaded the hotel to open the residents bar for a sing-song – 3 a.m. and she was standing on a stool with my Don, their arms around each other, swaying as they belted out 'The Wonder Of You'. If I didn't have those memories, I wasn't sure I could cope with what was happening to me now. Aye, this week was all fun and games, but I wasn't kidding myself – I knew what I'd be facing when I went home after this list was done. But that worry was for next week. Today... or rather, tonight... well, that was for a party and it was time to get started.

I'd already put my gambling money in my purse. A full month's pension. It felt shocking to be wasting that much money, but it was all coming out of the holiday fund that Josie and I had been saving for years before she died.

On the gaming floor, I whipped out the cash, all flash, as if I did this every day. That was as far as I got. 'What do I do now?' I hissed to Carly. She'd been in a casino or two over the years, so I'd promoted her to trusty advisor.

'Let's start with blackjack first,' she said, steering me over to a table that had five folk sitting at it. Three of them soon told me they were on a stag do from Michigan and they were already three sheets to the wind but still determined to party. The last two, well, he was a bit of a flash git in his sixties, all gold watch and expensive-looking suit, and she was a young woman, in her late twenties, maybe. It was hard to tell with all that lip filler and Botox these lassies used nowadays. Father and daughter, perhaps?

Jess and Carol went away for a wander and to make another one of those Tok Tak videos Carol was always doing, but Carly stayed at my side as I laid twenty dollars down on the table the way I saw the others do, and the croupier picked it up and swapped it for a pile of chips.

She pushed them towards me and I sent a message heaven-wards. *Right, Josie, let's go, ma love.*

The dealer started dishing out cards, and I glanced up at Carly for guidance. She leaned towards my ear. 'Remember that weekend in Blackpool when it rained every day and we played one card game morning, noon, and night?' she whispered. 'That's what this is, Aunt Val. It's pontoon. You know exactly what you're doing.'

Well, I almost puffed out ma chest and punched the air. I was a master at pontoon. Oh, my God, the number of holidays we'd been stuck inside because the rain was peeing down outside, and the cards had come out. Don and I had played it every day of our honeymoon in a caravan at Ayr beach. It was that or constant sex, but the sweet wee elderly woman in the next caravan kept knocking on our door for a chat and we didn't want to give her the shock of her life.

I focused back on the game, and soon got the hang of how the betting worked, and how the cards were dealt. After an hour or so, I had a big pile of chips in front of me and I'd sussed that the older bloke and the young lassie next to me were a couple. And not a very happy one at that. He barely spoke to her, didn't crack a smile, but he kept an eye on every single thing she did, ordered her drinks for her, told her what to do, what not to do.

At one point, one of the guys on the stag party made an innocent comment to her and the boyfriend put his hand on her leg. I was sitting right next to her, so I was the only one who saw that his knuckles turned white from squeezing so hard, and all at once I saw exactly what was going on here. It was a warning to her. A threat. I'd seen that kind of thing far too many times before. Sherilee Roberts from two doors along from us had a man like that and he terrorised her for years. She wasn't allowed to speak to anyone, to leave the house on her own, and if she did, she felt the back of his hand when she got home. My old pal, Nancy Wright, was in a similar situation. Her man, Franny, was a demon on the drink and that poor woman was forced to sit there, head down, and let him say whatever he wanted to her without reproach. And the things he got away with. Josie and I heard it one too many times before Josie cornered him in the gents' one night at the social club and told him that if he so much as laid a finger on Nancy again, or said one more nasty word to her, Josie would break into his house and beat his willy to a pulp when he was sleeping.

Thankfully, the old bastard died soon afterwards. Last time we heard from Nancy, she was using Franny's life insurance to go off to Benidorm with her sister and she planned to do whatever the hell she pleased.

The one that was closest to home, though, was our Sarah. She'd been Carly, Carol and Jess's pal their whole childhoods, but she'd dropped off the radar when she went to university. Turns out she'd met and married a horror, who had controlled every move she made. He'd made her life a misery and it was only by some miracle that she'd managed to break free from him and gone on to marry Nick and have a great life. She didn't forget though. After that, she raised every penny she could for womens' shelters and family refuge centres. The world lost a great person when that lass died. She never, ever walked away from someone who needed help. And I had no bloody intention of turning away from this lassie either.

Another hour passed and Jess swapped places with Carly, who'd gone off to play on the roulette thingamajig with Carol. Jess joined in the game, taking Carly's seat. Next to an empty one left when a bloke from the stag party had keeled over and fell off his stool. His pals had carried him off somewhere and we hadn't seen him since. A couple of strangers sat down at the other empty seats, leaving Mr Flash, his very quiet girlfriend – or should that be hostage – and Jess and I, all sitting together in a row. I'd struck it lucky. My twenty quid had not only lasted that long, but it had multiplied.

'Bloody hell, Val, you've got about two hundred dollars there,' Jess whispered, taking in the pile of chips in front of me.

Two hundred dollars. I'd already increased my money tenfold. That's what some divine intervention from Josie and living a life in Scotland's wet climate, with nothing more than a pack of cards for amusement, did for a gambler's skills. This was crazy. The whole point of the mission Josie and I had talked about was blowing the cash, not making more. The idea was to be stupid and crazy with money for the first time in our lives, after spending decades watching what we spent and guarding every penny like it was a pound.

Yet... none of that mattered to me right at that moment because

I could barely concentrate on the game now for watching the lass to my right. Sometimes, when her man lost a hand and his anger showed all over his face, I could see her visibly shake. Eventually, I couldn't take any more. Staring straight ahead, acting as if absolutely nothing was amiss, I reached my right hand down and touched the side of her arm, making sure that I was subtle, so he wouldn't notice. For a moment, I thought she hadn't realised what I was doing, until I saw, out of the corner of my eye, that she'd taken her hand off the table and put it down by her side where it met mine. I squeezed her fingers. This young lass and I were having a silent conversation, and not a single other person – least of all that big bastard she was with – realised it.

Letting my hand go, she put hers on her lap and then did a weird thing with her fingers. She tucked her thumb into her palm, then tucked her other fingers over it. I wasn't sure if I was reading this right, so I nudged Jess on the other side of me, and made a gesture with my eyes in the direction of the lassie's lap. Jess's gaze immediately went there too, just as the girl did the same thing again. Thumb into her palm. Then her other four fingers folded over it. This time I wasn't wrong, and Jess's wide gaze told me she had sussed it too. It was a sign for help. We'd all learned it on one of my great-niece Toni's – that's Carol's daughter – social media posts about abuse, when she filmed us all demonstrating the gesture. Thumb in. Fingers folded over it. It was a way of saying you were in trouble. In danger. A silent cry for help. I wasn't wrong. And if I was, I'd pay for the dry cleaning. Because right then, I did the only thing I could think of to do.

I knocked my drink all over the poor lassie's lap.

20

JESS

Monsters – Katie Sky

Fuck. To the untrained eye, I knew Val's slip of the drink seemed like an accident, but I knew better. Val had never been that careless with vodka in her life. I'd seen the hand gesture too. Carol's social media content might be full of superficial things like shopping, entertaining and going on luxury holidays, but Toni's online platform had a real message behind it. She talked about bullying, about sexual harassment, about self-harming and mental health. One day, a few months ago, we'd all joined in her video about signs to look out for if you suspected a friend, or even a stranger, was in an abusive relationship, or in distress of any kind, and how to signal to a stranger that you needed help. That's what this woman was doing now.

'Och, come on, love,' Val said to the young woman. In her late twenties, if I had to guess. Let's get you to the toilets and get you dried off.'

Her partner didn't look pleased, but what could he do? He couldn't insist that she sat there, soaking wet, covered in vodka, in the middle of the casino.

Val clocked his expression too, and went straight into harmless old lady mode. 'Don't you worry, pet, we'll bring her right back to you, all cleaned up and dried off,' she told him, with an expression that would melt the heart of a third-world dictator. The woman was a piece of work. Or a work of art. Or maybe a bit of both. Either way, she was fricking sensational and I had never been more glad that she was one of us. She scooped her chips into her handbag and off we went to the toilets.

As soon as we got inside the marble-tiled opulence of the loos, the woman began to tremble from head to toe. 'I shouldn't have done that. I shouldn't have made that sign. I'm fine, honestly. I am. I'd better go back.'

Val put her arm around her and guided her to a velvet chair in the corner of the room. 'I know you are, love, but just sit down a wee minute and let's get you dried off. I'm Val, pet. What's your name?'

A couple of years after Val's daughter, Dee, died, Val had gone to work with the Samaritans, on their helpline for people in pain or desperate situations. This Val was the flipside of the raucous, hilarious woman she showed to the world the rest of the time. She might not know one end of a tweet from the other, but when it came to human beings, she had a lifetime of knowing what to say and do.

It took her twenty minutes in all to get the whole story out of her. Twenty minutes in which Kimmy told us how she'd left Idaho and come to Vegas to be a dancer when she was twenty-one, had made enough to survive for a few years, but then the guy who owned the bar, that tosser she'd been with, had taken a liking to her and she'd moved in with him.

At first, she'd been relieved to stop working there and be his girlfriend instead, but it hadn't taken long for his control to become all-consuming. She couldn't go out alone. Couldn't speak to anyone. Couldn't call anyone. Couldn't breathe.

'You need to get out of there, ma love,' Val told her, voice full of compassion.

Kimmy shook her head. 'I can't. Where would I go? I don't have the cash to go home to Idaho. I can't get a job without an address. I promise that I'm not the kinda girl who gives up but...' The tears streaming down her face told us everything. She was all out of options. And in the harsh light of the toilets, the bruises we could see around her wrists told us even more.

Val and I met each other's gaze and we both knew what we were thinking.

'I've got about two hundred dollars upstairs and I can take more out of the cash machine,' I said. 'The others will help too. Let's go get them. Kimmy, wait here...'

The young woman was shaking her head. 'I don't have time. I need to go back. He'll come looking for me. Just because it's a ladies' toilet won't stop him. You don't understand...' Her voice cracked on every word.

'Oh, I do, love. I understand completely. Right, come with us.' Val took Kimmy's hand, and we left the loos, all of us scanning the games floor for any sign of him. In the distance, I spotted him, still sitting at the table, and I nudged Val and gestured over. Val immediately cornered a security guard standing at a nearby exit.

'Excuse me, son, but there's a bloke over at the pontoon table...'

'Blackjack,' I corrected her.

'Aye, blackjack,' she carried on, pointing through the crowds to the table in question, 'And he just asked me if I wanted to buy drugs.'

I'd pulled Kimmy out of sight behind me, but I heard her gasp as she listened to Val's utterly convincing story.

The security guard was listening intently now.

'The thing is,' Val went on, 'I've heard all about the drugs these people sell. They can turn you into a zombie and then these men have their wicked way with you. Monsters, so they are. I'm so shocked, I'm going off to my bed, but if this guy isn't punted straight out of here immediately, I'll be speaking to my lawyer.'

The security guard went straight onto his walkie-talkie, filled someone at the other end in on the story, then we watched from a distance as another two men in suits approached Kimmy's boyfriend. It was all the diversion and time that we needed. Val feigned upset to get away, and we went on the hunt for the others. We found them at the roulette table.

'Girls, don't ask, but this lassie is in trouble and needs money quick. She's in the same situation our Sarah was in.'

From their expressions of concern, I could see that Carol and Carly had caught on straight away and they immediately snapped to attention.

'How much can we rustle up between us?' Val went on.

'I can get a few hundred on my card, but I can call Sam...' Carly began, no questions asked.

'And I can get the same now, and go to the bank in the morning and get whatever you need,' Carol jumped in.

I'd never been prouder of my pals, but I saw that Kimmy's eyes were jumping from place to place, worried that he'd appear at her side at any minute.

Val had sensed it too. I saw that she'd stopped listening and was looking at the LED numbers on the post beside the roulette table, the ones that showed which number the ball had landed on after the last dozen or so turns.

She tipped her handbag onto the table and there were a couple of raised eyebrows and much curiosity from everyone around who saw a pile of chips fall out. Val bundled them up, and then pushed them all on to number ten, black. It took us a moment, but we soon got there. Josie was born on the tenth of October – 10/10. It had been her lucky number all her life, the one she picked in a raffle, in a tombola, and even in the Grand National every year. If there was a gamble to be had, Josie's number was ten.

'What we can rustle up right this minute isn't enough to get this lassie very far tonight, but maybe…'

She didn't finish the sentence because I could tell that even Val knew how crazy this was. Two hundred dollars. On one number. With so much more at stake. This was crazy. Insane. This was the kind of stunt that only worked in some imaginary movie like Ocean's 23, and even then, only because Brad Pitt had some kind of magic button that stopped the wheel at the right place. This wasn't the movies, it was real life, and this girl had no chance…

The dealer chirped, 'No more bets, please, no more bets,' and spun the wheel.

In that moment in time, everything else cleared right out of my mind. I didn't think about Arnie. I wasn't furious, or sad, or heart-broken or homicidal. I didn't care that my life had been trashed, my future decimated. All that mattered was the spinning wheel and the ball that was bouncing along it. Carol, Carly, Val, Kimmy, everyone else at the table were all staring. Ball number 10. Ball number 10.

The wheel began to slow down and the ball made popping sounds as it began to hop from number to number, each time slower than the one before. Slower. Slower.

Until, it stopped. Number 25, red. Right next door to…

Another very slight movement and it moved again. Black. Number 10.

The whole table erupted, even the dealer cheered, and I was pretty sure the people in the security room were staring into the cameras above us and scrutinising every movement. I didn't care. This wasn't cheating, it was divine intervention.

'Can I cash this in, son?' Val asked the dealer, still completely unaware of the ways of the casino.

He shook his head, swapped her pile for a few higher-value chips and handed them over to her, with directions to the cashier.

The four of us, plus Kimmy, bustled over to the cash desk and watched as Val cashed in her chips. Two hundred dollars. At thirty-seven to one. That made $7400 dollars and she handed every single one of them over to Kimmy.

'There you go, love, take this. Go home. Go somewhere safe and start again. This should be enough to get you on your feet.'

'I can't take it. I just can't...'

'Of course you can, love. It's a gift – from all of us, and a couple of pals who couldn't make it here tonight.'

That did it. Carol burst into tears – it wasn't her contact lenses this time – and Carly grinned and whispered a triumphant 'Yasssss.' And me? I went for the usual pragmatic approach. It was crazy how we all reverted to type in every situation.

'If you go now, you'll make it to the airport before the last flight out tonight. Do you have your driving licence with you?' I asked.

Kimmy nodded and gestured to her small clutch bag. 'Yes. I always carry it in case I get a chance...'

We all knew what she was saying.

'Okay, good – that's all you'll need. A flight is probably your best bet, so he doesn't catch up with you. Fly to LA, and from there, you'll be able to get a connection to Idaho or wherever you want to go. Here's my card. If you get stuck or in trouble, call me and we'll help.'

'I can't take this money. I just can't,' Kimmy argued. 'Things like this don't happen to me. This can't be real.'

'I promise it is,' I told her gently, but with urgency. I had no idea if the security team were still keeping the boyfriend busy or if he'd come charging over here any second.

Val reached over and took her hand. 'On you go, love. It's all yours. I just want to ask you one favour.'

Kimmy stared at Val like she was crazy. 'Any... any... anything.'

'One day, you'll find a decent bloke – or a nice woman if that's your thing – and maybe you'll have a family. If you have ever have a girl... can you call her Josie Sarah? It's a bit of a mouthful, but trust me, she couldn't have a better name than that one.'

Kimmy nodded as we rushed her outside, helped her into a taxi and waved her off.

As the lights disappeared in the distance, Val looked upwards and began talking to the stars.

'Aye okay, I'll give you that one, pal – that was some stunt. So what have you got next for us then?'

21

CARLY

4 Non Blondes – What's Up

'I'll miss you,' I whispered in my husband's ear. It was 9 a.m., we'd got in from LAX an hour ago after taking the first flight out of Vegas, after about four hours sleep, and now I was sitting on the marble top of his kitchen island. I mean, our kitchen island. I kept forgetting this was my house too now and wondered if it would ever feel like it. I shrugged off the thought for a later time. It wasn't long until we were going to head back to the airport for our flights to New York, where we planned to tick off a few more items from the bucket list. Josie would be so proud of our stamina. Although, I was exhausted, Carol was wilting and Jess had been beginning to get snappy when we sent her to her room for a nap. In fact, Val was the only one still going strong. She says it was down to years of conditioning, letting it rip on the dance floor at the community centre cabaret nights.

I focused back on the moment. I wanted to enjoy every second of the fact that my gorgeous husband was standing between my legs, his arms around my shoulders, his lips turning now to mine, closer, closer...

'You absolute fucking fuck of a fucker!' Jess wailed as she stormed in while simultaneously pounding the front of her mobile phone with her palm.

Sighing, my head flopped against Sam's chest. I was so knackered, I could just have left it there and gone for a snooze. 'Please call Arnie. Tell him I'll give him every one of my internal organs if he comes back and makes her happy again.'

Jess spun around, shooting fire from her narrowed eyes and spoke in a tone that could wilt the plants on Sam's windowsill. 'What did you say?'

'I said Arnie is a dickhead for leaving you and I just want you to be happy again,' I bluffed, shifting the narrative. I was too young to die. 'What's your phone ever done to you to deserve that kind of beat-down?' I asked, trying to sidetrack her and move on from the flashpoint. Jess in a temper is not someone I ever want to irritate. It's not so much poking a bear, as hitting it with a taser and then watching as it fries yet keeps coming at you.

'First of all, I put a few calls in for you to try to find out where these pics are coming from...' she raged.

Now I felt bad.

Sam gave me an amused, raised eyebrow of condemnation for slurring my friend when she was actually trying to help me. I felt suitably chastised.

'I love you,' I grovelled in her direction.

Sam folded his twenty-one-inch biceps and leaned against the counter, like something straight out of the (Aging But Still Got It) Hot Hunks edition of *GQ* magazine. His hair was longer now than the buzz cut he'd sported when I met him, but he still had shoulders like anvils and abs that I could file my nails on. Not that I was shallow about all that physical stuff. Okay, I was. But thankfully, he wasn't, because the other night I'd worn a pair of black, wet-look jeggings and from the back I'm pretty sure I looked like two bin bags full of baked potatoes on a vibrating power plate.

'Then I got a cease and desist from Dax Hill's people, in response to the text messages between him and Hayley that we released. He's also put in six calls to Entertainment LA, to try to stop the interview they're doing with Hayley today.'

'Did they drop it?' Sam asked. 'Because I'm happy to call Sally Marshall over there.' I had no idea who that was, but I was guessing she was the boss. My husband had that kind of clout. I, on the other hand, couldn't muster up a power play if my life depended on it. Being a small-time writer, with a few books under my belt and a twenty-year history of writing an obnoxious newspaper column, had paid the bills, but it carried no political weight whatsoever.

'No, they're sticking with it for now, but I don't know how much longer they'll withstand the barrage of threats.'

'Is he still denying that he had an affair with Hayley?' I asked, incredulous at the audacity of this guy. He'd had a six-month illicit relationship, and now that he was in a sticky situation he was denying all knowledge and saying it never happened. And his wife believed him and was standing by her man.

'He is. But he's also still refusing to consent to the DNA test and releasing false stories to the press at every turn. The guy is a snake. Hayley's lawyers are working on the legal stuff, but what's the use of a payout if he's put a whole load of shit out there about her? She'll never work again and she'll have to live with the notoriety for the rest of her life. I'm not fucking having it. Oh, and speaking of noto-riety... Don't freak out when you see this...'

Oh bollocks. Bollocks. Bollocks. If Jess was telling me not to freak out, then whatever was going on was definitely worth freaking out about.

She turned the screen around and there it was – a video of me, shaking my bits as I danced on top of a bar.

That moment had been number four on Val's bucket list. After we'd given the cash to Kimmy and put her in a taxi to the airport in Vegas the night before, we'd been crossing the hotel lobby, heading to our rooms, when Val had diverted to the concierge. She'd caught up with us at the elevators five minutes later.

'Change of plan, girls! We're going out.'

'In the name of all that is holy, someone take her batteries out,' Jess had groaned.

Val had ignored her and carried on. 'Ernest over there at the concierge,' she'd turned and given a smiling, twenty-something guy at the desk a wave and he'd responded with a cheery smile and thumbs up. 'Ernest tells me there's a country music bar about fifteen minutes from here by taxi.'

'But we're leaving tomorrow morning at the crack of dawn, Aunt Val,' I'd pointed out.

'Exactly! That's why we're going now,' she'd said, linking her arms through mine and Carol's, swinging us around and marching us across the lobby towards the door. 'And you'd better get a move on too, Jess Latham!' she'd shouted behind her.

Jess had reluctantly caught up with us and a little over ten minutes later we were climbing out of the cab in front of the kind of bar that usually featured at the beginning of an episode of any show involving forensic investigations.

The sign above the door had announced it was called Alabama Sweet. Didn't look that sweet to us until we opened the doors. It was like stepping into a Garth Brooks video. All the men were wearing Stetsons, jeans and cowboy boots. The women were in denim and boots too, and on the, admittedly dusty, wooden dance floor... well, I'd never seen anything like it. Actually, that's not true. When I was growing up in Scotland, all the aunties and grannies would hit the dance floor at any party and split into lines to do a synchronised dance called the Slosh. It was a rite of passage where we came from. You were born, you went to school, you had your first period and you learned to do the Slosh.

This was the chest hair and blue jean swagger version. About forty men and women, all moving at the same time, thumbs tucked into the front pockets of their jeans, kicking up their heels and twirling.

We'd headed towards the bar, and of course, Carol had whipped her phone out and snapped a quick selfie to let all her followers see where she was.

I was first at the bar, so I'd ordered up four Jack Daniel's and Coke, because it didn't seem like the kind of place that would stock Prosecco.

'Right, we're staying for ten minutes, drinking these and then escaping back to the hotel before someone realises that we've gate-crashed the Marlboro Man's house party,' Jess had hissed.

'You might want to tell her that,' Carol had countered, pointing to the dance floor, where Aunt Val was inserting herself between two guys, while watching their feet and trying to copy their steps.

'Oh, for fuck's....' Jess had begun.

But Carol and I were way ahead of her. We'd both ditched our drinks on the bar, and we were making a beeline for Val. Just as we reached her, I heard her shout over the music to the cowboy on her left.

'Right, son, don't let this ancient face fool you, they used to call me snake hips back in the day.'

I'd laughed until my sides hurt.

Right now though, in the cold light of the next day, faced with video footage of yours truly, it didn't seem so funny.

I groaned out loud. 'Why is this happening to me? Why? Who is doing this?'

As if it wasn't bad enough that I didn't want to live here because of a million things I'd miss about home, it was almost as if someone was trying to make sure I was as unhappy as it was possible to be by humiliating me.

'For what it's worth, I think you all look great,' Sam shrugged, watching the video of a later moment that showed me with Val, Carol and Jess, my dancing partners in crime, as we kicked up our heels on the bar top. It was another tick on Josie's bucket list and, up until five minutes ago, it had been an absolutely hilarious memory that I would treasure for ever. I just didn't want photographic evidence of it.

I batted him in the rock-hard abs. I don't even think he felt it.

'That's because you're biased. I could roll in here in a sumo suit and you'd still think I was cute.'

Sam laughed. 'What? You're saying sumos are not cute?'

Before I could answer, he switched his focus to Jess.

'Look, who can we speak to about getting this taken down?'

'Sam, it's on YouTube and a dozen blogs have already picked it up. You know better than anyone that when something is out there, it's impossible to control. It's like playing fricking whack-a-mole. As soon as you get one site to drop it, another ten pop up. And that's not to mention the tweets and the Insta posts and the Facebook shares. Basically, when it's out there, it can't be stopped.' She turned back to me. 'At least they're not saying you're a former stripper who is lying about being pregnant with the baby of a Hollywood agent so she can hustle him for money.'

'No, they're saying I'm a gold-digging, party girl who needs to cut down on the pies.'

'That's my kinda girl,' Sam joked again, unhelpfully. He wasn't taking this seriously, mainly because, after more than twenty years in Hollywood, and considering his big break was an autobiographical movie about his previous life as a high-class male escort for extremely rich women, the man was practically bulletproof when it came to this stuff. There was a double standard there, for sure. Male escorts? Studs. Female escorts? Held in utter contempt in this town. Except Julia Roberts in *Pretty Woman* and no one believed she was actually a hooker anyway.

I sighed again. 'Like I said, I just don't get it. What possible motivation could anyone have for running this sort of shit about me? I mean, who actually cares?'

The sound of approaching heels clicked louder and louder and I glanced up at the door, expecting to see Val tottering in on yet another pair of her rainbow spectrum of furry mules, but no...

'Good morning, everyone. Sam, I still have a key and the code for the gate, so I just let myself in. I knew you wouldn't mind,' she chirped. Sam shrugged. He never sweated the small stuff. 'How are we all today?' she went on.

Estelle Conran spoke to us as if she was opening an interview with Oprah on prime-time telly. The wide grin. The perfect teeth. The modulated voice. I'd seen old videos of her from when she first came to Hollywood, and she sounded like Minnie Mouse off her face on helium. She'd clearly done work to lower her register and perfect the cool, neutral, slightly husky tone she spoke with now. I was a woman who firmly believed in lifting other women up, but the only way I could possibly bring myself to raise Estelle would be if she sat on the opposite end of a seesaw, in which case I pretty much hoped that our weight difference would come in handy and I'd catapult her into space.

I realised that I'd gone so far into that little imaginary scene, that I'd almost missed her coming over all fake concerned and faux sympathetic. 'Oh my goodness, Carly, are you okay? Are you ill?'

Here we go. Jab, swing, jab, jab. Why did I never have a fricking seesaw when I needed one?

'Nope, Estelle, this is how I look in the mornings.'

'Oh. Well. I think it's wonderful that you're brave enough to embrace your natural look.'

I glared at Sam, who was struggling to keep a straight face. Again, he refused to get involved in this nonsense, so he dismissed it completely. As far as he was concerned, he'd lived with Estelle for a year or so, they'd had a perfectly okay but pretty-surface level relationship. During that time, I'd come here as a friend of twenty years, he'd realised that he'd never stopped loving me, so he finished with Estelle, and we'd got it together because we were meant to be. Now he and Estelle had a friendly working relationship. He'd moved on. She'd moved on. End of story.

I had a very different take on things. Less of a romcom and more of a psychological thriller where the psychopath ex-girlfriend ingratiates herself into her ex-lover's life, murders his new wife in cold blood, then steps over her body on the way to seduce him.

However, I wasn't giving her the satisfaction of showing her my insecurities or worries, so instead I threw out a beaming smile. 'Thank you. It helps when my husband thinks I'm perfect the way I am.' It really didn't, but she didn't need to know that.

Anyway, shots fired, psycho ex-girlfriend wounded but not down. She flashed her veneers at Sam. 'Are you ready, Sammy? We should really get going if we're going to make the call time at the studio.'

Sammy. He'd never been called that. It must be her pet name for him. Strange, because my pet name for her was Stella The Deranged Cow.

Sam gave me another kiss on the lips and I wrapped my arms around his neck and made it last just a little longer than a goodbye peck. If he noticed, he didn't comment. 'When will you be back from New York?' he murmured.

'I'm not sure. A couple of days, maybe.'

'Don't worry, Carly. I'll take really good care of him while you're gone.'

With that, and a flick of her baby blonde extensions, the two of them exited the kitchen, leaving Jess and I open-mouthed. Estelle Conran was fricking shameless.

Jess was the first to find her voice again. 'Carly, you know how you were wondering who could possibly have a motive for making your life here hell?' she asked, still staring at the door.

'I think I might have an idea who that could be.'

22
———

CAROL

Sabotage – Bebe Rexha

There were already 56,798 views of the video of me dancing on the bar with Val last night. The woman had footwork skills that made the crowd gasp. It was mormonising. I mean, mesmerising.

We'd been so careful not to get Carly or Jess in the shot that I posted online, because neither of them wanted to be filmed, so I could see why Carly was so pissed off that someone else must have been recording us and uploaded the clip of her to the internet. It was so bizarre. The irony wasn't lost on me. There I was, filming everything, uploading this 'inverted commas' brilliant life, when all she wanted was to be completely anonymous.

One of the comments on my Instagram today really got to me. 'I wish my life was like yours! Normality is so overrated! We love you!' I wanted to write back and say I'd give anything for a bit of normality. I'd give anything to wake up one morning and not have to act, not have to pretend, not have to adopt this happy, positive, cheery, completely bullshit personal. I mean, persona. Shit, why wouldn't my brain work properly?

'I've just had an idea,' Carly said, just as the 'fasten seatbelt sign' was switched off after taking off from LAX. 'Can I see your phone a minute? Mine is out of charge and I'm just thinking maybe your video has the image of someone recording us in the background. God, I'm a genius.'

We huddled together as I replayed the clip. Las Vegas. In a run-down line dancing bar just off the Strip at 3 a.m., after two or twelve drinks too many. We'd just watched Val give away seven thousand dollars because she was, quite truly, the loveliest, most big-hearted woman who had ever... I glanced over at her in the next row of the plane before I finished that thought, ...worked blue eyeliner, white patent boots and a pink feather boa into her daytime chic wardrobe.

'Can you see anything dodgy?' I asked my sister-in-law.

'I'm not sure,' Carly croaked. 'I'm so tired I'm having difficulty forcing my pupils to unblur the image. I think Val's broken us.'

A sudden bump of turbulence made me gasp and grip my seat handles.

'Are you okay?' Carly asked, concerned. 'I've never known you to be a nervous flyer.'

'I'm fine,' I blustered.

I wasn't. My heart was beating out of my chest, and I had a cold, prickly sensation burrowing its way under the skin on my arms, legs and stomach. As a model and later, as an influencer, I'd taken thousands of flights, on everything from a helicopter to a puddle jumper, to a huge bloody great big plane, to a private jet. I'd been in storms, in snow, in winds that made my glass of bubbly splash all over my tray table. Not once had I been scared. Not once, that is, until about six months ago, when I spent the whole of a mildly bumpy flight to Paris with fear gripping my chest, fighting the urge to vomit.

Thank God for Carly's short attention span. Her focus already returned to the screen of my phone.

'Nope, can't see anyone filming us. Must have been from another angle. Or maybe from the bar's security cameras.'

Jess overheard that and piped in. 'Carly, the toilets didn't have locks on the doors and the bourbon was pure moonshine. Somehow, I don't think their budget stretched to security cameras.'

At the other side of Jess, Val leaned forward. I noticed now that she'd put on sunglasses in the shape of huge white hearts. 'Could you keep it down please? Us elderly folks need an afternoon nap. Some irresponsible good-time girls kept me up half the night, last night.'

Carly almost spat out her drink. 'You got us into this! Let me ask you, who dragged us all to that bar? Carol and I nearly ended up in A&E.'

She wasn't kidding. At one point, before we'd even climbed on top of the bar, Carly had grabbed my hand, pulled me onto the dance floor, and we'd joined the end of the line, where we spun, we hollered and we fell over our feet because we went the wrong way more times than we could count. But not Aunt Val. She'd mastered the whole thing in about two minutes, and her furry mules and the cowboy boots were a-tapping in perfect sanitisation... Nope, that's not it. Simplification... Aaaargh, crap.

The memory blank snapped me back to the plane, thousands of feet above the ground, somewhere between LA and New York.

I nudged Carly. 'What do you call it when you're dancing and everyone is doing the same thing at the same time?'

'A fricking miracle?' she suggested, unhelpfully.

I rolled my eyes at her, then flopped my head on to her shoulder. 'Take pity on me, I've got a total brain freeze.'

She stroked my hair. 'Aw, petal, I think you mean a total hangover. Is synchronised the word you're looking for?'

'Yes! That's it. And you're probably right about the hangover. Do you think Aunt Val is on drugs? I've never met someone with such a high tolerance for alcohol and such a low requirement for sleep.'

Carly yawned. 'Maybe. I refuse to believe that she's powered solely by Jaffa Cakes. Whatever she's on, I want some of it.'

We sat like that for a few minutes, until I was just about dropping off. I shuffled into a different position, and as I lifted my head from her shoulder, I saw that she had her earphones in and was watching *Real Housewives of Beverly Hills* on her iPad.

I nudged her, then popped the earphone nearest me out of her ear. 'Trying to pick up tips?' I teased.

'This is sooooo not my world,' she countered, and as she said it, a frown went right across her face and jogged a memory in my mind. A couple of mornings ago. At the Regent Beverly Wiltshire. I'd walked in and she was talking to Jess, and they were saying something about secrets, and she had that exact same expression. I'd meant to ask her about it yesterday but – shocker – it had completely slipped my mind. Just for a change.

I turned in my seat so that I was facing her. 'Are you okay, honey?'

Whatever was going on, she shook it off. 'Yeah, of course. I'm fine.'

I knew her better though, and I wasn't letting it go. Carly rarely got pissed off, especially since she'd got back together with Sam. Another twist of anxiety flared in my stomach.

'Okay, don't make me torture you,' I said, lots of things dropping into place in my head. Now that I thought about it, she'd been acting a bit weird for the last couple of weeks. She'd been weirdly quiet since we got here. There was a sadness about her. And I hadn't really registered any of it because I was too busy feeling shit and thinking I was losing my mind. But now... Now, she met my gaze, held it.

'What would you say if I told you that I didn't want to start a new life in Los Angeles?'

The truth was out of her mouth before she could stop it.

'I'd say I'd swap places with you in a second. I mean, as long as Callum could come too,' I added quickly. We were friends first and sisters-in-law second, but this was too close to home. How could I tell her how I was feeling about Callum, my marriage, my life, when it involved her brother and her family? It would be putting her in an impossible position. Besides, right now, I wanted to go through the door she'd just opened.

'I always thought you were joking about not wanting to move here?'

She shrugged. 'I think I was just trying to say the words out loud and that was the only way to do it. The truth is, I love LA for a holiday. It's fun and it's a novelty, but it's not my life. Not the life that I want, anyway. You know, when I was married to Mark, I went along with it all. He worked obscene hours and I just took everything on and juggled my work, my boys' lives, money, time, our home... I did it all myself and I figured that was the deal. Mark's job was important to him, so I just had to get on with it. And the truth is, part of me loved the independence because I could spend my life with you guys and my boys and plan whatever I wanted. Sure, I was knackered and prone to the occasional bout of motherly martyrdom, but I had the life I loved, even if Mark and I had grown apart. Now I've got the guy I love, but when I think about living here, I just think how lonely it will be. I'll have Sam, but he already has so many other commitments. I've had twenty years of chaos that I thrived on, but here I'll have no boys and no close friends, especially now that Jess is going back to London.'

Wow. This wasn't the first time I'd heard this, but I'd never taken her objections to living here seriously, maybe because I couldn't believe anyone wouldn't want this life. I should have known better. Carly didn't give a crap about money or status or celebrity. Sometimes I wondered if it was a result of the way she and Callum had been brought up, with an alcoholic dad and a disinterested mum. All they both wanted was the people they loved around them and to live in the moment. They were never happier than when they were surrounded by a full squad of family and pals, hanging out in the garden or at the pub. Why had I not thought this through? Now that she'd pointed it out, it was obvious.

'I really don't want to come here, Carol,' she cut to the chase.

I cut to the chase too. 'Not even for Sam?'

I saw the flicker of pain cross her brow.

'For Sam, I'll do it. I love him more than I can say. But what if love isn't enough?'

23

VAL

The Story – Brandi Carlile

High above the clouds, the sky outside the airplane window was dark now, with just spots of gold here and there. That made me smile to myself. After Josie passed, it gave me comfort to sit out on my back step with a cup of tea late at night and look up at the stars. Just like my Dee, Josie was one of them now, I'd tell myself. They were the brightest ones.

Next to me, Jess was sleeping, a blanket over her right up to her shoulders. We were in business class for this flight, courtesy of lovely Sam, who'd once again upgraded us all. Return flights, because we were going to spend a couple of days with Carly back in Los Angeles, ticking off the final things on the list. She was a lucky woman, our Carly.

I glanced over at her now, deep in conversation with Carol. They were as close as real sisters, those two, and I was grateful for it. No matter what came their way, they'd have each other. That's how me and Josie were too. We'd had no idea that time would run out and one of us would have to face stuff alone. That's what was going to happen when I got back home – I'd have to face what I knew was coming alone.

But not yet, Josie. Not yet. Because I know yer still here, pal.

I picked up my pen, opened my notebook and flicked to the next blank page, then inhaled and changed my mindset while I was at it. I wasn't going to waste a moment of this trip with sorrow or dread. This wasn't a misery memoir I was writing here.

Right, Val. Deep breath. Slap a smile on. Pen to paper.

Dear Josie,

Oh, ma love, I think I've pulled a muscle with all that dancing. Another one off the list, ma darlin. Actually, two more, but I'll get to the other one in a minute. First, I just want to tell you that just in case yer not watching, one day, somewhere, if you spot a wee lassie called Josie Sarah, well, she's down to you. And, by the way, I absolutely know you are watching, because that stunt you played with the roulette table was class. If you could do the same with ma lottery numbers next week, that would be smashing. Especially since there's a cowboy in Las Vegas called Hank and I think I owe him a new pair of boots because I danced his legs off last night.

I paused to run back through everything that had happened in my mind, so that I didn't miss out any of the highlights.

We'd danced, we hollered and we yeehah'd, just like we used to do in my kitchen when Josie and I were practising our moves. Only this time I didn't knock over my fruit bowl and send my plums scattering across the room. I nearly pulled my back out picking them all up.

It was pretty safe to say my snake hip days are over and my

bunions were killing me, but it was just as much of a laugh as we'd thought it would be.

I'd have been happy with the gambling and the dancing, but somewhere along the line I got talking to the owner of the bar, a lovely bloke called Jerry. Well, when I say lovely... he had hair like straw hanging out of a bin, and his teeth looked like they were strangers to a tube of toothpaste, but he was a decent enough chap. I got to telling him all about our bucket list and he got right into the swing of it. First of all, he bought us all a couple of drinks. I was a bit suspicious at first, because you know, maybe he thought he was going to get my body in return, but he didn't make any demands, so we charged on with it. Turns out his grandfather came from Glasgow and he'd always wanted to go there. I think after the third drink I might have told him I'd get the spare room ready and he was welcome any time. Thankfully, the girls were too busy drinking and dancing to realise I'd practically adopted this bloke after knowing him for fifteen minutes.

Next thing I knew he was stopping the music and climbing up onto the stage with the microphone. There were a few moans and heckles, but he soon shut them up.

'Ladies and cowboys,' he'd announced, and that got them all cheering again. Apart from the girls, who were now watching proceedings with mild terror on their faces. Honestly, that lot need to get used to living in the moment.

So Jerry was still at the mic. 'We've got a very special guest here from Sc-a-t-land.' If his grandfather was still alive, I've no doubt he would have given him a scud across the back of his head for pronouncing it like that.

'And my friend from Sc-a-t-land has a very special favour to ask all of you... That's her over there, the swell-looking one with ma hat on.'

Aye, I'd borrowed his Stetson. I don't even want to think about what I could have caught from that. There was a big cheer from the crowd though, apart from our Jess, who had her eyes closed and seemed to be shaking her head – like I said, far too serious.

Jerry was still talking. 'On you go there, Valerie. We're all yours.'

Well, I didn't need asking twice. Although, I did need a wee leg-up onto a chair so that I could see everyone and get it all kicked off.

'Ladies and...' I caught myself before I came out with the wrong terminology. '... Cowboys,' I said, and how they roared. After that, it was plain sailing. I was sure to give Josie a mention though.

I went back to my letter.

After the dancing, I climbed up on the bar and made an announcement.

'Folks, me and my dearly departed friend used to say we'd come to America one day and that we'd have a wee sing-song in a bar. None of that karaoke stuff though. If you don't know the words off by heart, you shouldn't be singing them.' They knew I was kidding, but I kept my poker face on. 'So tonight, I thought that, in memory of my friend, I'd give you all a wee song, and yer welcome to join in.

'And before you ask, her name wasn't Caroline. It was Josie. She just had a wee thing for Neil Diamond. Right, here we go... one, two, three, four...

'Where it began...' I opened up my pipes and let it rip and, Josie, the most amazing thing happened. By the time we'd got to the chorus, they'd all joined in. Folks ten miles away must have woken up this morning thinking they'd had a dream about Neil Diamond and had 'Sweet Caroline' in their heads all day. It was bloody magical. So much so, we sang the whole thing twice. And you know how Westlife and Boyzone did that thing where they got up off the stools halfway through a song? Well, just as I got to the second chorus, I used Jerry's head to steady maself, and

*stepped up from the chair to the top of the bar. I was a bit
worried that my vertigo and the Jack Daniels would kick in and
I'd end up swan-diving on to the sawdust, but I managed to stay
upright.*

*And when we finished the song, there was a huge cheer and
the next thing I knew, the music was back on and the lassies
were up on the bar with me and we were shaking our wobbly bits
to one of those Billy Ray Cyrus songs, then that Carrie Under-
wood one where she takes a baseball bat to her man's car.
Remember, Agnes McGinty did that? Only it was a cricket bat
and her man's Ford Fiesta, but it was the same kind of thing.*

*So there we go, ma love. What a riot. What a laugh. And I
swear I felt you with me for every second of it.*

I paused again, and I leant over to shake Jess. The trolley was
coming with the dinners and she said I was to make sure she got the
chicken. Big mistake. It looked like it had been regurgitated. She
wasn't impressed.

I left my food unopened for now and picked my pen up again.

*Josie, just one more thing. I know I've asked before, but can you
look in on Don again for me, just check he's okay? I still haven't
heard from Michael for a day or two, so they must be out of
signal. He warned me that would happen, so I'm trying not to
fret. But I just feel better if I know you're keeping an eye on it all.*

*I'll keep you posted on what happens next in New York, ma
love.*

Keep dancing, keep laughing… and be happy up there.
Love you,
Val xxx

I tucked my pen inside my pad and slipped it back into my bag.

Beside me, Jess still didn't look impressed, even less so when I took the foil off my dinner and found I had a lovely bit of salmon with roast potatoes.

I glanced over to check on Carly and Carol and saw that they were still locked in conversation. I made a mental note to find out later what was going on there. If something was wrong with one of them, I wanted to know so that I could help. Privacy was an over-rated notion as far as I was concerned.

'Seriously?' Jess challenged, staring at my food with pure evils now. The lassie had never cornered the market on sweetness and light, but I'd realised on this holiday that she was even sharper than usual when she'd just woken up. 'How did you manage to get salmon, and I got chicken stew that looks like it came out of a tin?' she moaned.

'I slipped the captain a tenner on the way in,' I told her, straight-faced.

'I think you've gone power crazy now that you're flying business class,' she harrumphed. 'The old Val was perfectly happy with a packet of pretzels and a cheese and ham toastie on Ryanair.'

'You're right,' I went along with her teasing. 'From now on, I'll expect bed seats on every flight and I'm not leaving home without my tiara.'

'I bet Don will love that,' she joked. 'Although I'm not sure he's got the cheekbones for a tiara.'

Somehow, I managed to laugh, but in my head it sounded hollow. It wasn't Jess's fault – she wasn't to know – but her comment brought a terrible realisation slamming down in my mind.

Don and I would never fly again together.

In fact, there was a really strong chance that my flight home from America would be the last flight I would ever take.

24

JESS

Tears Dry On Their On Their Own – Amy Winehouse

Bloody hell, New York in November was freezing. This wasn't exactly a newsflash – I'd been here a few times before in the winter – but I'd gone soft after living in the warmth of LA for so long. Even Val had changed her mules for her white patent boots and produced a padded coat from the depths of her carry-on luggage. I've absolutely no idea how it fitted in there, unless she sucked every bit of air out of it and vacuum-packed it. It was one of those duvet coats, in a very snowy shade of cream, and it went from her neck to her ankles.

'Jesus Christ, I look like a single bed,' she whistled as she caught her reflection in a mirrored panel on one of the terminal walls.

The corridor up from the plane to the terminal had felt like it was about minus two degrees, but I told myself that the endless walk to the baggage reclaim – I swear it was in New Jersey – would at least heat us up a bit.

The conveyor belt hadn't even started spinning when my phone sprang into life and the notifications began pinging one after another after another. Email. Email. Email. Text. Text. Text. Missed call times four.

I checked those first. One of them had a prefix I didn't recognise, so I looked it up. Ojai. So Arnie had the absolute audacity and scumbaggery to call me from his ex-wife's home? Really? Was he that low? Obviously, that was the case. No thank you. I pressed delete.

Another missed call, this time from my client, Hayley. I quickly called her back, but it went straight to voicemail, so I left a message. 'Hey, honey, hope you're doing okay. I've just landed in New York, but I'm here if you need anything at all. Just give me a call back.'

The next one was a voicemail, and as soon as it started to play, I almost dropped the phone. 'Hello, Miss Latham, this is Dax Hill. I believe you're working with Hayley Harlow, and that you've been handling her image control for the last few weeks. I think it would be useful if we could talk. Please call me back when it's convenient.'

Holy. Shit. Dax Hill was calling me. That meant one of two things. Either he wanted me to call off the dogs and was therefore going to either threaten me or incentivise me to do so. Or else he was planning to drop the animosity to Hayley, accept his responsibilities and he was calling to broach a truce. I really hoped it was the latter.

There were a bunch of work emails, a few unimportant texts and a message to say my dry cleaning was ready. I deleted that one too. Everything I'd left at the dry cleaners belonged to Arnie. It could rot there for all I cared.

But Dax Hill had called me.

Shit.

Carol plonked her carry-on bag next to me and stretched upwards. 'Hey, luvly. You good?'

I rolled my eyes at her. 'Nope, I have a stick up my ass because I'm raging about the injustices in life. Like how you can get off a plane with no crushed clothes whatsoever. I look like I've slept in a tumble dryer.'

'That's because you actually got some sleep,' she countered. 'Carly and I ended up chatting for the whole flight. Erm, has she spoken to you?'

I took in the loaded question, the worried expression and the anxious glances over her shoulder to make sure no one could hear us.

'About?' I asked.

'About the fact that she's—'

Dammit! The ring of my phone cut off the conversation, but I made a mental note to follow it up. In the hotel room in Beverly Hills, Carly had been about to tell me something, but we'd been interrupted that time too. I really needed to get a life and a job where conversations with my friends weren't constantly cut off by intrusions. I should have asked her about it again, but with everything else going on in our lives right now it had completely slipped my mind. I was a shit friend.

The conveyor belt crunched into action, and suitcases began to flop up from the bowels of the terminal and thump down onto the moving rubber, so I wandered away from the others to take the call.

'Jess Latham Associates, how can I help you?' I had no associates. It was just me. But I liked that my company name gave the impression that I came team handed.

'Miss Latham, I finally tracked you down.'

My heart stopped. Then started beating again on supersonic speed. At first, I'd thought it was my long-lost fiancé – he often called me Miss Latham when he was mocking me in a playful way. But no. This voice was too smooth, too sleek and it had an altogether more refined tone than Arnie.

'This is Dax Hill. You're a tough lady to get a hold of.'

'I'm not really. I'm just very choosy about who I speak to.' Coming out guns blazing was always my plan of action – it generally put dicks like this on the back foot, if only for a split second.

Not this guy though. His laughter suggested he was either a really good actor (in which case he'd be a movie star instead of an agent) or he absolutely didn't give a toss. The hackles on the back of my neck began to creep up.

'I'd very much like to meet with you to discuss your client.'

Right then. I could have asked him why, or said that I'd only see him if he did the right thing and owned up to being the father of Hayley's baby, but that wasn't how this game was played. I wanted to get him in a room, look him in the eye and persuade him to be decent. Negotiating was my superpower. And I couldn't do it on the phone in the middle of an airport terminal thousands of miles from my target.

'I'm out of town at the moment, but I'll meet you at the Peninsula Hotel, next Tuesday at 10 a.m.'

'I'll need to check my—'

'No need. Come or don't. Up to you. But in the meantime, if you release anything else that's remotely damaging to my client, I won't be there either. Goodbye, Mr Hill.' With that, and a tiny surge of accomplishment, I hung up. He'd come, and I was determined to get a good deal for Hayley out of him.

The phone rang again immediately, and I answered it. 'I said there was no need to—'

'Jess?'

I almost dropped the handset. I definitely dropped my jaw.

A few metres away, I could see Carol and Carly looking at me quizzically and then reading my face and realising, with wide-eyed surprise, that it was Arnie on the phone.

'Jess, we need to talk.' Feck, I was in demand today. 'I need to explain. We need to sort things out. We need to—'

'Peninsula Hotel, next Tuesday, 9 a.m.' I spat. May as well get both over with on the same morning.

'Jess, I can't—'

'Then neither can I.' With that, I hung up, rammed my phone back into my pocket and tried to breathe slowly to sort out my racing heart.

Next Tuesday. Four days away. Part of me couldn't wait. Part of me wanted to stay away and ignore them both. And the other part of me? I looked at Carly. Then Carol. Then Val. And I remembered Josie and Sarah, who would both have given anything to be here with us, and that's when I decided I was going to park every single problem and just enjoy my friends for the weekend. Val obviously had a similar idea.

She appeared in front of us, her duvet coat shining like a beacon of light, grabbed her trolley case and then stuck her hand up like an overenthusiastic tour guide. 'Are we ready, girls? Let's go take a bloody big bite out of the Big Apple.'

25

CARLY

Empire State Of Mind – Alicia Keyes

Early morning, sitting on a bench on Fifth Avenue and my eyes felt like someone had poured grit into them, then given them a good rub-down with an electric sander. I shouldn't be awake right now. We should still be in our beds, like any bloody normal person would be after landing in New York at 10 p.m. last night, then checking into their hotel, before heading straight back out and ending the night in tears.

'Whose idea was it to go back out again last night?' I checked with Jess.

'Yours,' she croaked, sounding just as wrung out as me. Not that I'd change anything if I could go back.

We'd checked into our rooms at the Plaza around midnight (courtesy of Sam – and yes, I planned to reward him with energetic naked stuff), and we'd pretty much done an instant turnaround and piled into a cab.

That's how, at 1 a.m., the four of us had ended up standing in the middle of the walkway on the Brooklyn Bridge, with two bottles of wine from the Plaza minibar.

We'd FaceTimed Kate back in London. It was 6 a.m. her time, but like Carol, she was one of those nauseating people who sprung out of bed at 5.30 a.m., ready to start the day.

'Are you there?' she'd asked, and I could hear the emotion in her voice. I'd panned the camera around so she could see everything. The last time we were here, she'd been with us.

This was the place where we'd scattered our friend, Sarah, and her husband, Nick's ashes, years before. Sudden deaths. A plane crash while Nick was taking a flying lesson Sarah had bought him for his birthday. It had been the biggest tragedy of our lives.

Since then, we'd all been back once together, two years ago, to toast their memory right here, at Sarah's favourite spot on her favourite bridge. It felt only right that we did it again now. New York was Sarah's city, where she'd lived for almost two decades before she died. We were just dropping in on an old friend.

'Okay, let's go before our faces fall off in this cold,' Jess had said softly, taking over. She took a swig of wine. 'Hey, Sarah, it's us,' she'd said, eyes up to the sky. 'We miss you, darling.'

Kate went next, sending her thoughts via cyberspace. 'Sarah, I told Hannah we were doing this. She's here and staying next door with the girls for a few days. It scares me how much like us they all are,' she'd said, vocalising what the rest of us felt. Five young women together, taking on the world. Once upon a time, we were those girls.

'But we're taking care of Hannah and Ryan too, so don't worry,' Carol had added, tears streaming down her face. 'They're amazing and you'd be so proud of them. You always were.' Her turn to knock back a drink. She'd passed the bottle to me.

'To friends. And to forever love,' I'd said, quoting one of our old toasts. 'To Sarah and Nick, who'll always be together.'

The bottle went down the line to Val.

'And to us,' Val had added. 'Sarah, pet, if you're up there, give Josie a hug from us. And don't listen to her if she has a moan that we spend way too much time talking to dead people these days. It's just our way of keeping you here with us. Of letting you know that you mattered. You still do. We love you, sweetheart.'

More cheers, more smiles, more tears. We'd said another good-bye, then returned to the hotel, cold but strangely peaceful, despite the sadness.

I was glad we'd gone there. Just not so glad that I was already out of bed and starting off the day in such a brutal fashion.

'Here you go, ma love,' Val said, as she delivered the package to me. 'And here's yours, Carol,' she said, handing over another one. 'And, Jess Latham, get that frosty look off yer face. One dodgy meal won't kill you.'

'I just don't ever want to read that I was killed in the street by a hot dog. You know, this wasn't what I was expecting when you said Breakfast at Tiffany's,' Jess challenged. Carol and I acted like we couldn't hear her. She was way braver than us. I'd rather take on an armed mugger on the New York subway than my Aunt Val when she was on a mission.

That said, Jess did have a point. Breakfast at Tiffany's evoked all sorts of glamorous connotations. Audrey Hepburn. Little black dresses. Pearls. Those big long cigarette holder thingies and maybe the odd tiara. The reality? 9 a.m., it was minus four degrees, and there was a mild flurry of snow in the air. However, none of that mattered because the Christmassy feeling in the air was palpable. It was only the last week of November, but already there were blazes of lights in the shop windows, and from somewhere nearby, Mariah

Carey was singing about what she wanted for Christmas. 'Yoo-oo-oooooo,' Carol and I crooned, joining in.

The streets of New York were already awake with early-morning pedestrians, trainers on feet, eyes straight ahead, with places to go and people to see. And us? We were sitting on a bench outside the iconic Fifth Avenue Tiffany store, looking at a backdrop of scaffolding, eating hot dogs that may or may not have come from a hygienic source. I unwrapped the foil and took a bite, figuring I might die of salmonella, but at least the food would heat up my insides.

'Aye, well...' Val shrugged, 'just one of those things. When we made the list, we had no way of knowing that the café in there would be closed for renovations. We can have a wee wander around the shop later when it opens, but let's face it, I'd need to sell ma best china to afford anything. So this is what's called "improvisation". Hot dogs and coffee and a wee bit of Tiffany glitter behind us. Now straighten yer face, Jess, and get into the spirit of this. Look around you...' she said, throwing her arms wide and splodging a huge dollop of mustard on to the pavement. 'We're in New York, it's almost Christmas, and we've got each other.'

She inhaled deeply. Oh crap. I knew that mannerism, it meant she was going to join in with Mariah.

'All I want for Christmas, is yooooooooo,' she sang at the top of her voice.

Several early-morning commuters charging along the street changed their trajectory to give her a wide berth.

I nudged Carol, who was next to me on the bench. 'If I'm not exactly like Val when I'm older, just shoot me.'

Just like too many times over the last while, Carol's smile didn't quite reach her gorgeous big eyes. Not that anyone else would notice. There she was, looking effortlessly stunning in a Tiffany blue ski jacket (chosen for today's theme), flawless makeup, her long blonde hair accessorised with a white fur hat. She'd already posted a dozen pics of her outfit for the day today. As I watched all the images of her pop up on my Instagram feed, it struck me that anyone seeing her life would think it was perfect. Yet, for some reason, that I couldn't quite get to the bottom of, she was emanating sadness. Or stress. Or some other kind of negative force that I'd never seen before on my happy-go-lucky, eternally cheerful, wonderfully dippy sister-in-law.

But at least now, I had an inkling what the problem was – she was having marriage problems with my brother. It had almost floored me when she'd said on the plane that she'd swap lives with me. She'd immediately recanted, and said something about Callum coming too, but I saw the hesitation and I had a horrible feeling she hadn't meant that. Even more so because for the next couple of hours, there I was, soaring through the skies, pouring out my heart to Carol and yet she was the one with a tear-stained face and white knuckles from gripping the armrests on the seats. I'd tried twenty different ways to ask her if something was wrong, but I got nowhere and yet... That nagging feeling again. And my spider senses were telling me not to ignore it. There was only one course of action. I needed to speak to my brother.

'Right are you all ready, girls? Start spreading the news...'

Oh dear God. Val was now standing in front of us, conducting us with a hot dog in one hand, held aloft like a baton and she'd moved on to a less Christmassy rendition of a Frank Sinatra classic.

'We're leaving today...' I joined in, giving it my full Sinatra dramatic effect. Fuck it. There was a freedom in being in New York, because no one knew me, no-one knew I was married to Sam Morton, and there was no way whatever tosser had posted those dodgy photos of me had followed me thousands of miles to the east coast. Unless Estelle did in fact have something to do with it and she was right now hiding behind that hot dog cart. Surely not. She'd never go that close to processed food. Anyway, she was working in LA, so she was otherwise engaged. As soon as that thought permeated my brain, I felt myself relax. Time to live in the moment and just enjoy this, and not waste a single second worrying, because...

'Sarah would have loved this,' Carol whispered when we sang the last line, reading my mind. Sarah had moved to New York, with her husband Nick, and brought her children up here. She adored this city. New York would always be bittersweet, but that didn't matter, because it was also the place, more than anywhere else, that we felt Sarah with us. Right now, I knew she'd be hoarse with laughing, with chatting, with singing. This was her city. I wasn't going to let her, or Josie, down by getting distracted by my own personal dramas. That said, Josie never held back from getting into other people's business, so I had to brush away any hesitations about dipping into my sister-in-law's relationship with my brother.

I got my chance at lunchtime, when we made it back to the hotel, and Val steered us into the Champagne Bar, just to the left of the gorgeous, ornate entrance foyer, with – naturally – a stop at the stunning tree that soared towards the artfully painted ceiling so that Carol could take a pic and upload it to her Instagram.

The seats at the bar had a mishmash of people that were so typically New York. Two women in power suits groomed to perfection, with glasses of lunchtime rosé already in front of them. Three guys with slicked-back hair and sharp suits, all speaking in that slightly aggressive, raised way that New Yorkers considered a gentle whisper. And next to them, an elderly lady, in elaborate make-up, tracksuit trousers and a fur jacket, who had perched her small furry dog on a blanket on the bar stool next to her. If Val had an NYC equivalent, this woman was it.

A suited waiter showed us to one of the marble tables, placed Champagne Bar coasters and cocktail napkins in front of us and took our orders, over the background music of a classical 'Jingle Bells'. A gin and tonic for me, Kir Royals for the other three.

'I'm just nipping to the loo,' I announced, discarding my jacket, but grabbing my bag. I held my breath in case one of them decided to come with me, but thankfully the prospect of the imminent Kir Royals kept them in their seats.

I cut out of the bar, and instead of going to the loos, I turned left, into the Palm Court, gasping at the beauty of the stunning pillars, the elegant cream marble arches, the incredible artwork on the walls, all of it crowned by the most breath-taking, utterly magnificent, stained-glass domed ceiling. I was suddenly conscious that my boots had cost twenty quid from Matalan and under my TK Maxx jumper and jeans, my pants didn't match my bra. That seemed like the kind of thing that would matter in a room like this.

Most of the tables were already occupied but I spotted one in the corner with a single empty seat and made a dive for it, registering the disdainful glances of the rather snooty-looking trio of elderly women at the next table. I had a good mind to phone PETA and report those stoles that were hanging over the arms of their chairs. There was no way they'd picked them up on a three for the price of two deal in the Matalan sale.

But I had more important things to do. I pulled out my mobile phone, slotted in my ear buds and FaceTimed my brother. He answered on the second ring, and I could see by the background and his attire that he was out running around Richmond Green. I made a quick calculation and opened with, 'It's 6 p.m. on a freezing winter night and you're exercising. I absolutely refuse to believe we share a gene pool.'

He stopped, breathing heavily as he grinned. 'I got the exercise gene, but you got all the wit and charm,' he said, grinning. It was only funny because we both knew it wasn't true. Callum Cooper had the easiest smile, the most laid-back nature and the biggest heart. He also took nothing seriously, refused to stress and wouldn't notice an emotional situation or tense undertone if it smacked him in his beautiful face with a shovel. He also – prior to Charlotte and Toni moving into my house – lived with three women, so those characteristics had served him well.

'How's it going, sis? Everything good?'

'I was going to ask you the same thing,' I blurted, then shrivelled as three more disdainful glances came my way from the next table. Clearly mobile phones weren't the done thing in the Plaza's Palm Court.

He was stretching now, one arm straight up in the air, the other reaching over and clutching the straight arm's elbow. I'd only been in that position once in my life and it was when I'd got stuck trying to take off an anorak after a drunken night in the pub. I had pins and needles in my arms for two days afterwards.

'Why? What's going on?'

'Are you and Carol in trouble? Are you splitting up? You know you can tell me and, yep, it'll break my heart and, whatever has happened, I'll take her side, but you need to give me a heads-up so I can take care of her. And you, obviously. But more her, because she's my pal and you're only my brother, so she ranks way above you on my love list.'

Why, in the name of the holy rant, did I have to blurt out every single thing I was feeling the minute I got scared or worried? It was an affliction. My name is Carly, formerly Cooper now Morton, and my gob would appear to be on steroids.

'Woah, woah! Have you been drinking? You're making no sense. Why would we be splitting up?'

I knew that expression. It was the one he'd adopted every time in our whole lives when I'd got myself into a complete drama or I was having an emotional crisis and he had absolutely no clue what I was on about or how to handle it.

I took a step back from the edge. 'Oh. So you're not splitting up then? Or having problems?'

He'd lifted the phone again, and was now sitting on a wall, trees behind him. 'No, of course not. Why would you think we are?'

'Because, Dr Phil, your wife is completely miserable. There's something wrong, and she won't tell me what it is, so I thought it had to be something to do with you. It isn't, then?'

'No. And what's wrong with her? I haven't noticed anything. Are you sure?'

I may have been the first customer in the Palm Court's history to put their head on the table and gently bang it a couple of times. 'Yes, I'm sure. And call this a long shot, but I would hazard a guess you haven't noticed because... you're a fricking Cooper male.' I hissed the last part. Honestly, the men in my family were a breed of their own. Callum, my other brother, Michael, my dearly departed dad – all very good and decent men, but they needed something to be posted on a billboard before they noticed it.

'Shit. Honest to God, sis, I've not noticed anything. I mean... I don't know...' He was running his fingers through his immaculate greying hair. He'd always done that when he was thinking or perplexed. 'Should I be worried?'

'I think you probably need to talk to her, Cal. I can't put my finger on it. That's why I called. She just seems sad and wound up and anxious and none of those things are like her. Look, don't worry about it. If you do speak to her, just tread lightly. Don't make a big fuss. Maybe she's just having an off week or she's missing the girls or something. I'll keep trying at this end to get to the bottom of it. I'm glad you two are okay though, because you know if you two ever divorce, then I'm keeping custody of her. You'll find another sister.'

He grinned. 'I'd rather keep you now that you've got a house in Pacific Palisades.'

'Ah, there you go. Shallow and shameless. Maybe we're from the same gene pool after all.'

I wasn't sure if I felt better or worse when I hung up. I'd probably just scared the crap out of him for something that wasn't even tangible, yet, on the other hand, I felt reassured that whatever was going on, it wasn't some big issue between them. Maybe I should just back off and stop worrying. Perhaps it was nothing. Maybe Carol was just having one of those cycles that we all go through where we feel a bit crap for a while. Yeah, that must be it.

I got up and made my way back through to the bar. The best thing I could do for my pal right now was just to lighten up, drop the drama and focus on having a great day.

That's exactly what I planned on doing... until I got back to their table and they all turned to look at me with stricken expressions.

I spotted the phone in Carol's hand and I knew straight away what had happened.

Bugger.

26

CAROL

White Winged Dove – Stevie Nicks

As soon as Carly spotted the phone, I could tell that she'd sussed the situation straight away.

'More photos,' she said. It was more of a statement than a question.

I turned the phone to show her. It was the same website, a pretty popular celebrity blog, that featured images of famous faces caught in unfortunate moments, and plastered salacious headlines above them. It would be easy to dismiss if each post wasn't getting almost half a million views, and then retweeted and shared for the rest of the world's amusement.

'I'm not even a fricking celebrity,' Carly said weakly, as if arguing with the screen. She still didn't get it. When George Clooney married Amal, it sparked a wave of curiosity because everyone wanted to see who had finally made one of the sexiest men in Hollywood settle down. It was exactly the same thing with

Carly and Sam. If it were me, let's be honest, I'd be loving every second, gliding in and out of Mr Chow's wearing Gucci, and snapping up free invitations for front-row seats at Paris fashion week. Carly? Hating every second of being in the limelight.

I was still struggling to accept that she genuinely didn't want the five-star fairytale ending where Cinderella moved to Pacific Palisades and lived happily in the same street as several A list celebrities. I realised that was shallow, but I'm pretty sure 99 per cent of my followers would agree. Not Carly though. Worst thing was, I didn't know how to help her. I'd never discuss it with Sam, because that would be crossing boundaries. I couldn't persuade her it would be fine, because she'd already decided it wouldn't be. These photos didn't help that argument either.

'Shame of Sam's Wife's Time On The Streets' screamed the latest headline. Which, to anyone glancing at it would suggest Carly was either sleeping rough, or on the game and hustling tricks on Sunset Boulevard. It was absolute miso... miso... I searched my brain for the right word. You know, when women are treated unfairly. Urgh, nothing. I gave up and went with offering sympathy instead.

'I mean, they're not that bad,' I tried to console her.

Carly shot blades at me. I mean, daggers. 'I'm on a New York Street at 9 a.m., singing Frank Sinatra songs, holding up what was, in reality, a hot dog, but from that angle and blurred out like that looks like alcohol in a brown paper bag.'

All of that was true, so I stopped trying to make her feel better. She was right. It didn't look good.

'If I took that phone and kicked it across the room, would you hate me?' she asked, through gritted teeth.

My fingers held on to my handset a bit tighter. It had been part of an endorsement deal... an iPhone 12 pro, in a case I'd designed myself. It was one of a kind. 'Erm, can you kick Jess's phone instead? She saw the photos first.'

At least that made her laugh. She picked up her G&T and downed it in one, then put the glass back on the table. 'You know what? Don't show me any more. I've no idea what's going on, but it's making me crazy. I'm starting to look at everyone around me suspiciously. I mean, what's that cockerpoo doing over there at the bar? He definitely looks dodgy to me. Can someone go see if he's taking pics on a concealed phone?'

Everyone else was laughing now too, but I realised that my knuckles really were gripping my phone and my stomach was in knots. It had been a joke. I knew that. My phone was going nowhere. It was okay. I tried to take a breath, but it wouldn't come. Then suddenly, my phone buzzed and the noise made my heart thud.

Callum, the screen said. Why was he calling? What was going on? Why did he want to speak to me? Why couldn't I breathe? Was my scarf too tight? I wasn't wearing a scarf. Was it hot in here? Was it...

'Carol! Come on, luvly, let's go. Quick freshen-up before we go to the Rockefeller Centre, then the Empire State Building. Josie hates to be kept waiting.' Val took my hand and if she noticed it was trembling, she didn't say anything. Carly and Jess grabbed their bags, and we went upstairs.

In the safety of the room, I went straight to the bathroom, leaned against the marble vanity unit, staring at myself in the mirror as sweat ran down my back. What the hell was that? It felt like I couldn't breathe, like I could pass out at any second. This anxiety was getting worse and all I knew was that if this had happened at any other point in my life, Callum would be the person I picked up for, the one who would make anything better, yet now... I didn't want to speak to him. To anyone. I didn't want this trembling woman, with all these fears and worries, to be me.

I stared at myself in the mirror. Who was she? The Botox and the filler and thirty years of daily facial exercises might be holding back time, but they weren't fooling me. I could see under all that to the woman who hated this life she was leading. It was all fake. Fabricated. I wanted to take my iPhone and grind it under my Louboutin heel, to tell my friends exactly how I felt. I'd never hidden anything from them before but this was different. I kept telling myself that if I didn't share it, then it wasn't real. Maybe that was the only way I could deal with it.

My gaze met the one in the mirror again. *Come on, girl. This isn't where you are going to fall apart. You are the glittering one. The star of your own show. You have a living to earn, an image to maintain. Deep breath. You can do this.*

Carly banged on the door. 'Carol, sweetheart, you okay?'

It was the woman in the mirror who answered. 'I'm fine!'

You're not, I told her silently.

Not for the first time, I thought about making another appointment to see someone when I was home. A doctor. I'd gone to one a few months ago, and he'd palmed me off with some happy pills. They obviously weren't working. They hadn't made a difference to how I felt at all.

Maybe I needed a therapist. But again, that would make this all real. How could Happy Carol, Instagram influencer with the wonderful life, possibly be unhappy enough to need some kind of counselling? No, no, no. That wasn't what I was selling. Didn't fit with the brand.

Carly interrupted my train of thought and it vanished into the air.

'Are you ready to head back out?' she asked, and I could hear that she was right outside the door.

Tell her. She wouldn't judge. She has loved you every day of your life and she will help. She'll know how to make this stop. Tell her you're not okay. You're anxious. You're overwhelmed. You can't think straight.

The woman in the mirror got there first. 'Give me two minutes,' she said, in a sing-song voice. 'Just touching up my make-up.' She looked straight at me again, and this time she was talking to me. 'You've got this. Just keep smiling, keep it together and you'll be okay.'

She was right. I was fine. This would pass. Maybe I just needed sleep. A whole night. Where I didn't wake up two or three times and spend a restless hour trying to nod off again. I just needed to be here and to act like Carol, because as long as I was doing that, life wouldn't fall apart.

I fixed my face, said goodbye to the woman in the mirror, put my smile on and left the room. I was good. Back in control. I snapped the phone on and called Callum back. No answer from him this time and somehow that made me relieved. Lifted another little bit of pressure.

'You ready, babe?' Carly asked, distracted by throwing things into her handbag.

'I am. Let me grab my jacket and I'm good.' Crisis averted. I was good. I was good. I told myself.

Twenty minutes later, we were back out on the city streets. 'Can you take some pics?' I asked Carly, giving her my phone and then automatically striking a pose. It was second nature to me.

To go with the winter/Christmassy theme of the day, I'd changed into a scarlet Dior ski jacket and black jeans, with my new Skechers black snow boots and a bright red Revlon lip. I was going for the high fashion/high street combination that was my trademark. I'd tied my hair in two low bunches and added a red bobble hat that I'd picked up earlier in Saks Fifth Avenue. Carly and Jess had both changed their jumpers, but kept on the same jeans, jackets and boots they'd worn earlier, and Val... well, she was a spectacle of glam now that she'd added a huge white fur hat to her ensemble and, the star of the show, a matching white furry muff that dangled from her neck. She explained that it was multipurpose. It kept her hands warm and also gave her somewhere to store the small flask of brandy that she was carrying around 'in case she needed to warm up her old bones'. She'd taken at least two slugs before we left the hotel lobby.

I quickly uploaded the pics, with links to all the clothes, and then switched the phone on to silent so the pings of the unstoppable wave of comments wouldn't be the soundtrack to the day.

We could have taken a taxi, but walking gave me so much more content to load to my social media as we made our way back down Fifth Avenue. I began with a video in front of Gucci, then wandered around Sephora, highlighting and tagging all the brands that I'd worked with over the years, including the ones I still endorsed now. I pouted for the camera in my Revlon Red lipstick. I sucked in my cheeks as I applied a little Charlotte Tilbury contour and posed with the latest collection in Prada. And my followers kept clicking, kept watching, kept leaving the comments for the person they saw on the screen. They had absolutely no idea that the smile fell off my face as soon as each clip was uploaded. Insta Carol was the happiest, most together woman in the world, living a fairy tale life. Once upon a time, I recognised her. I wasn't sure that I did any more. #blessed? #whoamI?

It was dark by the time we got to the Rockefeller Centre, maybe eight or nine o'clock, and there were crowds of people milling around. There were gorgeous lights in the plaza, Christmas music was blaring and the smell of sweet things – churros, pretzels, waffles – made it feel even more festive. The huge Christmas tree was up, although it wasn't lit yet. We were probably a week or so too early for that. No matter. What was important to Val was that we got to the ice rink.

I'd been there before, years ago, when I was still modelling, and I'd booked a job in New York in the middle of December. A swimwear line, if I remember correctly. I'd spent a good three days freezing my tits off on a roof garden in the Upper East Side. When it was over, Callum had come to meet me and we'd stayed here an extra few days, revelling in the sheer joy of New York in December. We'd stayed up in a little boutique hotel near Central Park and every day we'd walked, we'd talked, we'd danced and we'd made love all night long. It had been magical. I'd never have believed that one day the magic would disappear, but now I couldn't remember the last time I felt it.

'It's this way,' I told the others, shaking off the memory and concentrating on the layout of the Rockefeller Plaza. We were on the same level as the tree and the ground floor of the centre, with a glass balustrade all around the rink, which was in the middle, but maybe half a level below. It gave everyone on this level the perfect vantage point to watch the skaters, while taking in the perfection of the beautifully lit plaza. 'The staircase is over here,' I shouted back to the others, who were following behind. We located the steps and went down them to the next destination on the bucket list, the iconic landmark that was full of romance, that conjured up the absolute joy of winter in New York, the ice rink that was... that was...

'Suffering Jesus, it's shut,' Val wailed, stopping dead in the street and almost causing a concussion to Carly and Jess, who were right behind her. The fur on her hat was quivering as we huddled beside the lower-level barrier.

Jess's eyes darted to Carly, and then to me. 'Did no one think to check what date it actually opened to the public?' Every word was steeped in irritation. This was the Jess that could make grown men cry.

'No.' I spluttered. 'I haven't been dealing with this side of things because, you know... too many cooks spoil the...' Brain freeze, brain freeze... '... trifle.'

Carly rounded on Jess. 'Eh, is there a reason you're laying this on us? Aren't you supposed to be Miss Organised around here?' I could tell by her tone that she was only half joking. There was a point being made in there too.

'Last time I checked, I was a bit busy with trifling things like, oh, I don't know, GETTING MY FUCKING HEART BROKEN AND HAVING MY LIFE TRASHED.'

Several people walking by turned to stare, but Jess just stood there, eyes blazing, waiting for Carly to react. I said nothing. There were many wars I didn't want to get involved in. The Cold War. The Middle East. Jess versus Carly.

'Oh, for Christ's sake, I think you two need a nap,' Val interjected. 'This is like listening to you both fighting over which one of Take That you were going to marry. Now, sort yourselves out and let's see if we can rescue this situation. Follow me.'

Carly and Jess glared at each other but did as they were told. If I wasn't feeling highly anxious about the tension in the air, I'd have thought it was hilarious. We were middle-aged women, but throw in a quibble and we were right back to the teenagers who squabbled over anything and everything but loved each other above all.

Val, however, was ignoring them and focussing on her mission. We clambered down the steps to the large sheet of ice.

'Excuse me, son,' she shouted to one of the security guards strolling around the perimeter of the rink.

The portly gentleman glanced around, realised she was talking to him and made his way over, his walkie-talkie crackling on the chest of his leather jacket, his pistol bobbing up and down on his waist holster as he walked. Val versus a bloke with a gun. Another war I didn't want to be in the middle of. Although, my money was on Val.

He opened the gate and took the few steps forward to where Val was standing. 'Yes, ma'am?'

'Sorry to bother you, son, but will the rink be opening tonight?'

'No, ma'am. It opens next week. We're just preparing it and testing everything at the moment.'

'Next week?' Poor Val slumped, then made a quick recovery. 'Look, the thing is, I've come all the way from Scotland and I'm here for my pal. It was her last wish to skate on that ice, and we've come to do it for her. I don't have a week. I could be dead by then.'

The guard's eyes widened but, credit to him, he held firm.

'I'm sorry, ma'am. There's nothing I can do about it. We don't open until next week,' he repeated. He took a step back, as if he was about to turn away, but Val wasn't finished with him.

'Can I just check if a bribe or a bit of flirtation would do the trick?'

Jess's eyes closed and Carly's shoulders began to shake as she tried to control her laughter. I just glanced around anxiously in case anyone was filming this or calling the police for reinforcements. No one seemed to be paying any attention at all. They were all just going about their evening.

In fairness to the guard, he found her funny. It was probably the first time he'd been propositioned by a sixty-something woman who looked like a cross between an explosion in a paint factory, Doris Day's twin and Madonna if she'd never had surgery. 'No, ma'am. We're not allowed to take bribes and I'm a happily married man. But I appreciate the offer.'

'Och, well it was worth a try. Thanks anyway. Yer wife's a lucky woman.'

'I tell her that all the time,' he replied with a grin, before sauntering off.

The four of us stood in silence for a few seconds as we watched him go, before Carly sighed and gave Aunt Val a hug. 'Don't be too disheartened. It's only one thing. We'll do everything else on the list, so I'm sure Josie won't mind. Look at all the fun she had with the cowboys the other night.'

Val gave a sad smile, but she didn't make a move, just continued to stand still and stare straight ahead. Poor soul was obviously heartbroken. I knew how much this meant to her.

I reached for her hand and wrapped it in my red woolly mitten. 'Carly's right. Come on, let's go get some hot chocolate to warm us up.'

Still, she didn't move. I was beginning to think she'd taken unwell when she finally nodded in the direction of the gate. 'Do you see what I see, ladies?' she whispered.

We all zeroed in on the focus of her stare. The gate. Or rather, the black steel sliding bar that locked it. The one that was still slightly raised, because the security guard hadn't closed it properly. I had no idea what the significance of this was. The ice rink was closed. We had no skates. There were people crowded around us everywhere. What could she possibly want to do? It didn't take her long to tell us.

'Carol, pet, hold ma muff. I'm going in.'

27

VAL

Nowhere To Run – Martha and the Vandellas

It wasn't a secret that I didn't have the kind of body that was built for speed – unless I was trying to get to the bar in the bingo before they called last orders – but I put it down to that power that women have inside them at critical moments. You know, the same one that gives Wee Ina from Denniston the strength to carry her man home from the pub on a Saturday night, despite the fact that he's double her body weight and left her pure mortified when he tried to chat up Senga from number 42 who was sitting at the next table.

But back to the point. That superpower was the only explanation I could come up with for the uncontrollable urge I had inside me right at that moment. It was either that or Josie pressed some button up there that made me Usain Bolt from the waist down. I let go of Carol's hand, and I lurched forward, ignoring a simultaneous gasp of 'Oh shit' from Carly and Jess. I crossed the two or three metres to the gate so quickly, I was probably a blur to the human eye, which might explain why no one got there fast enough to stop me.

The whole time I was talking to Josie in ma head. *Don't you worry, pal, I'm not letting anyone tell me I can't do this.* If I'd just shirked the challenge and walked away, I'd never have forgiven myself. Josie Cairney was the bolshiest, bravest, most unstoppable force on God's earth. In all the years that I knew her, the only thing that ever beat her was fecking lung cancer, so I wasn't going to let something as trivial as a closed gate get in the way of the list that we'd promised ourselves we'd conquer. I was never going to get another chance to come here. This was it. Now or never. I chose now.

I got the gate open, I pushed it forward, I took two long strides onto the ice and suddenly I was soaring, like Jayne Torvill in that Bolero lark, gliding forwards, arms wide, head thrown back, propelled by nature, a magnificent study in movement and grace... for about three seconds, before the rubber soles of my boots came to a swift stop on the frozen surface, and I fell forward, face-planted on the ice and skidded like a speeding torpedo on my front before I finally came to a stop about twenty metres from where I'd started.

What happened next was a blur. There was shouting. There were flashes. There were gasps and shrieks. Some of those might have been mine. But the strangest thing. Even as I lay there, my cheek stuck to the ice, I couldn't help but smile because I knew this was exactly what my pal would have done. *I didn't give up, Josie. You'd have been proud of me.*

'I swear to God, Aunt Val, if you're not dead I'm going to kill you.' That was our Carly's voice. She'd somehow reached me and she was on one side of me, Jess was on the other and they were both manhandling me up, while doing their best not to fall themselves.

'How much of that fucking brandy did she drink?' Jess shot back. The mouth on that lassie would make yer frozen toes curl.

Somehow – I've no idea how – they got me up and, slipping and sliding the whole way, got me back to the gate, where Carol was standing on firm ground, holding back the security guard, while reaching forward to pull me in.

I heard the crackle of the security guard's radio as he called for help and that's when the chill set in. Bugger. I might have pushed this too far. I had a vision of me in handcuffs, getting marched off to jail and I didn't even have a clean set of pyjamas with me.

'Are you okay?' Carly gushed, sounding a bit frantic. 'What were you thinking? Aunt Val, you could have killed yourself.'

Carol was patting me down, trying to brush the ice off my body.

Jess had gone straight into damage limitation and was trying to appease the guard. 'I'm so sorry. It's her age. She gets confused sometimes and I think she thought you'd left the gate open for her and...'

On and on she argued, while I just tried to get my breath back and process what I'd just done.

Only a few seconds had passed, but it seemed like hours, when another security guard appeared on the scene. 'Ma'am, you're going to have to come with me...'

'No,' I answered calmly.

'She's an elderly woman!' Carly objected. 'She's not going anywhere. Look, I'm so sorry about this, and I know she shouldn't have done it, but I'll take her back to our hotel and I promise she won't cause you any more problems.'

'Ma'am, she just trespassed on New York City property,' the second guard argued.

'I might need you to faint in a minute,' Jess whispered in my ear, before stepping forward to enter the fray again. She put on her most authoritative voice, and I got a flashback to when she played one of the wise men in her school nativity play in primary three. Carol was Mary (naturally – she was so beautiful she always got the starring role) and Carly was a sheep who just had to baa to cover up the silence when anyone forgot their lines. Problem was, Carly got too over enthusiastic about the whole baaaa-ing thing, couldn't stop, and had to be yanked from the stage because she was drowning out Away In A Manger. Anyway, Jess took her role as a wise man extremely seriously and gave Joseph a bollocking for holding the baby Jesus by the ankles. It was the same tone she was using now, but without the swear words that got her grounded for a week.

'Officer, we don't want to cause a problem here, but the fact is that she wouldn't have got through there if the gate hadn't been left open. I know it was a harmless mistake, but she could have been hurt or even killed out there. Now, all we want to do is take the old dear home...'

I made a mental note to have a stern word for calling me both elderly and an old dear in the same night.

'... And wrap her up warm and make sure she's okay. I can assure you, we have no wish to take things further and we'll waive any right to pursue legal action in regard to the open gate.'

I marvelled at how she turned things around like that. It was exactly the same back in primary three. Joseph had held the baby Jesus entirely upright for the next two shows.

'And we promise that you'll never see us again, I swear,' Carly added.

I took advantage of that moment to lean forward into Jess's hair. 'Shall I faint yet?'

She gave my leg a swift jab and I retreated. It was only now I realised that the second man had a suit on and appeared to be someone in charge. He was speaking into his walkie-talkie now, relaying everything back to some invisible judge and jury, when the most extraordinary thing happened. Someone in the crowd that was gathered around the rails above the rink began to clap. Then another. And another. Then the cheering started. And pretty soon I couldn't hear myself think for the noise all around us. It was like an impenetrable groundswell of sound that was almost jubilant, the kind of uproar that happened in a football game when Scotland scored a goal.

I raised my eyes, not to Josie this time, but to the lights and the level above us. They were cheering for me. And for Josie. And for these girls that were fighting my case. I was the Rockefeller One and these were my supporters. And all of them, every single one of them, helped me secure my freedom. The authorities – or, as I began to call them in my head, my suppressors – got incredibly flustered and immediately changed their attitudes towards us. We became less of a threat and more of a rescue mission, as they made a big play of gently escorting me to their security office, while I waved at my fans. Now I knew how the strippers at Twickenham felt as they were carried off by the cops who'd wrestled them to the ground at the halfway line. I was a rebel with a cause. Although, I was mighty glad I'd kept my clothes on because that ice would have had the nipples right off me.

It took another hour or so in the security office, where Carly discussed, Jess argued, and Carol placated, but eventually, with a stern warning and a couple of signatures that confirmed I waived all legal rights to sue anyone within a ten-kilometre radius, they let us go.

As we made our way out of the square, the atmosphere between us reminded me of all those times I was dying to give my son, Michael, or my Dee, a good talking-to for bad behaviour, but I had to wait until there was no one in earshot so that my name wouldn't be muck all over our village.

We'd just got back on to Fifth Avenue, and were on a side street across from Saks, when Jess slumped against a wall. I waited for it. Nothing. Carly bent double, her hands on her knees and I expected her to explode. Nothing. Our Carol sat on the windowsill of the little boutique behind us and exhaled deeply. Still nothing. I wasn't sure what to do, so, without thinking, I pulled my flask out of my muff. 'Anyone want a wee drink?'

That broke something in all of them. I expected tears and recriminations, but it wasn't that. It was laughter, loud, cackling, coming right up from yer boots kind of laughter, along with streams of water coming from all our eyes. It lasted until we were breathless and then there were a few gasps as we tried to regain our powers of speech.

Jess got there first. 'I swear to God, Val, you're going to be the death of us.'

'Honestly, my heart can't take it,' Carly agreed, her voice a little hysterical as she teetered on the edge of laughter again.

Even Carol was joining in, the first time I'd seen a real, genuine laugh from that lassie since we got here. 'My cheeks are sore,' she chirped, her eyes still glistening.

'Sorry about earlier,' Jess said to Carly, reaching over to give her a punch on the shoulder. It took me a second to catch up with the reason for the apology, but then I remembered them yelling at each other. This was the way of it with these two. They fought like sisters but adored each other.

'I'm sorry too,' Carly replied. 'I mean, you're still a stroppy cow, but I love you.'

That set them off again.

'Right, let's get back to the hotel, have a drink in the bar and get Shawshank Redemption there to her bed.' She pointed at me when she said that, but I chose to ignore it and, instead, I opted to pick my battles. Right now, I had something else on my agenda. I checked my watch.

'Erm, I don't think so, ladies,' I objected. 'I believe we still have another item to cross off on the New York list.'

Carly led the arguments for the prosecution. 'But, Aunt Val, it's eleven o'clock, we've been out all day, you almost got arrested and I'm pretty sure when the adrenaline wears off, you'll realise you've popped both your hips out of their sockets and there will be friction burns in unmentionable places.'

'Exactly!' I agreed. 'Welcome to the city that never sleeps. And neither do we. It's eleven o'clock. The Empire State Building is open until 2 a.m. And if you remember correctly, Tom Hanks and Meg Ryan met there late at night in *Sleepless In Seattle*, so is one of you going to hail a taxi, or will I skid across the road and do it myself?'

Two minutes later, we were in a taxi headed downtown.

I closed my eyes. *Don't worry Josie, we've got this. But if you could help me out with a bit of pain relief for these hips, that would be grand.*

I opened my eyes and stared out of the window. In that movie, the two of them had got a miracle when they finally found each other. I thought about me and my Don. The wonderful life we'd had and the uncertainties of the future that was mapped out in front of us now.

I could do with one of those miracles myself.

28

JESS

Sorry Not Sorry – Demi Lovato

If you'd asked me before I'd got there, I'd have said that the observation deck of the Empire State Building would have been deserted at almost midnight on a freezing cold November evening, but I'd have been so wrong. Clearly, that movie had more fans than I realised, as that was the only explanation I could come up with for the place being packed with snogging couples and groups of tourists taking pictures at the edge of the deck at this time of night, with the NYC skyline in the background.

We could see the stunning blue lights of the Chrysler Building, the kaleidoscope of colour from the top floors of the latest viewing attraction at One Vanderbilt, and in the distance, the lights around the top floors of The Edge at Hudson Yards. But even in the midst of all these glorious buildings, there was something special about the art deco lines and historic magnificence of the Empire State. I lived in a fairly perpetual pit of jaded cynicism about most things in life, but this was one of the few places on earth that gave me goosebumps.

Carly and Val were already out at the barriers, looking over the side, while Carol hugged the wall behind us. When we'd first arrived, she had, of course, made a video for her Instagram. I'd filmed her while she raved about her night, making the cheeriest, most enthusiastic, joyous celebration of one of the most fantastic buildings in the world. Five minutes later, the camera was off and her worried expression was on, as she held onto the wall, refusing to go anywhere near the edge.

I tried to persuade her to join the others.

'Weren't you the one that made us go to the top floor of the Eiffel Tower and wave our bras at Paris?' I asked her, referencing a trip that, granted, was twenty years ago, but still. She'd definitely never shown any signs of a fear of heights back then.

'Yep, but that was before...' she said simply.

The wind got my hair up and I had to hang on to my hat. 'Before what?'

'Before I was scared of everything.'

The only thing I could do was hug her. I didn't want to make a huge fuss, or try to talk to her here, because this wasn't the time or place, but I'd speak to Carly about her again when we got back to the hotel. Something wasn't right with our friend, and it was up to us to find out what it was and fix it. Not for the first time, I wished that Sarah or Kate were here. Those two were the most emotionally intelligent ones in our group and I was missing them both. Of course, Sarah would never rejoin us, but that's why it was up to us to make the most of our lives in her honour. And Kate... another note. As soon as we got back to London, we were going to take her for a weekend away somewhere and make up for the fact that she'd missed out on this.

'Uh-oh, you look deep in thought there,' Carly said ominously, as I reached her and Val at the edge of the deck. 'Everything okay?'

Like I said, this wasn't the time or the place. 'Yeah, of course. Shit, the wind could cut you in two out here,' I blustered, changing the subject. I hugged myself, trying to stop the air getting in through the seams on my jacket. 'How long do we have to stay up here?' I asked Val, wondering if I could remember how to treat frostbite. A million years ago, we'd watched an educational film in school about how to handle hypothermia. Although, if I remembered correctly, that situation was on a snowy mountain and the solution was something to do with sharing a sleeping bag, exchanging body heat and sending up flares. I was pretty sure at least one of those things broke NYC rules and laws, and we'd already done enough of that tonight with the Rockefeller One.

'Until the job is done,' Val said.

I almost forgot I'd asked her a question, so I had to rewind to make sure I understood what she'd said. We had to stay up here until the job was done?

'What job?' I asked, perplexed.

Carly was grinning, so I knew whatever was about to come next was going to be either hilarious or ridiculous. Turns out it was the latter.

'The thing is, Josie had this image of being up here and snogging the lips off someone she'd never met before.'

If I wasn't so cold that I could no longer feel my face, I was pretty sure I'd be frowning with confusion about now.

Nope, I still didn't understand.

I went back in again, while I could still get my jaw to function. 'So this only gets ticked off the bucket list when you snog someone up here?'

Val's expression was aghast. 'Of course not! I'm a married woman.

I can't go around laying lips on other men. That's ridiculous.' This is the woman who glided across an ice rink like a speeding otter just a couple of hours ago, and now I was the one being ridiculous?

'And I can't do it either, because I'm married too,' Carly added. It was only then that the clouds in my brain began to clear.

'And Carol can't do it, because she's over there hanging on for dear life,' Val went on.

'So we were just chatting about the fact that there's only one option left...' Carly couldn't keep the amusement out of her voice or off her face when she said that, and beside her, Val was chuckling away too.

'Oh no. No. Absolutely not. No way,' I objected. 'That's ridiculous. We are grown, mature, sensible women.'

'Have you met us?' was Carly's retort to that one.

'That's the whole point,' Val argued. 'Josie and I were fed up of being seen as past-it old bags when that wasn't how we felt on the inside. We wanted some fun. A bit of adventure. We *wanted* to be ridiculous. And just because we were in touching distance of the finish line didn't mean we couldn't be as wild as we were when we were younger. That's what the bucket list was about. It wasn't about doing things before we died. It was about doing them while we still felt alive.'

It might have been the wind, but there was definitely moisture in Val's eyes when she said that, and the tears, combined with her words, added up to a big fat guilt trip and sense of obligation for me.

'I can't believe I'm even thinking about this...'

'Yaaassss!' Carly cheered, punching the air and almost losing a pink furry mitten over the edge.

'I knew you'd do it,' Val winked, just a wee bit smugly.

'Yeah, well, you just hang on to your muff there, old lady,

because I'm only half the problem. Who am I going to snog?' I cast a glance around me and there were no obvious candidates.

'Leave that to me,' Val wittered.

Moving a few feet back from the edge, she took up position in the centre of the deck. Oh bollocks, what was she going to do now? It was bad enough having to snog a stranger, but if Val made a scene, I'd be mortified.

'Excuse me!' she yelled, turning heads for the second time tonight. 'We are conducting a poll. How many of you here have seen *Sleepless In Seattle*?'

Well, hello mortification. Where were the exits? Other than the obvious one which required a parachute?

After a bit of a pause, while people tried to work out if they were walking into a scam or encouraging someone who was slightly bonkers, a few hands went up. Then a few more. The incredibly slow Mexican wave carried on until almost all hands were in the air.

'Okay, well, here's the thing. We have a bet on with our lovely friend here...' she pointed at me, and I felt a red rash of shame rise. This was crazy. Mad. But yet, it was kind of hilarious too, and as soon as I realised that and decided to go with it, my face defrosted enough for me to laugh and bow to my audience. That threw up a few sniggers among the crowd too.

'And to win the bet...'

I was glad she wasn't going with the truth about the bucket list. The last thing I needed was someone sucking the face off me because they were concerned that I was on my last legs and about to pop my wellies.

'... She has to kiss a stranger up here at midnight, which is in exactly...' Now that she'd added a time crunch, she took her hands out of their protective white fur for long enough to check her watch. 'Two and a half minutes. She's very nice, there will be no inappropriate touching and she brushed her teeth before she came out tonight. So, do we have a volunteer to pucker up and do the job?'

Oh. The. Holy. Mortification. If I got through this night without ending up on a register, it would be a fricking wonder.

Carly, Val and I, cast our eyes around the crowd, my toes curling with every passing second. I suddenly realised that the only thing worse than doing this, would now be not doing it. It would be the biggest public rejection I'd faced since my twenties, when my much older MP boyfriend chucked me as soon as our relationship leaked to the press and I was left heartbroken, jobless and destroyed. I swore then that I'd never put myself in that position again. I hadn't counted on Val doing it for me.

Still no response. Hardly surprising. Most of the people up here were in couples. There were a few groups of women, and to be honest, I would have been just as happy to pucker up with a female as with a male, but there were no takers. I was about to give up and make some pathetic speech about it all being a joke, when the wind made a noise around my ears.

At least that's what I thought it was the first time. The second time, I realised it was a low Southern drawl, and it belonged to a tall man who'd stepped forward from behind a crowd to my right. Please make him be clean. And someone who brushed his teeth and flossed twice a day.

'I'll do it,' he repeated, earning a cheer from a few people behind him – I was guessing those were the folks he was with. Either that or he was just a weirdo who hung around up here every night, hoping some windswept romcom fan would come and ask him to pucker up.

Again, for the second time tonight, we'd stopped a crowd, and they were all staring at us, loads of them (including Carol) with their phones out, ready to capture the action. As Val would say, Suffering Jesus.

'I bloody knew someone would be daft enough,' Val cheered, before hastily adding, 'Sorry, Jess,' at the end of it. 'Son, yer a marvel,' she told the guy, who'd taken a few more steps forward and was standing in front of me now.

'I'm Greg,' he said, putting his hand out to shake mine.

'Jess,' I responded, unable to resist checking him out. He was taller than me, and I'm five ten, so given the height difference, I was guessing he was about six three. He was maybe somewhere between thirty-five and forty and he was wearing decent jeans, and a navy Canada Goose jacket, topped with a beanie, so I couldn't see what his hair was like. But I definitely appreciated what I could see. He was cute. No, not cute – attractive. Handsome. In a two-day stubble, cute creases around his eyes when he smiled, kind of way. I just had to check he wasn't a weirdo. Not that I exactly had the high ground on that possibility, given that I was the one being pimped out by my pals.

'Do you come here often?' I asked, trying to suss why he was there.

'Only when my brother is proposing to his girlfriend,' he answered, earning another cheer from the people he was with, one of them a guy who bore a very obvious resemblance to him.

Okay. I liked that. He'd come to support his brother who was asking his girlfriend to marry him. That was sweet.

If he was in, so was I.

I stepped forward, my gaze locked on his.

'Hang on, hang on,' Val yelled, looking at her watch again. 'Okay, here we go. Ten. Nine. Eight…'

The crowd cheered again, as Greg leaned forward, dipped his head down and kissed me.

At that very moment, the stroke of midnight, fireworks went off.

I just wasn't sure if they were in the New York skyline or in my mind.

29

CARLY

Something's Gotta Hold On Me – Etta James

'I just putting this out there again, I want to be exactly like her when I'm that age,' I murmured to Jess, as we both took in the magnificent spectacle that was Val Murray, cosmopolitan traveller, in first class on the flight back to LA, wearing her complimentary socks, eye mask and lip balm while still managing to somehow get her vodka tonic to her mouth.

Carol was sitting next to Val, but her head was turned away from us, seemingly staring out of the window into the nothingness.

I sighed, exhausted but unable to sleep. 'I'm worried about her.'

This time, Jess lolled her head around, so that she was facing me, and pulled her earphones out of her ears. 'Worried about who?'

'Both of them,' I said honestly. 'Carol is so anxious, so uncomfortable in her skin, and we both know she's never been like that before. It's as if there's something playing on her mind, or something is causing her to be at, like, 90 per cent stressed all day long, and the smallest thing is sending her into full-scale panic or shut-down. And can you take those sunglasses off? Now that your hair is short, you look like Kris Jenner with those on.'

Jess pushed her glasses up on to her head, then flinched. 'Ouch, the daylight. Do we need to have a deep and meaningful conversation right now or can I go back to sleep and ponder the fact that I had incredible sex with a complete stranger last night?'

'Nope, we're being deep and meaningful. But I'm happy for you with the whole sex thing.'

Just at that, the beautiful flight attendant, who was looking after our cabin came by and I saw the corners of her mouth turn upwards. 'Champagne, ladies?' she asked, clearly cheering on Jess's nocturnal achievements. Actually, it wasn't so much nocturnal as night-time, morning time, and well into the afternoon. Turns out that Jess and Greg from Texas had taken that bucket list kiss and turned it into a fourteen-hour marathon interlude of bendy stuff. We'd had to pack up her stuff, then stop by his hotel, the St Regis, to pick her up on the way here.

'Yes please,' Jess replied at the same time as I said, 'No thank you.'

My hangover wouldn't allow it. 'How come I went back to our hotel, admittedly tipsy, at 3 a.m. and got seven hours sleep and feel crap, yet you got no sleep and feel great?'

'I sweated it out,' she answered, with deadpan nonchalance. For years after her divorce, Jess had very happily stuck rigidly to a regime of casual one-night stands of her choosing. No relationships. No ties. No risk of getting hurt. Seemed like now Arnie had broken her heart, she was returning to her former game plan.

'So how are you feeling about Arnie now then?'

'I don't care. I really don't.'

Her hesitation was brief, but I knew her well enough to see it.

'Which I would absolutely believe, if you hadn't spent half of this flight rubbing the ring on the chain around your neck.'

It had been the first ring Arnie gave her. A copper twist they'd picked up on a trip with Sam and me to Yosemite not long after they got together. She'd been wearing it on a chain since they got engaged and I'd noticed she hadn't taken it off.

'Okay, so maybe I care a bit, but only because we haven't had closure. I need to meet him tomorrow and make him say everything to my face, make him tell me he's back with Myrna, make him squirm. Then I'll close the door and I won't look back. Done. I'll go back to the UK, carry on working, rustle up a few more British clients and life will go on. I'll be fine.'

I knew she would be anything but fine. I reached for her hand and interlinked my fingers with hers. 'I'm sorry, Jess.'

Her bottom lip quivered just once, then she brushed it off by nudging me and forcing a smile. 'Yeah, you're only saying that because I was going to be your only friend in the whole of LA and now I'm leaving.'

I got the message. She didn't want to talk about this any more. Walls up and, under pain of death, do not show so much as a chink of vulnerability. I went along with it. For now.

'You're absolutely right,' I breezed. 'It's all about me. Completely fricking rude of you not to consider that in your decision-making process.' That made her cackle and propelled us back to her safe space of non-personal, non-emotional, neutral ground.

She took another sip of her champagne. 'Talking of which, we never finished the conversation we started that day in the Beverly Wiltshire.'

Pin out. Grenade thrown. I was hoping she'd forgotten about that. She'd been so overwrought that morning after she got back from her stakeout, and we'd been so busy ever since, that I hoped it had slipped her mind.

I thought about taking the more measured and middle-of-the-road approach, but then I remembered I'd never been measured or visited the middle of the road in my life.

'I don't want to live here. In America, I mean. I want to go home.'

Her gasp made the bloke in the seat in front of her startle himself awake and he scanned the cabin like a periscope trying to work out what had woken him up.

'You're leaving Sam? For fuck's sake, Carly, you've only been married five minutes and you're calling it a day and—'

'No! No! I'm not leaving Sam. I love him, I want to be married to him, I just don't want to live here.'

'Because of those stupid photos on the internet?'

I could see she was grappling with this and trying to make sense of it.

'No. I felt like this before I came here. I was dreading it and I don't see how I can fix it. I live in the UK, I don't have Sam. I live here, I don't have my boys, my friends, the life I have back home.'

'But surely Mac and Benny can visit?'

'More champagne, ladies?' the flight attendant asked, reappearing from behind us.

Jess met my gaze and we passed a subliminal message. This conversation called for harder stuff.

'Two bourbon and Cokes, please,' she said.

'And any kind of chocolate, please. I'm comfort eating,' I added weakly. I was sure she'd had stranger requests in first class.

'Where was I?' Tiredness and a bloodstream that was already mostly alcohol made it difficult to retrace my thoughts. Eventually I got it. 'Like I said, it's not just my boys, it's my whole life back. I love it there, I love my friends, I love my home, I even love the fact that the fridge leaks and I'm on my third Flash mop. That's my life. This...' I gestured to our surroundings '... this isn't me. And I know

I'd have what loads of people think would be this awesome, flashy, want-for-nothing life in LA, but that's not me either. I like having coffee with Kate in the morning. I love it when everyone piles over for Sunday lunch. And then doesn't complain when I burn it. You'll be back home too, so we'd all be there together again, all the time. That's just... my happy place.'

The attendant delivered our drinks and a bowl with some Lindt chocolate balls in it. I considered asking her to marry me.

Jess took a large slug, before she returned to the conversation. 'What are you going to do then? Is there a plan B?'

'No. I don't know. Talk to Sam. Try to make him understand. I can't ask him to move his life to the UK, because he already stayed over there for nearly two years for me, and he was desperate to get back here. And I know he won't do the long-distance thing. That would be okay for a few months, but we're talking about forever. I just can't see a way forward that would make both of us happy. You're the problem-solver in our group, Jess. Help me,' I pleaded.

She thought about it for a few moments, then just when I thought she was going to hit me with some genius solution that would save the day, she shrugged helplessly.

'I'm sorry, Carly, I've got nothing. I mean, look at the clusterfuck that I'm calling my life right now. I don't think I've got a right to preach on anything. The only thing I do know is that Sam loves you and you love him. The universe will work this out.'

'That's all you've got?' I asked her, astonished. 'The universe? Not entirely strategic and logical, is it?'

My first reaction was despair, but then I reined myself back in. Jess had lost the man she was going to spend the rest of her life with, and here I was, moaning about where to live with my new husband. This was the last thing she needed right now. Bloody hell, I was being selfish. I decided to put my relationship struggles to one side and go for more superficial stuff instead. Nothing like a mutual irritation to get us on to safer ground. 'Urgh, Estelle would fricking love it though.'

Jess nodded ruefully. 'Yes, she would. I still reckon she's behind the photos, you know. It seems like the kind of nasty cow thing she'd do.'

I bit into my chocolate ball. 'I don't think you're wrong, but I can't exactly accuse her of it with no proof. It would make me look like a complete tit.'

I'd seen the expression Jess was now wearing. It was 'deep in thought, with an edge of malice and an overtone of don't you fucking dare'.

'Leave it with me and I'll get to the bottom of it,' she promised.

I took her hand again. 'Thank you. You're a pal, Jess Latham, and I love you.'

Right on cue, the PDA rattled her cage and she went for bluster and deflection to cover the moment of heartfelt emotion. 'Yeah, you're not bad either. Now please stop speaking so I can go to sleep, otherwise I'll hate you and I'll plant photos of you in shoulder pads from 1986. It wasn't your best look.'

With that, she rolled over and dozed off, and not even the sound of me sucking my chocolate disturbed her.

Hours later, the sound of the landing gear crunching down woke her and, weary and desperate for showers, we trudged through the terminal building, collected our bags and made for the exit. Jess and I walked in front, Carol and Aunt Val somewhere behind us, lagging a little because, as always, Carol was filming an Instagram Live post.

Jess took the opportunity to make an attempt at hatching a plan. 'Listen, what you were saying earlier, about Carol. I think we need to talk to her. Find out what's going on. And we should do it here, because if it's anything to do with Callum, it's going to be easier to talk to her before we go back to the UK. I know you said he denied having problems in their marriage, but maybe he doesn't know. It could be all on her side, and if that's the case, we need to support her and help her through it.'

The doors from the baggage reclaim to the concourse slid open, and we started up the walkway, ignoring the dozens of people who were standing waiting for loved ones or corporate pickups.

'I think it's too late for that,' I said, stopping dead and almost having my ankles taken from under me by the laden trolley of the man right behind me.

'Why? Do you think she's already made up her mind?'

I was still rooted to the spot. 'I've no idea. But I think there's a bloke over there that might.'

Jess turned to see where I was looking and spotted the guy who'd almost reached us now.

'Hey, sis,' my brother Callum said, throwing his arm around me. 'I'm scared to ask, but what have you done with my wife?'

30

CAROL

Because Of You – Kelly Clarkson

I raised my iPhone, made sure I had good angles, then pressed record on my Instagram Live and chatted as I walked. I'd already changed my outfit before we got off the plane, so that I could squeeze in another endorsement for Yawn & Yoga. 'Hi, guys, Carol here! So New York was amazing – thank you to everyone who left such lovely comments. I'm back in LA now, and I want to thank American Airlines for the wonderful service in first class. I can't be completely sure, but all I'm saying is that there was a passenger a couple of rows in front of us who bore a stunning resemblance to Jon Bon Jovi.'

I didn't mention that Val had tested the theory by humming 'Livin' On A Prayer' for ten minutes in the hope that he'd join in and give himself away. He didn't. But I recorded her doing it, and I was saving it for my prime upload window for my UK followers later tonight because it was absolutely hilarious and I was fairly sure it would get huge traction – maybe not the same volume as her gliding across the Rockefeller ice rink on her belly, but hopefully it would be close.

I was still filming as we exited the baggage reclaim. I liked to keep the videos running for as long as possible at LAX, because, well, you just never knew who you would see, and all it took was a minor celebrity to open the door to a shared collab and a ton of new followers.

'Right, I'm going to go track down my ride back to the Palisades. If you want to get this look, my top and pants are from the new line at Yawn & Yoga. I'll put the link in my bio, and remember, as always, you get a 10 per cent discount on your first order if you use my name as a promo code. Have a great day! Love you all and…!' My words trailed off when I saw him.

The rest of the world disappeared, swept into the ether by complete shock, because there, hugging his sister, was my husband. Callum was here? Was something wrong? Was it the girls? Oh, God, had something happened to my girls? Sweat beads started popping out of my pores, a roar of thunder shut down my brain and something was on my chest, pushing it into my ribcage, squeezing my lungs. I wanted to run to him, to ask, but my legs wouldn't work. They couldn't hear the signals my brain was sending as they were frozen, rooted to the tiled floor of the terminal building.

He spotted me, he turned, but I couldn't read his face. The girls. Definitely the girls. Were they gone? An accident? Worse? Had someone hurt them? That couldn't happen. Not to us. Didn't everyone always say we had the perfect life? Still couldn't breathe. Couldn't think straight. Couldn't move. Couldn't speak.

Suddenly, his whole being reacted to seeing me, he opened his arms and came towards me with a bashful smile. 'Surprise!'

He wouldn't be saying that and grinning if something was wrong.

I wanted to throw up. To gasp. To scream. But then I realised that my live video was still running and that this was the kind of spontaneous content that people loved, so I flipped the screen. Everyone watching saw Callum Cooper, my handsome husband, saunter towards me with that easy-going walk of his, that adorable grin, that husky voice. 'Hey, babe, I missed you...'

It was a beautiful, heartfelt, thoughtful, sweet surprise. As he reached me, picked me up, twirled me around, I laughed, kissed him, got us both in the shot as we hugged each other and in that moment, I knew... I knew I didn't feel a thing. Nothing at all.

I looked up at him, channelling the JLo/Ben Affleck adoration vibes. 'I love you, baby,' I murmured. Then back to the camera, 'Sooooo, I love you all too, but I have to go and thank this amazing man for making me the happiest woman ever. I might be a while,' I joked, then waved and cut the feed.

I could already see the comments flying up the screen.

OMG I want your life!

#truelove #couplegoals

When you're finished with that man, send him my way.

I locked the phone and pushed it into my pocket, the sick feeling in my stomach kicking me right back into the fear and anxiety ballpark. 'What are you doing here? Is everything okay? Are the girls okay?'

'Yeah, they're great. Everything is fine.' I saw his eyes flicker to Carly, but didn't think anything of it. Those two had such a close relationship, they communicated on some weird, submarine level. Sub... Subliminal. Dammit!

He took my bag and slipped his arm around my shoulders. 'I had a few days off, so I thought I'd come hang out with you guys. Don't worry, I won't cramp your style. I'll force my brother-in-law to play pool and drink in bars. It'll be tough, but we'll manage it.'

A million years ago, I was on a shoot in the Maldives and

Callum showed up just as we were wrapping. He'd whisked me away to a bungalow on stilts in the deep turquoise ocean and we'd lost ourselves in a bubble of bliss. It was one of the happiest moments of my life. Another time, only a few years ago, I'd surprised him by rearranging my schedule so that we bumped into each other at Heathrow. Instead of going home, I took him straight to Terminal 5 and we flew to Paris for a two-day break. We walked, we had amazing sex, and I thanked the gods of romance that I was still so in love with this man after twenty-five years of marriage.

What had happened? Why didn't I feel any of those things now? Where had all that joy and passion and love gone? Why did I feel so empty?

In the limo, I managed to keep the smile on my face and the pretence of happiness going all the way back to Sam's house. Jess was quiet, but Carly, Val, and Callum chatted and there was much laughter as they filled him in on everything that had happened. I was with them, but at the same time, I wasn't. I felt detached. Disjointed. Like an outsider to this family that I'd been a part of for most of my life. But still, I kept smiling, held my husband's hand, tried to make him feel like I wanted him to be there.

I only managed to keep it up until we got back to our room at Sam's house. As soon as he closed the door, Callum came to me, put his arms around me and for the first time ever, I froze. I just couldn't. I didn't want him to hug me. I didn't want him to touch me. I definitely didn't want to have sex.

He frowned, held me out at arm's-length and searched my face for answers. 'Babe? Carol, what's going on?'

I wanted to answer him, but my mind was racing. Did he really mean it when he said the girls were fine? Should I call them and check? Perhaps something was going on that none of them were telling me?

'Carol! Jesus, you're shaking. Honey, talk to me. What can I do?'

I could hear the panic in his voice, but at the same time I wanted to block it out. Why was he stressing? What did he have to worry about? Why was he even here?

The maelstrom in my head was so loud and distracting, I barely realised that I'd vocalised that thought.

'Why are you even here?'

He was staring at me like he'd been slapped and he didn't recognise the person who'd just hit him.

'Carol, what's going on? I'm worried about you.'

For some reason, his tone permeated the panic in my gut, and the anxiety and adrenaline that were coursing through me began to subside a little.

Shaking him off, I took a step back and sat on the edge of the bed. *Get a grip, Carol. Pull it together. Don't let him or anyone else see how you're feeling.* It was like I was a kettle, on the point of boiling over, and I'd just managed to switch myself off.

'I'm sorry, I'm just tired. It's been a bit of a hectic few days and I'm wiped out.'

He knew I was lying, but he didn't call me out on it. Instead, he did the worst thing of all – he was kind to me. He kissed the top of my head, then put his hands on my face, gently stroking my cheeks with his thumbs. His tenderness almost broke the barrier of normality that I'd just slid into place.

'Babe, you know you can talk to me about anything. If something has happened, you can tell me. I'm here. I was thinking on the plane over that maybe we've not been great lately. I guess we've slipped into a bit of a rut. Maybe taking each other for granted. If that's what's bothering you, we can fix this. I've got you. I've always got you.' Everything he was saying was spot on. We had definitely got lost somewhere in bringing up the girls, my career shifting in a new direction, getting older, but not much wiser. This should have been the opening for a heartfelt, honest conversation about making things better, checking in on our marriage and forcing one of those shifts that couples make over the years to ensure they go the distance, but all I wanted to do was drop his hand, pick up my phone and run off the twisted knot of terror in my gut.

He was trying to make me get real. I just didn't remember how to do that. It had been too long since I felt anything more genuine than the number of likes that clocked up on one of my posts.

'I'm fine. Honestly. Just a bit overworked and overwhelmed.'

The fog that had been coming and going in my brain for months came back down and acted like a blanket, suppressing my thoughts, wrapping me up against the anxiety that kept taking hold.

Callum knew nothing of that though. He gently helped me down onto the bed, snuggled next to me and rubbed my hair as my face lay against the rise and fall of his chest.

'Okay, babe, but I'm here if you need me. Bloody hell, I was worried there for a minute. Don't you go falling out of love with me, Carol Cooper. I'm not always great at making an effort, but you know we're keepers, right?'

It was our little saying, one we'd told each other a million times since we met. We're keepers.

His question replayed in my ears. *We're keepers, right?*

My mind was playing my honest answer. *I don't know. I really don't.*

My mouth was saying something altogether different.

'Of course we are.'

31

VAL

Ariana Grande – Get Well Soon

I was fresh out of the shower, smelling of that lovely coconut body lotion that was in my en suite. Get me with the 'en suite' stuff. Don and I had managed to live our whole lives and raise a family in a house with one bathroom, and now I was saying en suite like I'd never lived a day without such luxury. Ah well, better late than never. And never was coming straight towards me.

I opened my notebook and shot off a quick letter to give my pal an update.

Dear Josie,

Well, pet, we're almost done with the bucket list and it's been a blast. You'd have loved every crazy, mad, unexpected moment of it. And I really hope you're watching what's coming next. Josie, I'm going to be acting in a movie. I'm only getting one line – that's all I need – but it's in the new Sam Morton action thriller,

so everyone at home will see it at some point. Can you imagine
their faces when they sit down next Christmas for a wee film with
their tub of Quality Street, and there I am, in full glory? I hope
those bloody big flat-screens don't make ma arse look huge.

Anyway, doll, my part is in a reshoot of a scene with Estelle
Loveherself (that's her Scottish name, you know, the ones we
made up by taking your first name and then adding your
strongest personality trait or habit – mine was Val Eatsmanybis-
cuits and yours was Josie TwoCigsandabitquicktempered). My
line is, 'Sugar and cream with your Americano?' Yup, the Oscar
for Best Actress in the category of Sassy Waitress In One Of
Those Fancy Coffee Bars will be coming my way. Before you
know it, I'll be the mysterious older woman that Matt Damon
sweeps of her feet in his next movie. Actually, sweeping off the
feet might be a bit much. I'd settle for sharing a cup of tea and a
fruit scone.

Anyway, doll, I'd better go.
Keep dancing, keep laughing… and be happy up there.
Love you,
Val xxx

I put my pen down, and raised my eyes upwards. *Are you watch-*
ing, Josie, love? Are you proud?

Right at that second, my phone buzzed with one of those texts,
and for a moment it startled me because I thought it was Josie
answering the question. But no. My boy, Michael. When I say 'boy',
I mean a forty-year-old man, but he'll always be my firstborn kid.

Hi Mum, all good with us, so don't be worrying. Just came to top of hill
to get signal. We're going to head home in few days. Dad has had a
good time and I've kept him busy. Did you get everything done? Are you
ready to come home now? Love you, Mike.

I'll confess I had a wee wobble of the chin now that there was a finish line to all this. It was strange, but somehow having the bucket list to look forward to gave me a reason not to think, not to dwell, not to face what was coming. That time – *my time* – was running out.

I texted back. Took me ages using one index finger, and even then my new nails kept pressing the wrong button.

Aye, son. Wikk be hone bu satirday. Love yoi ans givr yer fad a huy fron me. Mun xxxx

Send.

Saturday. Today was Monday, so I had five more days to get the rest of the bucket list done and get home. It would be easy to slip into a downer right about now, but that would defeat the purpose. The last couple of weeks and the next few days to come were about living. And I wasn't going to give a single one of them up to worry or stress. Instead, I chatted all the way to the studio, and took in every sight, every conversation and every feeling, right up until I was sitting in a chair, in a fancy dressing room, getting ready for my close-up.

'Right, are ye sure that's ma best angle? I'd asked the photographer, who was taking pictures of me – the kind that shot right out of the arse of the camera and developed in seconds. They were for something called continuity. No idea what it was, but I was going along with it because Sam had been kind enough to set up this acting gig for me and I didn't want to blow it.

I stared at Michael's text again.

'Aunt Val, what are you thinking? You're miles away,' Carly asked, making me sit up a little straighter and pay attention. Carly, Jess and Carol were sitting over on the white leather sofa that was up against the other wall in the dressing room. I was pretty sure

that actresses with one line didn't normally get this level of facili-
ties, but my niece was sleeping with the producer.

'I'm thinking that these Spanx are cutting off the circulation to
ma toes, is what I'm thinking. What waitress would wear these to
her work?'

'Take them off then,' Carol suggested. She was looking awfully
pale, that one. I'd have thought that my nephew turning up would
have cheered her up, but the sadness was still seeping out of her. I
planned to sit her down and make her tell me what was wrong. But
in the meantime, I wasn't going with her commando suggestion.

'I will not!' I replied, horrified. 'Me and Isa McGlinchy have
been up at that Slimming World every week for the last year and
there's no way I'm letting her think she's lost more than me. The
humiliation would kill me. The pants stay on. I'll put up with the
suffering.'

Just at that, Sam and Callum came in. Och, those men. Granted,
I was biased, because one of them was my nephew, but the two of
them were thoroughly decent blokes. Funny too. If Ant and Dec
were a foot taller and good-looking, they'd be dead ringers. Callum
leaned down to kiss Carol, then perched on the edge of the sofa
next to her. She still didn't crack a smile, the poor lass. Meanwhile,
Sam came up behind my chair and looked in the mirror, his hands
on my shoulders. 'Ready for the big break?'

'Son, I was born ready. That Estelle one should be shaking in
her boots in case I outshine her.'

'Did I hear my name being mentioned there?' Estelle Lovesherself swaggered into the room and came up behind me, stopping
next to Sam, so that they were both looking at my reflection as she
spoke to me. That lassie was way too fond of herself, if you asked
me. Aye, she was stunning, but so was my toaster, and it didn't have
much of a personality either. Our Carly was warm and caring, and
God, she was funny and a joy to be around. This one, on the other

hand... well, if I could feel my buttocks, the irritation would be making them clench.

'I was just saying how I could never outshine you, sweetheart,' I told her. I knew she'd believe it. If she was an avocado, she'd eat herself.

My reply made Sam grin and shake his head. 'I'll see you on set, in ten minutes,' he chuckled, and off he went, our Callum going with him. They'd been such good pals since they met when Carly and Sam were together the first time round. I was fond of Carly's ex-husband, Mark. He was a decent bloke, but he'd never got his priorities right. For him, work was top of the list and Carly just had to put up with that while they were married. Sam was different. I could see that, for him, the sun rose and set on Carly, and the lass deserved it.

All those bulbs around the mirror in front of me were gleaming, and maybe that's why, despite not having my specs on, I noticed in the reflection that Estelle was carrying a pile of papers – her script, maybe – but on the top was one of those tabloid magazines that I'd seen in stands at the airport. It was the front cover that made my chin drop though. Estelle. Sam. And a headline, 'Are Hollywood's Bolden Couple Back Together?' I processed that for a minute, then realised it said Golden. Like I mentioned, I didn't have my specs on.

Oh, suffering Jesus, this would break our Carly's heart, even though we all knew without a single doubt that Sam would never touch this lassie again with Johnny Depp's bargepole, never mind his own. I think that's what did it. That, and the fact that I'm fairly sure Josie Cairney inhabited my body right at that second and took charge of the matter in exactly the way I'd seen her do so many times when she was alive: confrontational and taking no prisoners.

I squinted and saw that the photo showed the two of them in a car, coming out of Sam's gates.

'Well, that was convenient, wasn't it?' I said, harrumphing my bosoms. 'I mean, imagine there being a photographer hanging about outside on that day you came to pick Sam up. What a coincidence.'

Behind her, I saw Carly, Carol and Jess stop what they were doing and look up, startled, recognising my tone as the special one I saved for working up to a bollocking. They'd all heard it the time I had to pick them up from a nightclub at 3 a.m. when they were sixteen and they'd sneaked out of Carly's house during a sleepover. She'd called me instead of her dad because she knew I would cover for her. I did. But only after reading them the riot act all the way home.

Unfortunately, Estelle Lovesherself didn't recognise the tone and tried to bluff her way out of it.

'Oh, it's just one of those things. These photographers are always lurking around. I'm a big pay cheque for them if they get me. It doesn't mean anything at all,' she purred, all sickly-sweet.

'Och, I know – it must be terrible for you. I wonder if that was the same photographer who took those photos of our Carly and plastered them all over the internet?' I could do sickly-sweet too.

Estelle's expression was beginning to change though, as she was getting the gist of what I was implying. The Three Degrees over on the sofa were keeping schtum though. They knew better than to interrupt me – and Josie – when we were on a roll.

'I don't think so,' she said, and behind those big blue eyes, I could see her brain spinning like a whirligig in a hurricane.

'Because that would be such a coincidence, wouldn't it?' I chirped. Still sickly. Still sweet. You could hear a peanut drop over on the sofa in the gallery at the back. 'I mean, that would almost be like it was planned. Like someone tipped off a photographer to take a photo of you and Sam at the exact moment you left his house. And then also tried to make a right fool of his wife by getting all those dodgy pictures and stories out there. That would be terrible. I wonder who would have an interest in doing that though?' I twisted my head so that my gaze met Carly's wide-eyed reaction. 'Who do you think would do that, Carly? Someone with a grudge? Someone...' In my mind I was pulling the fingers of my gloves, ready to take them off. '... Who thinks that they should be with him instead of you?'

At that, I returned my stare to Estelle, keeping my smile on my face.

'Are you implying that I did that?' she said, catching on.

'Of course not!' I said, then paused. 'There's no implication there at all. I'd bet my best Wonderbra that you're not involved in this, love, and if you are? Well, I feel sorry for you, because you're on to plums. And not Sam's plums.'

Too late, I realised that she probably wasn't familiar with that expression, but she seemed to catch on to the meaning of it when her beautiful features twisted into pure indignation.

'Lady, you've lost your damn mind,' she said, and I could hear tell-tale signs of a different accent, not the low, sexy LA one she used on screen. 'I don't need to make her look like a disaster – she's a train wreck all by herself.'

'You know I'm here, don't you?' Carly said, cheerily, as if she were talking about the weather.

We both ignored her, on my part, because I was raging. 'Don't you dare talk about my niece like that. Okay, so she might not look like you...'

'Still here,' Carly chirped.

'But she's one of the very best people I know...'

'Aaaaw, thanks, Aunt Val,' came from the background.

'And I'd much rather spend a wonderful day with her than a day with you trying to get that stick out of your arse. Sam is with her because of her personality and her heart. You might want to learn a thing or two about that. So back off, sweetheart. Leave them alone.

Because Sam is going to think even less of you when he finds out it was you who did this to the woman he loves.'

'Can we clap?' I heard Jess say to Carol. 'Because she's fricking mighty when she gets going.'

I paid no attention, still watching Estelle, whose eyes were blazing now.

'Shit, you must have been drinking the same Kool-Aid as Sam. Lady, I already told you, I didn't plant those stories. They were nothing to do with me. Trust me, if they were, I'd take credit, because they were the most amusement I've had in a long time. But the bottom line is that I'd lose my female fan base if I were portrayed as a homewrecker in the press and no man is worth that. Did you miss the whole Jenifer Aniston/Angelina Jolie debacle? The wronged, chirpy sweetheart always comes out on top. I'm Aniston, not Jolie. I'm the sweetheart and nobody will fucking say otherwise. Now, if you'll excuse me, I have a scene to shoot. I just wish it was one where I got a bitch of a waitress fired from her job.' With that, she turned on her fancy heels and marched out.

'I really wish you'd given me warning about that so I could have filmed it,' Carol murmured.

Carly's jaw was still going up and down and eventually she got the words out. 'Aunt Val, are you okay? I mean, that was completely spectacular, but you didn't have to fight my battles.'

'I know, love,' I told her, 'but it was out before I could stop it. It's my age. Both my bladder and my powers of restraint aren't what they used to be.'

That set them all off on the giggles, but I knew what I was going to say next would change that.

'Thing is, ladies, I hate to say it, but I believe her. My lie detector was vibrating like a toothbrush when she was talking about the magazine cover, but the other stuff? I think she was being truthful when she denied the rest. She's so ruthless, she wouldn't risk her career for anyone.'

That sobered them up. After thinking about that, Carly was the first to find her voice and it was thick with weariness. 'You know, I think you're right. She's not that good an actress. Aw, bugger. If she didn't plant the photos, then who did?'

32

JESS

Respect – Aretha Franklin

It felt strange to be wearing my suit of armour again after so long without it. I'd been working from Arnie's home for the last couple of years and everything was online these days anyway. It was so rare that I actually met anyone in person.

My favourite pale grey Armani suit still fitted like a glove (thank you, break-up appetite loss) and my charcoal suede Louboutin stilettos had only taken a couple of layers of skin off the back of my heels. It was a small price to pay to feel like I belonged here. Over the years, I'd had many meetings in the Belvedere Brasserie in the Peninsula Hotel, on Santa Monica Boulevard in Beverly Hills, and now I was back. Walking through the gorgeous entrance doors of the cream stone building, under rows of white windows with black steel balconies, it had felt like I was returning to a familiar, comfortable place. Which was just as well, because I didn't feel particularly comfortable on the inside. I was tired. I was apprehensive. And I was still in the fury stage of grief and looking forward to taking that out on someone.

That person was walking towards me right now, the maître d' bringing him to my table.

Arnie.

I'd wondered how I'd feel when I saw him and now I knew. No fucking suit of armour could stop the piercing dagger of pain that was ripping through my heart. He was wearing his armour too. One of the things I'd always adored about him was that he didn't play the Hollywood game, and even in the elegant surroundings of the Peninsula, he was still himself: grey jeans over cowboy boots and a black T-shirt that showed every single curve of his muscular frame. I knew we looked like an unusual pairing: this chic businesswoman and her muscle-bound guy who was a good ten years older than her. I used to think that was good. Now I thought we looked like a mismatch because we actually were. I understood fidelity. He didn't.

When he reached me, I didn't get up, just took a sip of my coffee. I couldn't risk my shaking legs giving way and landing me on my arse. He didn't even try to kiss me and I wasn't sure if that made me happy or even more pissed off.

'Hey, Jess,' he said, that low drawl, combined with those gorgeous brown eyes, doing something disturbing to my insides.

No. Enough. I wasn't giving him one ounce of control here. Time to take charge. Keep calm. Cool.

'Hi, Arnie. Look, I haven't got long. I've got a business meeting here in an hour and I've still got a few things to prep for it.' He'd probably know I was lying about the prep. When it came to work, I'd always been religiously organised and wholly prepared. Again, keep calm. Cool. 'And, to be frank, I don't think we've got much to talk about. You cheated…'

'I didn't.'

Calm and cool went right out of the fucking window. I leaned forward, keeping my voice barely above a whisper so that no one around us could hear.

'Arnie, I heard you on the phone to Myrna. I heard what you said to her. I heard your tone. It was everything you used on me and I was such a fucking fool I believed it.'

He leaned forward too, put his elbows on the table, dipped his head, then lifted it when he was ready to speak and when he did, I could hear the weariness in his voice. 'Jess, I don't want to be the guy who uses clichés, but it's not what it looks like. I know you need more than me saying that, so I need you to hear someone else.'

Who? What was he talking about?

'Hi, Jess.'

Aw, for fuck's sake. I'd been so engrossed in listening to Arnie, that I hadn't noticed his daughter, Talia, approach the table. If I was wearing my armour, she was too. I recognised the engraved V's on the buttons of her razor sharp Valentino suit and the signature style of her strappy Jimmy Choos. Every feature on her stunning face was perfectly contoured and today, going by the admiring glances, she owned the room. I was going to have to up my armour game.

'Can I sit down?'

Ambush. I'd walked right into it. What they didn't realise was that I would still come out shooting.

'Look, Talia, no disrespect, but if you've come to gloat or to put me in my place, don't bother. I know your parents are living together again. To tell you the truth, I'm not even sure on the time-lines of anything any more. Maybe I was just someone to keep him amused while he was in a long-distance relationship.' An hour and a half's drive wasn't exactly long distance, but Arnie's job involved living on Sam's estate, and he'd always said Myrna refused to move from their family home. 'So maybe they were together the whole time I was with him.'

'They were,' she answered calmly and the knife was plunged

further into my body, making my lungs collapse in a split second, letting every drop of oxygen escape. I had to get out of here. Had to leave. 'But only in her head,' she added, before I could get power to my legs.

'I need you to hear me out. Please.'

I didn't have any choice. I still couldn't feel my lower limbs. 'Okay.'

'I need to tell you a bit about my mother. She's a good woman, but she loved my dad more than life, so when they split up, she took it so hard and she started to drink. Somewhere along the line, the drinks turned to Oxycontin, prescribed by the doctor for the pain she told him she had in her back. When that dried up and she couldn't get any more, she found it somewhere else. Now...' There was a pause and I could see she was gathering herself, forcing herself to keep it together. Maybe we had more in common than I thought. 'She's a full-blown addict. Heroin.'

I shifted my eyes to Arnie, who locked on to my stare. 'Why didn't you tell me this?'

'Because I begged him not to,' Talia answered for him. 'My sister did too. We wanted to deal with this ourselves.'

I took stock. I was shocked and my heart went out to them, but none of this excused Arnie's infidelity. I was about to say that when Talia cut me off by continuing.

'A while ago, it reached a stage when we knew we couldn't, so we tried to get her to go to rehab. That didn't work either.'

'So you went back to her?' I challenged Arnie. 'Great excuse.'

Arnie leaned forward again. 'Jess, I know this is tough to hear, and your foot is probably shaking under this table because you're so damn mad...' How did he know that? 'But I just need you to hear everything. That's all I ask – then you can make up your mind about me.'

Deep breath. Steady. 'Okay, go on.'

Talia nodded. 'She wouldn't go to rehab, because somewhere in her drug-addled mind she was waiting for Dad to come back to her. She was convinced that they were still married and said she couldn't go until he came home. She said she needed to know he'd be waiting when she got out. That's why we asked him to go along with her delusions, and then to come back to the house, just to help us get her to the facility.'

Arnie took over. 'I know it sounds crazy, Jess, but I couldn't let the kids down.' For the purposes of this emotional, heartfelt moment, I decided to overlook the fact that his 'kids' were in their thirties. It was in the same category as Val calling us her girls, when not one of us was under fifty. 'I started calling her, went up there a couple of times. I swear nothing happened. It was enough that I was there. She was pretty gone by that time.'

'Where was I when all this was happening?' I asked, astonished. 'How did I miss this?'

'The birthday party,' Talia said. 'When I told you that you weren't invited. There wasn't a party.'

'And all the other celebrations and visits to your daughters and grandchildren in the last few months?' This was all clicking into place. I used to think there was no family on earth that celebrated more occasions than Arnie's brood, none of which I was invited to.

'All fake,' Arnie confessed. 'Look, I'm sorry I lied, but if it's any consolation, I didn't even tell Sam. He was still over in the UK, so I just told him I needed personal time and he didn't ask questions.'

The tables around us were still a hive of noise and industry. Yet, no matter how many people from the movie world were in here, I was pretty sure none of their pitches would be more convoluted than the real-life drama going on here. I had a flashback to just a week or so ago, when I saw his car in the driveway of their family home. This wasn't adding up. If she was in rehab, why would he stay there? I waited for a moment to hit him with that, but he was still talking, so I tucked it up my sleeve.

'That call you heard... she'd freaked out. She was smashing the place up and Talia called me and put me on the line. I was trying to talk her down. You were gone before I could explain, and I saw the flight you booked on the computer, so I thought you'd left the country. You wouldn't take my calls. The kids were desperate, so in my mind, the best thing to do was to go up there, to sort it out, then come to you, find you, explain.'

That was a light-bulb moment. That was exactly how Arnie's mind worked. Logic. Sort one problem, then the next one. My ability to multitask used to drive him nuts.

'But it didn't go smoothly. She overdosed before I got there that night, then she refused to get help, and it took us until the day before yesterday to get her into rehab. That's why I was blowing your phone up, trying to get you, to explain. We only got control of the whole situation when we finally got her admitted to the clinic for help.'

My ace fell out of my sleeve. And worse, the Joker took its place. Sure, he'd lied to me, but Arnie hadn't been having an affair. While he was dealing with a massive, life-altering family crisis, I was the one who was shagging fricking Greg from fricking Texas. Fuck. Literally.

'I need you to forgive me, Jess. And I need you to come home. Can you do that?'

Again, fuck. With a side helping of heartbreak, guilt and uncertainty over whether I could lie by omission.

'I need to think about it. Look, I wasn't lying about another meeting. This is a lot. I'll come back to the house tonight and we can talk.

I'd thought Arnie was the bad guy in the movie of our relationship. Turns out it was me.

33

CARLY

Just Give Me A Reason – Pink

'Seriously, Mum, it's like the highlight of our day. Isn't it, Benny?' Mac said. My boy's gorgeous face cracked wide with a huge smile as he glanced to his brother's equally gorgeous face for affirmation.

'Yup,' Benny agreed. 'We wake up in the morning, switch on our light, down some water, check what's happened on Tinder overnight, and then see what bonkers photos we can find of you on the internet. The one of you hugging Uncle Callum at the airport was a cracker. Although, obviously they have no idea who he is because they said he was your secret lover.'

There were so many things wrong with that sentence that I didn't quite know where to start, so I led with, 'What have I told you two??! Stop going on bloody Tinder! That's where serial killers stalk their prey!'

In the car beside me, Sam laughed. We'd driven down to the Peninsula together in my husband's inconspicuous black pickup truck. He drove that when he wanted to stay anonymous. Callum, Carol and Val were on their way in his other car, a classic, petrol-blue Mercedes convertible, after a touristy stop at the Hollywood sign, with Val behind wheel the whole time. The trip served two purposes. It ticked the convertible ride off the bucket list and it let Val get a fabulous photo up at the tourist landmark to send to Isa at her Scottish Slimmers class. She swore she'd dropped ten pounds after all our walking and dancing, and she said she wasn't letting it go to waste.

The plan was that Sam and Callum would then head out to do a bit of fishing on a boat out of Marina Del Rey, and I would take Jess, Val and Carol back to the house for a long-awaited day at the pool. I was counting the minutes. In fact, I'd quite happily have skipped this and just stayed at the house if Jess hadn't required us to be her backup here.

We'd arrived early and had just parked up when the boys had FaceTimed me and I'd taken the call, so we were still sitting outside the main entrance to the hotel. If we were anyone else, we'd have been moved on by the doormen by now, but as soon as they'd seen it was Sam, they'd told us to take as long as we needed. That's what star power got you in Hollywood.

Their laughter gave flight to a gut twist of missing them so strong that I had to stroke their faces on the screen.

'Mum, did you just do that weird stroke-y thing again?'

'Yes. Don't judge me. I'm happy in my warm and bubbly state of pathetic. I miss you two so much. I wish you were here.'

'Ma, you're supposed to be too busy shopping and flying across the world in a private jet and having dinner with Ryan Reynolds to miss us,' Mac pointed out. 'Uncle Sam, what's going wrong over there? You need to be keeping her crazy busy so that she stops calling us ten times a day and tracking our every move.'

They weren't wrong. I did do that.

Sam leaned over so that he was in view of the camera. 'Sorry, guys, you're right, I've let the side down. I'll do better. We do miss you guys though. Come over soon and rescue me before I'm lighting candles and having bubble baths.'

'Mum's rubbing off on you,' Benny teased. 'She's turned you into emotional mush and you've not even been away for two weeks.'

Almost two weeks without my boys. It already felt like a lifetime. I couldn't do this. I just couldn't.

'S'pose we'd better go,' Benny said reluctantly. 'Tabitha will be home from work soon and she's expecting us to do a yoga session with her and Dad. It was a novelty at the start but now we hate it and we're running out of excuses. Mac's been saying he's had a groin strain all week.'

'Too much Tinder will do that to you,' I joked, secretly glad that the novelty of Tabitha had worn off already. And yes, my joke was probably slightly inappropriate, but it made them howl and that was all that mattered.

'When do Aunt Carol and Aunt Val come home?' Mac asked.

My whole stomach flipped when he said that. I couldn't bear to think about them leaving. It was even worse now that it looked like Jess was going with them, unless some miracle had happened and Arnie was right now changing her mind in there.

'I'm not sure. Maybe Friday or Saturday.' My voice broke on the words.

'Okay, well, have a great time with them before they go. See ya, Mum. I'll call tomorrow. Try to be on a jet,' Benny demanded.

'I'll do my best, son. I love you both.'

'We love you both too,' Mac shot back, with a cheery wave before disconnecting.

For a moment I couldn't speak.

'Are you okay, darling?' Sam said, breaking the silence first.

'I'm fine,' I croaked, trying to hold it together.

'Carly?' he drawled. 'What's going on?'

"Nothing. I'm fine.'

'Sweetheart…' he began, and that was it. Someone put a stick of dynamite in Pandora's box and blew that shit wide open.

'Sam, I can't do this. I can't live here. I hate it.'

'Babe, if it's those photos…'

'It's not the photos. I couldn't give a toss about them. That's the point – I don't care what the world thinks about me. I don't care that it's all glam and flash here. I just want to live at home, with my sons and my pals and my kitchen table and my Aunt Val appearing when we least expect her with another daft idea. I don't belong here. And I know that sounds so ungrateful because anyone would want this life and it's amazing and I'm so proud of you…' I was aware I was doing the nervous rant thing, but as usual I couldn't stop. 'The only thing I'm here for is you. That's it.'

Nothing was said for way too many seconds before he came back with a quiet, 'And that's not enough?'

'Yes, it is! It's just… Sometimes, no,' I added weakly. 'I know your life is here and you gave up all this for two years to live with us, so now it's my turn but…' I bit my lip, trying to stop the words, but I couldn't hold them back. 'I don't think I can do it. I want to go home.'

Another crippling silence that was only broken when banging on the window scared the crap out of us both. Val. She'd arrived with Carol and Callum, and she was announcing it was time for us to go inside.

I feigned cheeriness and gave her a thumbs up, then searched my husband's face for a clue to how he was feeling.

He decided to make it clear by telling me.

'The thing is, Carly, this is my home. I thought that made it yours too.'

With that, he opened the car door, jumped out and then slid

into the seat Val had just vacated in the other car. My brother waved, completely oblivious, as my husband drove him away.

Carol stuck her head in to see what was keeping me and saw my face.

'Oh, honey, you told him?'

I nodded, determined not to cry because if I started, I wasn't sure I could stop.

'Don't be nice. Don't be nice. Don't be nice,' I begged, knowing that would tip me over the edge.

'Okay. Right. In that case, get your arse out of that car and let's go back up Jess. Right. Fucking. Now!' she stormed. Then immediately de-escalated and cagily asked, 'Too far?'

'You're never too far,' I told her, as I climbed out and fell into a needed but brief hug. 'Okay, let's go.'

I tossed the car keys to the valet, like I'd seen them do in a hundred movies, but my eyes were so shot with unshed tears that I went wide, missed altogether, and then scrabbled to pick them up, over-apologising profusely in case he thought I was a total dick.

More proof, if it were needed, that I didn't belong here.

In the hotel, we went straight to the brasserie. Jess had given us detailed instructions so we knew where to go. At the entrance, Carol took charge, while Val scanned the area. 'Bloody hell, it's not McDonald's, is it?'

If the maître d' heard, he chose not to comment, and instead, showed us to the table Jess had booked for us. I checked the time on my phone: 9.45 a.m. I felt like I'd lived a week already this morning. I scanned the room looking for her and there she was, sitting at one of the back tables on her own. Peering, I tried to suss how she appeared, searching for hints on how the meeting with Arnie had gone. She gave me a sad smile. Not good then. Crappola. Our merry little team was striking out everywhere this week.

She gestured to her phone, and then called me as soon as she saw us take our seats.

'Okay, are you all good. Is Carol recording this?'

Carol leaned into the phone. 'Sure am.'

'And I'm here in case it gets physical,' Val said. 'Unless I get distracted by people asking for autographs now that I'm an actress.'

I left the phone line open, and we ordered coffees and a selection of breakfast pastries while we waited. At exactly 10 a.m., the man I recognised as Dax Hill strutted into the restaurant and went straight to Jess's table, shaking hands and saying hello to various other diners as he went. Popular guy. For a snake.

When he reached Jess, he sat down and immediately took out an envelope from his inside pocket. The three of us watched everything unfold from across the room, while listening to the conversation on the open line.

'I'll make this quick,' he said to Jess, who now sported a contemptuous expression, complete with raised eyebrows and cool smirk.

'I'd heard that about you,' she said. If Dax Hill wondered why a woman of a certain age on the other side of the restaurant spluttered on her coffee, he didn't show it.

'Photograph,' he said. 'You. Empire State Building. I believe you're due to marry Arnie Deluca. Great stunt man in his day. Don't think he'd approve of this. Or the fact that you spent the night with this guy in the St Regis.'

Holy crap. Three sets of eyes at the other table were wide as saucers.

'Call off Hayley Harlow and make my whole situation disappear. If you do that, this will disappear too.'

'What the hell?,' Carol hissed in my ear. 'This is like the stuff that happens in movies. This is why I only watch romcoms.'

From where we were sitting, it looked like Jess met his gaze.

'Nothing is disappearing. You do what you have to do. And when you've done it, you can watch Hayley do a DNA test on Entertainment Tonight.'

'You're bluffing,' he replied. 'Because we both know this isn't worth it.'

'That's where you're wrong. To me, this is worth it all day long.'

'We'll see,' he spat. With that, he got up and walked away.

'That's a face I'd never tire of punching,' Val said as he passed.

As soon as he was out of sight, Jess got up and joined us.

'Did you hear all that?' she asked, disgusted.

We nodded. 'Val thinks she's in an episode of *Special Victims Unit*,' I told her. 'We're waiting for Ice-T to storm in and take prisoners.'

'What do you think he'll do? And what happened with Arnie?' Carol asked as we all got up, leaving cash in the wallet with the bill.

'I've no idea. To both those questions. Let's go home. It's not even 11 o'clock and I've already had enough drama to last me all day.'

'You might want to avoid asking me about the conversation I just had with my husband then...' I said ruefully.

'And the one I need to have with mine,' Carol added, absently.

I didn't even get a chance to interrogate her on that, because in the biggest shock of a totally shocking morning, Val sighed. 'And you might want to shut me up if I start talking about my Don too.'

34

VAL

Chains – Tina Arena

Jesus, Mary and Josie, what was I thinking? I almost blurted out all my business to the girls without warning. I blame the mental image of Ice-T bursting into the restaurant. I've always had a thing for him. Luckily, I think the lassies thought I was joking and didn't press me for more details. Instead, we headed outside and waited as the valet bloke brought Sam's pickup round to us.

I wanted to take that chap home with me. Isa from Scottish Slimmers would be pure jealous if I had a valet for my Skoda.

We climbed in – or rather, Carol and Jess got right under me and manhandled me into the back. I needed a set of steps to get up there on my own. Carly and Jess were in the front seats in the cabin, and Carol and I took the back two.

Carly stretched her neck as she turned to talk to Jess. 'Well, he was a peach. Are you okay?'

Jess nodded. 'I just need to process everything. I've dealt with a fair few scumbags in my life, but I've never had someone actually blackmail me. And to my face! This is nuts. Let's just go and we'll talk at the house. These shoes are killing me and my days of wearing grown-up clothes are over. I want my joggies.'

'I'll have the suit, if it's going free,' I piped in. Jess had looked smashing in it. It was like one of those shoulder-padded power suits that we'd worn in the eighties, when I could still walk in a pencil skirt without pulling a muscle. 'I mean, it'd be three sizes too wee for me, but I've still got those magic pants.' I waited for Jess to say that they were magic, not miraculous, but she didn't even come back with the obvious smart arse comment. That bastard had stolen my cheeky, insulting, brutally cutting Jess. I missed her.

We still hadn't pulled off from the entrance to the hotel, so I stretched forward to find out what was going on and saw that Carly had picked up the photo that Jess had tossed on the seat between them. Jess and that nice Greg bloke at the Empire State Building. Och, it was a lovely pic, with all those fireworks in the background. Apparently, there had been some official event on across the river and we'd just got lucky with the timing.

Carly was still staring at the picture. 'Do you know what's weird?' she said eventually.

Given the week we'd had, I could give her a list.

Jess put her feet up on the dashboard. 'What?'

'That photo looks exactly like some of the ones of me that got put on the internet. Is it not a bit coincidental that there are two lots of dodgy photos doing the rounds? God, this town is mad. What are we doing here?' she finished with a sigh, tossed the pic back on the seat and pulled off.

We weren't even out of the hotel driveway when Jess pointed out of the front window and started to mumble, almost to herself. 'I recognise that guy. Is he an actor? I think he was in *Grey's Anatomy*. Hang on, get closer. Yup, definitely seen him before.'

Carol and I stretched over to see who she was talking about. A guy in jeans and a hoodie. Standing about ten metres ahead, almost concealed by a fake conifer tree in a huge tub at the entrance to the hotel. Damn, I didn't have my specs on again.

'Yes!' Carol blurted. 'I've seen him too.'

I'm not being judgemental about my niece-in-law's perception skills, but I didn't hold out much hope that she was going to be the one to solve the puzzle. Yesterday, I caught her putting hairspray on her armpits because she'd confused the can with deodorant.

'The beach. I saw him at a beach. But when were we there?' Jess was still mumbling, giving us a running commentary on her thought processes. 'We were in swimsuits. The red ones. We were all there. The first thing on the bucket list. Malibu. That's it. Oh my God... HE'S THE GUY WHO STOPPED TO TAKE THE PHOTOS FOR US THAT DAY WE WERE IN MALIBU!'

The last part was a screech, a wail, a complete bloody distraction for Carly at the wheel. Not one who was used to driving a vehicle of that size at the best of times, she was clearly startled by Jess's screams. The shock, combined with straining to see who Jess was referring to, caused her to swerve the truck. Unfortunately, at that very same moment, the photographer raised his camera, stepped forward and our bloody great big vehicle ran right over his foot.

In the chaos of screams and yells, he went down like he'd been shot by a sniper. Carly then screamed again, slammed on the brakes and brought the pickup to a halt, barely missing the pot plant, but giving us all sure cases of whiplash.

For a split second, all was still, until Carly opened her eyes. That may have been a clue as to why we were now on the pavement. 'Did I kill him? Oh shit, is he dead?'

Jess was already out of the truck and standing over the bloke, shouting, 'Call an ambulance,' back to the gent at the hotel doors.

Time stopped. Started. Slowed down. Sped up. I've no idea how long it was – could have been minutes, hours, days – until we heard the sirens and saw the blue flashing lights. The photographer was now sitting up, but he was holding his leg, shouting threats and abuse. I could see now that Jess was right – it was definitely the man from our first day at the beach.

Carly was on the pavement, her head on her knees, Carol was beside her, hugging her and Jess was, as far as I could see, trying her best not to boot the injured bloke in the good leg for stalking us for the last fortnight.

The first thing the cop wanted to know was who was driving, but Jess had warned us. Back in the day, she'd seen every episode ever of *LA Law*, and she'd told us, under pain of death, that we should say nothing. Not. A. Thing.

'I'm sorry, but we can't say anything until we have a lawyer present,' she said solemnly, when asked. Carol said the same. And me. And Carly was too shaken to even speak. Carol had called Sam and Callum, but it had gone straight to voicemail. Apparently, their fishing trip must have taken them into international waters where there was no signal.

What would Josie do? It came to me straight away.

I tried to divert the officer's attention from the fact that we hadn't answered his question.

'Is Ice-T not coming?' I asked. I should have known better than to think he would have a sense of humour that was in line with that of an elderly woman from the other side of the world.

'If you'd just like to come with me, ladies. I think this is best sorted out at the precinct.'

35

CARLY

Roar – Katy Perry

'My TripAdvisor review of this place isn't getting five stars,' Jess muttered. 'Not even a bloody minibar.'

Yep, these were the things I learned today:

1. The American dream is only a couple of twists away from the kind of nightmare they make movies about. Right now, *The Shawshank Redemption* and *The Great Escape* come to mind.
2. I really need to brush up on my driving skills as at least one hospital admission in the LA area today was my fault.
3. Right now, out in the world, there's probably a lawyer already planning a court case against me that will destroy my life.
4. Oh, and a Los Angeles jail cell isn't that different from a

London one. Four walls. A locked steel door. And
despite ample padding in the posterior area, my arse is
not designed for a concrete bench.

A wave of anxiety made my stomach churn and my skin crawl.
Apart from the buttock area, which was comfortably numb. But
that wasn't the point. I was in jail. Again.

'I suppose there's no chance of room service popping in with a
gin and tonic and a Toblerone. Or a packet of cheese and onion
crisps.' Val lifted her legs and nodded in the direction of the totteringly high pink sandals on her feet. 'I'd give one of these furry
mules for a Greggs steak bake. I'd be walking in circles for the rest
of the day, but I don't s'pose it would matter in here.'

Carol closed her eyes and, for a second, I wondered if she was
upset or trying to contain her anger, but then I realised that she was
actually just committing every detail of this to memory to be
recounted later to her 1.2 million fans and followers.

'I'm so, so, sorry about all this,' I bleated, for the 234th time since
the metal door banged shut. 'I promise that somehow I'll make it up
to you all.'

'An invite to George Clooney's house for a pool party might just
about do it,' my Auntie Val demanded. 'I know you've got connections there.'

I decided now wasn't the time to let her in on my certainty that
I'll be about as welcome as a sausage at a vegan restaurant in A-list
circles after this. I appreciated her trying to inject some levity into
the situation, but it wasn't working. The reality was that I'd seriously messed up. I'd been a shit example for my sons. Pissed off my
friends. Enraged my brother. And served my ex with the perfect
excuse to call me irresponsible and feel smug about our parting of
the ways. Not to mention being an absolutely shit wife to the
husband that I adored.

I couldn't see how it could get any worse.

'Morton!' A shadow was cast across the floor as a muscle-bound guard the size of a Portaloo appeared in front of the gate.

'There's someone here to see you.'

He stood to one side and there was one of the best lawyers in the business – according to the role he once played in five series of an Emmy Award-winning legal drama.

Sam's eyes met mine, and I wasn't sure what I saw there, but the muscle that was throbbing on the side of that perfect jaw of his told me it wasn't happy thoughts.

'Are you here to get us out?' I asked weakly.

His beautiful green eyes darkened, that muscle on his jaw throbbed faster, and his head went into a slow-motion, loaded shake. That's when I realised our score on that marriage test was about to be an epic fail.

'Can't get you released until there's news from the hospital,' he said. 'They've only let me in here because the cop at the desk works security on sets and I said I'd hook him up. What the hell happened?'

'I don't know,' I answered honestly. 'The guy... he's paparazzi. We think he's the one who's been posting those photos. I got distracted and... and...' The trembling was starting again. 'Sam, is he okay? Tell me if I've killed him. I mean, he was alive after I ran over his foot, but shock can set in later. I saw that on *Holby City* once and...'

'Carly, stop.' His voice was soft and caring, but I knew that could be a ruse so that I wouldn't hate him when he divorced me. 'Listen, I have to go. They said I could only have five minutes. Try not to worry. We'll get you all out as soon as we can. We're on it. Trust me.'

With that, Sam Morton, the love of my life, the man whose heart I had crushed just a few hours before, left the building.

'Can he not call that bloke from *Prison Break* for tips?' Val asked.

I knew she was only coming out with lines like that to cheer us up. Val and Josie had coped with every crisis, every drama, every tear and heartache that way. 'Fuck all going for us, but we're still chipper,' Josie would say.

I slumped back down next to her on the concrete bench and hugged her. We sat in silence for a few minutes before she got fed up with that and decided to chat.

'Well, girls, we're not going anywhere, so we might as well make the most of this.'

Jess was sitting with her head against the cell wall, but she rolled it towards Val to reply to that. 'Are you going to make us start doing press-ups and crunchies? I've seen that on loads of prison shows.'

'I was thinking more of a wee chat about life in general,' Val replied. 'How are you doing over there, Carol?'

'I... I... don't know.' Carol managed to mutter. It was only then I saw that her hands were shaking and her colouring was a pale shade of grey.

Val smiled at her kindly. 'You know, you're going to have to tell us about it at some point, pet.'

'Tell us about what?' I asked, confused. Did Val have some secret info on Carol that I didn't know about? Jess and I had already talked about how worried we were, but Carol insisted there was nothing wrong. Was she leaving my brother after all? Was she sick?

'I hate my life,' she said eventually, so quietly that we had to strain to hear.

I must have made a mistake. Carol Cooper had the best life ever. That couldn't be what she'd said.

'I really, really hate my life,' she repeated. Shows you how much I know. 'I want to run away, and keep running and just not stop.'

I could see Jess was as shocked as I was. 'But why? Has something happened?'

Carol slowly shook her head, still staring into space. 'I don't know why. I used to wake up happy in the mornings. I used to love my life, my husband, my job. I don't know when that changed, but it did. Now, I wake up and dread the day.'

Her voice was still quiet, but it was steeped in such anguish, such unadulterated pain, that it made my heart ache.

I crossed the cell – not a sentence I thought I'd ever say – and sat next to her, took her hand. 'Carol, what can we do, babe? How can we help you?'

Two silent tears began to run down her perfect face. She even cried beautifully. Still staring straight ahead, she went on, 'I don't know. Nothing makes this better. Every day, there's just this knot of anxiety inside me. This dread. Fear.' She finally turned to look at me. 'I'm scared all the time, Carly. It's like I'm numb, but terrified too. There's a fog in my mind and it stops me from thinking straight. I can't remember things. I get everything mixed up. And then the fear comes again and shuts everything else down and only leaves room for panic and terror. Every day I'm scared something will happen to the girls. I'm scared I'll fail at my job. I'm terrified that I'm too old now and the endorsements will stop coming in. I feel old. Unattractive. Exhausted. Like my best days are gone and there's nothing ahead. I'm scared that Callum will stop loving me, yet I can't remember the last time I felt I loved him. Or wanted to have sex. Or to go anywhere. Everything now is just for content. It's all fake. All those people want to be me, and yet I'm a fucking mess who is falling apart. I don't know what to do.'

Rivers of tears were there now. Oceans. Sliding down her cheeks. Jess had moved to the other side of her, and we both had her, both holding on, as if we could somehow form a human patch over the wound that was causing the pain. How had I not known things were this bad?

'Have you been to see a doctor?' Jess asked softly.

'A while ago,' she whimpered. 'He said I was depressed. Gave me pills. I take them every day, but nothing has changed and I can't go back, Jess, I can't. I just can't do it, because I'm so scared he'll tell me that I'm losing my mind, or that something terrible is wrong with me, something that can't be fixed, that'll take me away from my family. I don't want to stay, but I don't want to go either. I just can't... just can't see how I can be happy.'

My sister-in-law and friend had always been the sweetest, most positive person of us all. We'd noticed that she wasn't her usual self but why had we not seen that she was struggling this badly? Either she was a great actress, or we were the crappest pals ever, and from ten years of watching her as Mary in the Nativity plays, I knew she was a terrible actress. The guilt was sending shock waves of sorrow riding under my skin.

'Why didn't you talk to us, sweetheart? Why did you keep telling us nothing was wrong? We would have helped.'

'Because I just couldn't say the words. I couldn't get them out. Talking would somehow make it real and I couldn't face that.'

Ouch, more guilt. I should have probed harder. No more. My crapness stopped now.

'Okay, when we get back to the UK, I'll come with you to the doctor and we'll get answers, Carol. I promise. We'll be there for you...'

Val interrupted us. 'Carol, love, when did your periods stop?'

It was such an unexpected question that all three of us took a moment to process it. There were two tiny, faint lines between Carol's brows. 'They haven't stopped yet. Why?'

'Because everything you've described is exactly how I felt when I was going through the menopause. Only, we called it "the change" back then.'

'But I don't get the sweats. Or anything else. I'm fine. I have no symptoms.'

'Everything you just mentioned can be the symptoms. I was exactly the same. It started about a year before my periods stopped. Peri-menopausal they call it now. I've got all the lingo now. Anyway, I was so wound up, my Don was for giving me away and I'd have let him. The brain fog was awful. I once came home from Tesco and realised I'd left my trolley of shopping in the car park. Completely forgot to put it in the car. I'd meet people in the street that I'd known for years and suddenly their names were a blank to me. I'd get my words mixed up...'

'In fairness, I have been doing that since we were about five,' Carol interjected, and we all smiled, because she wasn't wrong.

'Aye, true. That's nothing new right enough,' Val said, kindly, before returning to her point. 'It was like walking through fog every day. God, it was desperate. And the sadness... Sometimes it took everything I had just to get out of bed. I didn't want to go out, I didn't want to see anyone. And don't get me started on the lack of sex.'

'Oh, dear God, PLEASE don't get Val started on the lack of sex,' Jess begged.

Val pursed her lips and ignored her, before going back to Carol. 'All I'm saying, sweetheart, is that it might be what's going on here. That Davina McCall is always on the telly talking about it. Apparently, a lot of doctors don't fully understand it, so they prescribe antidepressants, which don't solve the problem. Davina says they can work miracles with that HRT stuff these days. She swears by it. So does Lorraine Kelly in the mornings. And that Carol Vorderman too. She says she put those patches, or maybe it was that HRT gel stuff, on her legs and she's like a new woman. Not that we want you to be a new woman, because, you know, we love the one we've got already.'

Carol blinked a few times, as if she was trying to assimilate this information. 'I don't know why I never thought of that. Maybe I was waiting for all the other stuff, the flushes and my periods to stop. I didn't realise this could all be connected to my age.'

'You'd think the doctor would have mentioned it though,' I said, shaking my head, exasperated.

Carol shrugged. 'He barely spent ten minutes talking to me. I'm not blaming him, though. I mean, it's my fault that I didn't ask. I should have made the connection. It's my responsibility to know what's going on with my body. I was just so down that the stuff he said about being depressed made sense.'

'I get that,' Jess said with uncharacteristic compassion. 'When I was depressed, I had a load of those symptoms too. Makes sense that you didn't challenge it.' Jess had suffered chronic post-natal depression after her son was born, and then had a couple of dark periods in the following few years. She had offered her services free to loads of mental health charities over the years and she was forever telling us that we had to take care of our minds as well as our bodies. 'Maybe if I'd been living back home I'd have spotted it, but you always seemed like your usual cheery self on our FaceTime calls.'

'Acting again,' Carol admitted sheepishly. 'Sometimes I had to hang up because I couldn't keep it up any longer.'

'So that time you said you had to go because you were interviewing Vivien Westwood for your blog?' Jess gasped.

'Lie.' Carol admitted.

'So there was no free frock for you to pass on to me? Aw, bollocks. Now I'm the one with the sudden mood swing,' she joked. Like Val and Josie, gallows humour had got us through most of life's struggles, and this wasn't going to be any different.

Carol's shoulders rose very slightly as she rolled her eyes, and there was a definite sigh of relief there. It wasn't exactly a hallelujah moment, but it was as if little nuggets of realisation were dropping in, making sense, and giving her hope that there was a logical explanation for how she was feeling and it could be treated. 'I can't tell you how much better I feel just for talking about this. I need to speak to Callum. I should have done it a long time ago,' she said simply, making my heart soar. No matter what this was, as long as they were talking about it, I was pretty sure they could deal with anything.

I hugged her. 'I used a couple of really informative websites when I was going through menopause. I'll send you all the links.'

'Thank you,' Carol said, almost managing a smile, then she groaned, 'I'm such an idiot. I should have sussed this out and done my research. And from now on, I will, I promise. Anyway, I can't talk about me any more. Jess, tell us about Arnie.'

She did. And just when we thought that Carol's revelations would be the second most shocking thing of the day, after a journalist with injuries that could kill him if he was on *Holby City*, Jess laid out the whole story that Arnie and his daughter had shared.

'Suffering Jesus,' Val said, shaking her head. 'How did you leave it?'

Jess shrugged. 'I said I was going to think about it, but then Dax Fucking Hill showed me those pictures and I realised I'm screwed. I thought Arnie was the unfaithful one, but it was me.'

'But you didn't know!' I wailed, raging at the injustice.

Jess shrugged. 'True. But I didn't exactly take my time getting over him, did I? Maybe that says something about how I feel about him.'

I didn't believe that for a minute. This was Jess Barriers Back Up Latham, the woman who acted like she was tough as nails, but who spent at least ten years of her life having no-strings, casual sex with strangers because, deep down, she was so scared of getting hurt again.

'Okay, well, since this place has turned into a confessional, I'm just putting this out there, but don't dare be nice to me because you know that will make me fall apart – I told Sam that I don't want to live here and I want to go back to the UK. I'm pretty sure he only pitched up here out of sympathy. He's probably already decided to leave me and he's halfway to Estelle Tart Face's house. I won't be discussing this further until I've come to terms with it and slashed her tyres.'

Joking on the outside, dying on the inside. They knew me well enough to understand that was just how I handled it and I'd crumble at a later date when I felt good and ready and there was chocolate in the vicinity.

'So now we've got all our revelations out of the way,' I went on, 'Can we have a sing-song? How about starting with "I Want To Break Free"?'

'Actually, there's another revelation or two that we haven't covered yet.' Aunt Val's cheeks were flushed and her shoulders slumped as she sighed.

'I think I should probably be honest about the reason I have to do all the stuff on our bucket list now. You see, I need to get it done before it's too late…'

36

CAROL

Thank You – Dido

I'd couldn't remember ever seeing Val cry, but I wasn't sure she could blink back the tears on her bottom lids for much longer. Carly was back over there hugging her again now, and my heart was thumping. Everything Val had said about the menopause made sense, and it had given me a tiny shard of light at the end of the tunnel, but every pore in my body was still oozing anxiety and fear. Something was wrong with Val. And I didn't want to hear it.

She took a deep breath. 'It's true that Josie and I made that list long before she died, and we had every intention of doing it all. We'd been saving for years, and we couldn't wait to get started. You all know your Uncle Don isn't one for travelling abroad, so this was my chance to have some incredible experiences while all the bits of me still worked. Except my common sense gene. That one's buggered.' she laughed half-heartedly, before carrying on. 'Anyway, after Josie died, well, I just couldn't face it. I shoved it in a drawer and thought no more about it until... until...'

The dread of what she was about to say made my teeth clench so tightly my jaw began to ache.

'Your Uncle Don is in the early stages of Alzheimer's. We've known for a while that something wasn't right, but in the last few months, it's become difficult to ignore.'

I gasped, Jess bowed her head, and Carly let out a low, tortured, 'No.' We all loved Don. He was a very typical Glaswegian man of his time. He liked his football, his work, loved his family, but wasn't one for talking about his emotions. He was, however, one for having a right good sing-song at the first bar of an Elvis tune. Val adored him. He adored her. The sadness of this situation was unbearable.

'When he started to decline, the two of us made a pact. He wanted to travel up north to the islands, to visit Skye and Isla, because that's where his family came from. And he wanted to go with our Michael, because he knows I won't go anywhere that'll ruin ma hair.' She patted her coiffure as she said it, emphasising the joke. 'That traipsing up hills in the cold and taking windswept ferries isn't for me. Michael agreed to come back from Australia for a few weeks and make the trip with his dad, and I came here because it's the last chance I'll have to see out Josie's wishes. We both know that when I go back, it'll be me and Don, and we're getting to the time that I won't be able to leave his side. And that's fine with me, because there's nowhere else I've ever wanted to be.'

I choked back a sob. 'I'm so sorry, Aunt Val.'

She put her hand up and spoke with a soft, sad smile. 'I know, pet. I'd love to come out with some wise, profound words, but the truth is that the disease is a bastard of a thing.

'That's why you lot need to live your lives, because you don't know what's in front of you. Carol, you need to talk about how you're feeling and get help because, lass, you have such a gifted life and you deserve to suck every bit of happiness from it. Carly, if you want to go home, then do it. Follow your heart. Because none of us should live with regrets and what's for you...'

'Won't go by you,' Carly finished the sentence, repeating the line used by every Scottish auntie over the age of sixty, especially after she's had a sherry.

'And, Jess, you have to let yourself love and be loved, pet. None of that bendy stuff makes up for spooning someone that you adore the bones of. And, let's face it, at your age, yer knees will be fecked soon and all that sex stuff will be out the window.'

Jess was stopped from returning the cheek by the sound of clanging metal. The door opened and a guard sauntered in. 'Right then, ladies, I've got a bit of good news, if you want to hear it.'

'D'ya think they're putting Tom Jones in the next cell?' Val whispered to Carly.

'Really, Aunt Val? That's where your mind went when you heard "good news"?' Carly shot back. Then, 'We are so related. I was hoping for Liam Neeson.'

'Let's hear it, please,' Jess replied, frowning at the other two.

'We've reviewed the footage from the security cameras at the Peninsula. Turns out the alleged victim was making a bit more of it than he should have. From what we could see, your tyre just missed him and the hospital have reported no broken bones.'

'He was faking it?' I don't know why that seemed shocking to me. I was a woman who spent her whole life faking just about every minute of every day.

'He was faking it,' the cop confirmed, swinging the door open with a flourish and letting us traipse out past him, exhausted yet jubilant, as if we'd just been released early from a ten year stretch. Jess's head was held high, Carly's smile was back, and even several hours in a cell hadn't knocked a single hair on Val's head out of place.

It took about half an hour for us to have everything returned to us, and then to be escorted down to the main door of the building and let out. We didn't exactly run blinking into the sunshine, but it was close. We linked arms, took a step forward and then nearly face-planted when Carly stopped dead in her tracks and caused a domino effect of staggers.

'I think my ovaries just threw a party,' she murmured.

I put my hand to my eyes and squinted to see what had stirred her.

The car park in front of us. Sam's convertible Mercedes was there, and leaning against it, arms folded, grins on their faces, were Sam, Callum and Arnie.

And to every single person's shock and surprise, it was big tough Jess who was off and running first. She reached Arnie and threw her arms around him, then kissed him with the suction of a Dyson. She was only just putting him back down when the rest of us reached them. 'I just had to do that because after I tell you what happened in New York, you won't want to do that again.'

Arnie pulled her back towards him. 'I know what happened,' he said, then kissed her again. 'And I'm gonna keep doing this anyway.'

As she roared with laughter, I slipped into the open arms of my husband. Callum kissed the top of my head, then whispered in my ear. 'You okay?' It wasn't *War and Peace*, but it was said with such tenderness that I melted even further into him.

'I will be,' I told him. For the first time in months, I believed it.

'Hey, Mr Morton,' Carly said, as she stood in front of Sam. 'You sticking around?'

Sam shrugged, but his wide grin helped. 'I'm here,' he said. 'That do for now?'

'Yeah, that'll do for now,' she told him, returning his smile. Something computed in her head at that moment. 'Wait a minute, how are we all getting home? There's seven of us. We won't all fit in your car. Crap. I'll call an Uber. Do they pick up from jail?'

'Don't worry, we've got it covered.' Sam leaned into the Mercedes and pulled out two motorbike helmets.

I thought Carly was going to burst a gut. Motorbikes definitely weren't her preferred mode of transport.

But instead of handing the helmet over to his wife, Sam turned and held it out to Val.

'I believe the only thing left on your bucket list is a motorbike ride. Shall we take care of that?'

'There's no way that helmet is going on over that bob,' Jess declared.

Val ignored her, then proved her wrong. Using some kind of technique akin to vacuum packing, she managed to get the helmet on her head, then took Sam's hand and let him lead her to a Harley-Davidson the size of a horse parked on the other side of his car. She climbed on behind him, wrapped her arms around his abs as far as they would go, and let out the most contagious cackle, before they roared off into the late-afternoon sun.

Josie would have been so proud.

37

CARLY

THREE DAYS LATER

It Hurts So Good – Millie Jackson

'Aunt Val, the van is outside,' I yelled, trying to hurry her up. If we didn't get her on the road soon, she was going to miss her flight. 'Come on!' I said, traipsing outside, pulling her screaming pink carry-on case with one hand, and carrying her life-size cardboard cut-out of Al Pacino in the other. We'd spotted it in a memorabilia shop on Hollywood Boulevard yesterday and she'd refused to leave without it. I had no idea if British Airways were going to demand that Al had his own seat, but Val wasn't leaving him behind.

Out in the driveway, I handed them over to the driver, Aaron, who put them in the boot. Val, meanwhile, was standing just outside the front door, hugging Jess. My friend's face was beaming. Pretty much three solid days of sex with Arnie, and the cherry on top of that cake was that Dax Hill had finally agreed to a paternity test and made a provisional offer to take care of Hayley and her baby. A few things had contributed to his decision. He'd realised that Jess was completely ruthless and wouldn't give up. She'd also told him she had a recording of their conversation, and it would be going out on Hayley's new podcast if he didn't concede. Oh, and that Arnie knew about the New York guy so she didn't give a toss if he showed her fiancé the photo. Having the photographer onside had helped too. Jess had threatened to press charges for falsifying a crime, if he didn't admit to it all. He'd given an affidavit saying he was hired by Dax to dig up some leverage on Jess. The photos of me were just a happy accident for a guy who knew that he could make pictures of Sam Morton's wife tell any story. He'd trailed us on Dax's dime, while flogging the pics of me to an unscrupulous website for clickbait and side money. I was over it. The main thing was that Hayley was thrilled with the developments and planned to name her baby son Jesse. It seemed fitting that Dax's son would bear the name of the woman who beat Dax at his own game.

Jess's relief was all over her face. Arnie's too. His ex-wife was doing well in rehab and his daughter, Talia, had brought the whole family over the night before to thank Jess in person for allowing them to make things right for their father. At the end of the day, now that their mother was safe and getting help, they just wanted to see their dad happy. They saw now that he could never be happy without Jess.

'You take care of yourself, love,' Val said, hugging Jess again. 'And take care of this man too,' she said, hugging Arnie now. 'And if the two of you can try to actually get that wedding arranged this time, that would be dandy. Any time before I pop my clogs will be just grand.'

Next in the line were Carol and Callum.

'Suffering Jesus, it's like Downton Abbey round here. I feel like I'm getting a royal send-off.'

'Nope, we're just making sure you actually get in the van,' my brother teased her.

Carol gave him a playful punch and hugged Val. My sister-in-law looked like ten years had been lifted off her. Which was a complete bummer because she already looked ten years younger than the rest of us. The day after we'd got out of jail – again, not a sentence I ever thought I'd say – she'd made an appointment to see a fabulous doctor who specialised in menopause. They'd run a whole battery of tests, and whilst all the results weren't back yet, everything pointed in the direction of her symptoms being down to being perimenopausal and they were considering a range of medicinal and natural treatments. We told her she could have saved the doctor's fees and just listened to Val instead. My brother was fully supportive, and they were going to stay out here for another couple of weeks to reconnect, talk and have a bit of fun, which would be easier now that Carol had suspended her social media accounts and taken a step back from the hamster wheel of the internet. She said that after the initial fear of shutting it all down, the relief had been instant and huge. No more fakery. No more pretending. No more pressure to perform. For the first time in years, she was allowed to just be Carol. The private one. Not the person who had to perform for the world every day.

'I'm so sorry Sam wasn't here to say goodbye, Aunt Val.' My husband was on set somewhere today. In fact, he'd pretty much been there constantly since he'd given Val a spin round LA on his bike. They'd been gone for hours, and apparently, they'd ended up sitting on Malibu beach, watching the sun go down and putting the world to rights. I wasn't sure they'd done a very good job, considering he'd pretty much been avoiding me ever since.

That was a problem for another day, though. Right now, I wanted to enjoy every moment of being with Val.

We gabbed all the way to the airport.

'You know something, love,' she said, when we pulled into the car park at LAX. 'I always thought Josie and I planned this trip for us. Now I'm beginning to think she made me actually take it for you lot. It's like you're all where you should be now, but only thanks to Josie's powers.'

'You're right. Do you think she'd approve of everything we did?'

Val nodded. 'Especially the last one.'

'The motorbike ride?'

I didn't understand why that made her hoot with laughter and I was even more perplexed when she dipped into her bag, took out another piece of paper and handed it to me. Straight away, I recognised Josie's flamboyant, curly handwriting. 'That was our original list,' she said.

I cast my eyes down.

JOSIE AND VAL'S BUCKET LIST

1.Go to a line dancing bar and snog a cowboy (a cross between Urban Cowboy, Saturday Night Fever and Dirty Dancing)

2.Act in a TV show or movie (A Star Is Born – the Barbra one)

3.Gamble a month's pension on a blackjack table in Las Vegas (Casino)

4.Shop on Rodeo Drive and stay in that hotel from Pretty Woman

5.Have breakfast at Tiffany's, then skate on the ice rink at the Rockefeller Centre in New York (Breakfast at Tiffany's and every romcom ever set in New York)

6.Run across the Malibu sands in slow motion like big Hasselhoff in Baywatch

7.Dance on top of a bar (Coyote Ugly) and give them a wee chorus of 'Sweet Caroline' while we're up there.

8.Snog a stranger at the top of the Empire State Building (Sleepless In Seattle)

9.Ride a motorbike (Top Gun) and drive a convertible (Thelma and Louise – but without the driving off a cliff bit at the end)

But it was the next item on the list that stunned me. There was a number ten, that was there clear as day, but hadn't been on the list Val had initially given us.

10. Get arrested (Chicago)

The giggle came right up from the soles of my boots. 'I can't believe she wrote that.'

Val nodded triumphantly. 'Yep. But I covered that one up in case it stopped you coming with me.'

'Of course it wouldn't! I already spent time in jail a couple of years ago. I'm like a hardened criminal now. Sam is giving me an orange jumpsuit for Christmas. Or a divorce. I'm not entirely sure yet.'

I forced myself to act like that last comment was a joke, but the truth was that it wouldn't surprise me if Sam was giving up on us.

I was still pondering that after we'd left the car, loaded all her luggage and Al Pacino onto a trolley and pushed it into the terminal building. It was still two weeks before Christmas, so the airport was busy, but not packed out with festive travellers yet.

'You know you said Sam might divorce you?'

'Ouch. Can you warn me next time you're going to mention Sam please?'

'Okay, I'm warning you now. Do you mean the same Sam that's sitting over there?' Val asked, pointing to a row of three seats by the check-in desk.

My heart swelled. Sam was sitting in the middle seat in a disguise of baseball cap pulled down firmly on his head, glasses and dodgy teeth. No Cher wig this time. But he'd come to say goodbye to Val after all. She'd be so chuffed.

It was only when we reached him, I realised that behind the false teeth, he wasn't smiling. He was, however, holding out a boarding card to me.

I took it and handed it straight to Val. 'Here you go, just show that...'

'Carly, it's not for Val.'

My head slowly rotated back to him as I absorbed what he was saying.

'It's mine?' I asked fearfully. This was it then. He'd made the decision for both of us. If that's how he felt, I wasn't going to argue with him in the middle of a terminal building surrounded by crowds of people. I'd learned my lesson. It would be all over the internet in minutes. And there was no way – no bloody way – I could let a single person watch as my heart disintegrated into tiny pieces. I only had enough air left in my lungs to utter a strangled, 'Sam...?'

He put his hand up. 'Don't say anything, Carly. There's no point. This is what you want.'

It was. But it wasn't. I wanted both options, but it was an impossible choice. I forced my lungs to refill so that I could say something. Anything.

'Sam, I don't know if I can do this,' I told him honestly. Stay. I should stay. Maybe I'd get used to it eventually. Make new friends. Buy new children on Rodeo Drive.

'You can,' he said, before reaching into his jacket pocket and pulling out another card. 'And so can I. I love you, Carly. And I love the boys. Life's nothing without you all in it.'

I shrieked so loudly I'm pretty sure many hands went to their phones to call security.

'You're coming? Are you sure?'

'I'm sure.'

Sam was a great actor, but even Al Pacino couldn't have faked the genuine happiness on my husband's face. He meant it.

'This is bloody brilliant. I'm coming over all giddy,' Aunt Val interjected, fanning the tears in her eyes with her hand. I gave her a squeeze too, as the technicalities popped into my mind. Big romantic gestures were one thing, but there were a couple of issues with this.

'What about our luggage? All our things? My passport?'

He was back in the pocket again, digging out my travel wallet, which he duly handed over. 'It's all in there. The luggage is already checked in.'

'But how did you know what to bring?'

'It didn't take a genius, my love. You hadn't unpacked. That should probably have been a sign I picked up on earlier.'

His laughter was contagious and he was so fricking adorable, I threw my arms around him. 'So what's next, Mr Morton?'

He shrugged. 'I've no idea, but I think we'll have a pretty good time figuring it out.'

I'd never felt surer that he was right. We had each other, and now we'd also have my boys, my pals, Aunt Val, Uncle Don and our happy, familiar, non-flashy lives back in the UK, with maybe just a bit of LA glitz every now and then.

As we walked towards the departure gate, I glanced heavenwards.

We'd also have a kick-ass woman up there looking out for us.

EPILOGUE

Ain't No Mountain High Enough – Diana Ross

Dear Josie,

Well, doll, this one wasn't on the bucket list, but oh, you'd have bloody loved it. A full-scale Scottish wedding, complete with a bloody big muscly American bloke in a kilt. I'm sure you once had a fantasy about a situation not too different to that. I think it was that night we overdid the home-made cocktails while we binge-watched a whole series of Outlander.

Jess's big day was nothing like originally planned. There was no posh wine in Napa, just a free bar and a marquee up in the back garden at Carly's new home. Can you believe it? Sam bought a bloody great big house just up the street from where Carly used to live, so she's still within a two-minute walk of Kate, and all the young ones who are still living next door in Carly's old house. They're like a commune, that lot.

Anyway, Arnie's whole family came over, and I've never seen that lassie look so happy. She's moving back to Los Angeles with him because they want to be close to his children and grandchildren. His ex-wife is doing much better now and Jess even let her stay with them after she'd been in rehab. We always knew there was a big heart underneath that veneer of cutting harshness. She reminds me a bit of someone I used to know... lol! (That's laugh out loud, not lots of love, just in case yer not up with the trendy lingo up there).

Who's next? Carly and Sam are still in the honeymoon phase. Turns out he missed Mac and Benny almost as much as she did, so they're much happier now that they're all here together. Sam doesn't half turn heads when he goes to watch Mac playing basketball or Benny at the swimming though. Even when he wears the baseball cap and the dodgy teeth.

Our Carol and Callum are doing much better too. Her HRT is making such a difference and she's got all that anxiety under control. She's even started a podcast just like the one Toni was doing, but Carol's is for the over fifties. It's called, 'Living Your Best Menopausal Life'. She only does it once a week, but she enjoys it much more than all that social media nonsense. Dear God, that lassie took more photos in a day than we took in the whole of the seventies.

You know, pal, I thought I'd be sad now that the bucket list is done, but I'm not. The girls have been brilliant. They got together with our Michael to make sure I've got all the help I could need with my Don. They all call me every day and they've worked out a rota so that at least one of them flies up and stays for a couple of days every fortnight or so, just to give me some support. On the nights I'm alone, though, I know you see me, when I shed a tear or two over the man he used to be, but, Josie, I'll still take the man that he is now over anyone else. It's not easy, but we both know that life isn't fair. If it was, you'd have been with me on every day of that trip to America, and we'd have had a blast, ma love.

I still tell myself that you saw it all and I know you'd have loved every second from start to finish.

Anyway, pal, time for me to sign off. I'll write again with all the gossip from this wedding as soon as my hangover wears off. It's the champagne that does it. Two glasses and I'm giddy these days. And I'm watching my weight so I can get into my frock for the premiere of the movie I was in. Can you believe it? It's at the Odeon in Leicester Square. I'm taking Al Pacino as my date if I can get him down from the loft.

So that's all our news then, my love. I hope you're here with us now, and every day forever, but if not...

Keep dancing, keep laughing... and be happy up there. And keep the space next to you warm for me. I'll join you one day, pal.

Love you,

Val xxx

ACKNOWLEDGMENTS

Thanks once again to everyone at Boldwood Books. I still feel so lucky to work with a team that is so creative, inspiring and just blooming brilliant at every single stage of the book process, from conception to the moment it reaches the hands of our readers.

Gratitude too to Jade and Rose for taking my words and making them so much better.

Huge appreciation to all the wonderful book bloggers who join our virtual tours - you make such a difference and I love hearing your thoughts.

And, of course, to every single reader who chooses to pick up my work. I'm beyond grateful that after twenty-one years, I still get to do this.

Finally, thanks to my family and my pals, who live through my deadline panics every time, and still come back bearing coffee, biscuits, and laughs.

And to John, Callan, Brad and Gemma who are, and will always be, everything, always... Sxx

MORE FROM SHARI LOW

We hope you enjoyed reading *What Next?* If you did, please leave a review.

If you'd like to gift a copy, this book is also available as an ebook, digital audio download and audiobook CD.

Sign up to Shari Low's mailing list for news, competitions and updates on future books.

http://bit.ly/ShariLowNewsletter

Explore more from Shari Low.

ABOUT THE AUTHOR

Shari Low is the #1 bestselling author of over 20 novels, including *My One Month Marriage* and *One Day In Summer,* and a collection of parenthood memories called *Because Mummy Said So*. She lives near Glasgow.

Visit Shari's website: www.sharilow.com

Follow Shari on social media:

facebook.com/sharilowbooks

twitter.com/sharilow

instagram.com/sharilowbooks

bookbub.com/authors/shari-low

ABOUT BOLDWOOD BOOKS

Boldwood Books is a fiction publishing company seeking out the best stories from around the world.

Find out more at www.boldwoodbooks.com

Sign up to the Book and Tonic newsletter for news, offers and competitions from Boldwood Books!

http://www.bit.ly/bookandtonic

We'd love to hear from you, follow us on social media:

facebook.com/BookandTonic

twitter.com/BoldwoodBooks

instagram.com/BookandTonic